PENGUIN BOOKS

RED ANGER

Geoffrey Household's life began innocently enough. He was born in 1900 in Bristol, England, into "a conventionally and mildly cultured environment," educated at Oxford University, and slated for a respectable career in international banking. But one day he jammed his umbrella into the grillwork of the bank's gate, placed his bowler on the handle, and boarded a night train for Madrid. In the years that followed this break for freedom, Mr. Household sold bananas in Spain and ink in Latin America and spent five years during World War II as a British Intelligence officer in Romania, Greece, Syria, Iraq, Palestine, and Germany. He is the author of many celebrated novels of adventure and suspense, including *Rogue Male* and *Watcher in the Shadows*, both published by Penguin Books.

Books by Geoffrey Household

NOVELS

AUTOBIOGRAPHY

SHORT STORIES

FOR CHILDREN

Red Anger

by

Geoffrey Household

PENGUIN BOOKS

Penguin Books Ltd, Harmondsworth,
Middlesex, England
Penguin Books, 625 Madison Avenue,
New York, New York 10022, U.S.A.
Penguin Books Australia Ltd, Ringwood,
Victoria, Australia
Penguin Books Canada Limited, 2801 John Street,
Markham, Ontario, Canada L3R 1B4
Penguin Books (N.Z.) Ltd, 182–190 Wairau Road,
Auckland 10, New Zealand

First published in the United States of America by
Little, Brown and Company in association with
the Atlantic Monthly Press 1975
Published in Penguin Books by arrangement with
Little, Brown and Company in association with
the Atlantic Monthly Press 1977
Reprinted 1978

LIBRARY OF CONGRESS CATALOGING IN PUBLICATION DATA
Household, Geoffrey, 1900—
Red anger.
I. Title.
[PZ3.H8159Re 1977]   [PR6015.O7885]
823'.9'12   77-10061
ISBN 0 14 00.4522 8

Printed in the United States of America by
Offset Paper Mfrs., Inc., Dallas, Pennsylvania
Set in Linotype Electra

Red Anger

Prologue

Extract of a letter from Mrs. Eudora Hilliard, dated
New York, June 17th, 1974

Yes, I agree with you. It is now nearly ten years since my nephew disappeared and we can try to clear his name without either of us having much fear of prosecution. But you should write the story, not I. Your tastes and character will carry conviction, and you have, thank God, no enemies — apart from your battles with Marketing Boards of which Tessa writes with a tempestuousness which you are too tolerant to feel yourself.

Me, I do have enemies who give other names to what I call my pro-American activities. So if I were to write the story of Alwyn's disgrace and escape it would be suspect from the start. *That* woman again, they would say!

3

You'll object that there are incidents which you are not all that keen to publicize. I can't help it. It's your duty to Alwyn. But it might, I think, be possible to get around the difficulties by presenting our story as fiction and disguising names and places as far as you can. Those who loved Alwyn Rory and served under and over him will see through it at once and at last understand what happened to him and why.

For the general public he is no longer news. So perhaps you should start with a reminder of the actual facts of the case of Lieutenant Mornix, generally supposed to be living it up in the paradise of the Soviet Union but undoubtedly frying in hell. We don't have to bother at all with Mornix himself — a traitor, a name, an obliterated ghost leaving behind him the malignancy in which you and Alwyn were caught up.

Your Government never said exactly what information this guy was selling to the Russians. Alwyn was too loyal a servant of the state to go into details, and even I do not know. But you can explain that it was to do with underwater listening and beacons on the sea bottom — with the possible landing of agents as a sideline — and that it was far more important to find out what the other side wanted to know than to arrest Mornix straightaway. So your British Intelligence hand-fed him with stuff they wanted his employers to believe, together with just enough truth to make it all convincing.

On the day when they were ready to arrest him Mornix vanished. It was the sort of failure that is part of the game — no general ever won all his battles — and nothing would ever have come out if it hadn't been for a fat slob of an MP trying to embarrass the Government. He asked in the House what action had been taken to explain the continued absence from duty of Lieutenant Mornix, and he got the answer that the police were following the usual routine for tracing a missing person. Then back he came with:

"Is it a fact that Lieutenant Mornix was employed in a secret naval establishment?"

4

The Under-Secretary replied that he was employed in H.M.S. *Nereid*, a shore-based establishment of no particular secrecy and open to the public.

That was a damned silly reply, because next day the news hawks were down at Portland in scores and they found that while the public could certainly stroll around the gardens of H.M.S. *Nereid* — a large country house, not a ship — that was about all they could do.

Naturally none of us ever knew what went on behind the scenes in, I guess, agitated meetings of the Cabinet, the head of MI5 and the Ministry of Defense, but the next front-page news was the resignation of a junior minister and the appointment of a Special Tribunal. The public always demands a scapegoat, Willie. One had been found. The other was on the way.

Here, verbatim, is part of the evidence given by my nephew to the Tribunal sitting in camera. And camera it sure was! Not a word, as you know only too well, ever leaked out. I never showed this transcript to anyone while I was in England, for I didn't want to spend the rest of my declining years in the Tower of London. You can safely swear you invented it. I believe forty more years must pass before the top-secret evidence given to the Tribunal is open to historical research.

Quote this transcript as an introduction to whatever you write! Without it nothing will make sense.

"Mr. Rory, I understand that it was known to your service that Lieutenant Mornix was in the pay of a foreign power?"

"It was."

"And it was your duty to supervise his movements?"

"Yes. But not too closely."

"So there was always a possibility that he might abscond?"

"My orders were that his suspicions should never be aroused. I therefore took risks which I would not normally have taken."

"Why were such orders given to you?"

5

"That question should be put to another branch of Intelligence."

"It has been stated in evidence that Special Branch had ample evidence to justify the arrest of Lieutenant Mornix when he left H.M.S. *Nereid* on May thirtieth. Would you agree?"

"Yes."

"And that you gave instructions that the arrest should be delayed until his return to Portland."

"I did. I had good reason to believe that his employers required him in person for consultation. If only I could find out whom he met and where, my case was complete."

"So you alone were in a position to decide whether he should or should not be arrested?"

"To some degree — yes."

"On arrival in London he was followed?"

"He was, but very discreetly. I have already explained that it was vital that he should have no suspicion."

"Where in fact did he go?"

"To Number Forty-two Whatcombe Street. He had some difficulty in finding the address, which suggests that he had never visited the street before."

"You think that was the rendezvous with his employers?"

"No. I think it was intended to check the hounds — like a fox going through a flock of sheep."

"What happened then?"

"My agents were able to watch the house, back and front, till dark, but Mornix never came out. Arrangements were then made with the police to raid the house on suspicion of a drug offense and check the identity of every person in it. He was not there."

"How do you suppose he left?"

"There was a continual coming and going of odd types, very hairy and — on such a warm day — half naked except for beads and fringes. I imagine that Lieutenant Mornix put on some such disguise, stood on the porch talking to other tenants, and simply walked off with them. Under those circumstances he would be hard to recognize even for an expert. My agents could not stop everyone and check whether whiskers and Afro-American hair styles were false."

"The escape of Mornix seems to have been organized by persons or a person with considerable experience, Mr. Rory."

"Of course."

"Could such a person have got him out of the country?"

"I doubt it, unless as diplomatic baggage."

"A rather bulky piece of baggage!"

"Not if divided into manageable pieces."

"Please be serious, Mr. Rory! Suppose he was assisted by someone with inside knowledge of the security controls?"

"Possible. But I do not believe such a traitor exists in my service."

"Let us return to Forty-two Whatcombe Street. The lady whom the Tribunal has decided to refer to as Miss X owned the house?"

"She did."

"Assuming for a moment the unlikely event of a Minister of the Crown frequenting a suspicious character, would her antecedents be automatically investigated by MI5?"

"I wouldn't say automatically. If there were a definite request, with some prima facie evidence that her contacts were undesirable, she might be discreetly investigated and the Minister warned."

"Was there such a request in the case of Miss X and from whom?"

"There was a request from the CIA."

"And was she in fact investigated?"

"No. It was considered unnecessary. The lady, her opinions and her contacts were all well known."

"You were on terms of friendship with the Minister?"

"We belong to the same club and have common interests."

"Was it you who introduced Miss X to the Minister in the first place?"

"It was. He told me he wanted to know more about the communal living and revolutionary idealism of the younger generation. As Miss X had let the lower flat of her house to

7

such a commune and as she was a woman of good family and high intelligence I suggested he might talk to her."

"You were aware of the more intimate relationship which developed?"

"From hearsay only. In any case it was a private and normal relationship between a young woman and an older man who found each other mutually attractive. In my opinion the Minister was quite wrong to resign."

"You still think then that it was nothing more than coincidence that Miss X lived in the very building where Lieutenant Mornix disappeared?"

"The fullest investigation is taking place."

"Shutting the stable door when the horse has bolted!"

"If you wish. But there is no evidence against her beyond some unconventionality in her politics and choice of friends."

"In forming your favorable opinion of Miss X had you anything to go on besides your personal acquaintance with her?"

"I had other sources of information."

"May the Tribunal know what they were?"

"Common friends. I don't want to drag in names which have nothing to do with the case."

"Mr. Rory, I am bound to put to you certain questions regarding your personal affairs. I must emphasize that you are fully entitled to refuse to answer them here and now."

"I will tell the Tribunal to the best of my ability anything it wishes to know."

"On May thirtieth, the date of the lieutenant's escape, your bank account was overdrawn to the extent of 1,560 pounds."

"It may have been."

"On June fifteenth the overdraft amounted to nearly 1,900 pounds."

"Probably. I had bought some claret I couldn't really afford."

"On June sixteenth your account stood at 89 pounds — in credit."

"Of course it did not! Well, I mean there must have been a mistake."

8

"You received no advice from your bank that a sum of 2,000 pounds had been transferred to your credit?"

"Not that I remember."

"It would have been your duty, I presume, to report such a large payment from an unknown source to the Head of your Department?"

"Of course, if I had known it was there."

"I must ask you again if you did not receive an advice from the bank that it was there."

"I don't know. I mean — I might have done."

"Could you be more precise?"

"Well, I might have thought a letter from the bank was about my overdraft and just stuffed it in a drawer."

"In any case your bank statement at the end of the month would have shown your account was in credit."

"I didn't look at it."

"Stuffed it in the same drawer, I suppose?"

"Well — I'm afraid — yes. I know it sounds silly but I always do when I know I'm badly over the overdraft limit."

"Did you not notice that no check of yours was dishonored?"

"Yes, but I supposed the Manager was being reasonable. He never bothered half as much about my overdraft as I did. And I knew he would telephone me if I had really gone too far and that then I would have to do something."

"What, for example?"

"Well, there's always something one can do."

"Yes, Mr. Rory, no doubt there is. Have you any idea where this money came from?"

"Not the least."

"I am instructed that it was passed through two foreign banks before reaching yours and that the order originated in a numbered account at a Swiss bank. I shall pass you a slip of paper with the number of that account. Please tell the Tribunal if it means anything to you."

"Good God — why didn't they pay cash?"

Willie, that was the impulsive exclamation which sank him. It sounded as if he was regretting the bribe had not been paid

9

in cash; but the question, in that moment of surprise and pros-tration, was addressed to himself, not to the Tribunal. What he meant was that if the spy-masters had paid cash in the normal way there would have been no trace of the origin of the pay-ment; therefore they intended it to be traced — not too simply but after weeks of clever investigation.

The Tribunal allowed him to explain what he meant, and he did it badly and incoherently. When he claimed that the pay-ment was an attempt to discredit him he was asked what the object of that could be, since everything he knew or suspected would be already on record in the files. He was then asked if he could give the name of any responsible person who knew of and could confirm this infantile habit of stuffing his bank statements into a drawer unread.

He could not, and that was the end. The duty of the Tri-bunal was to report; it had no power to decide criminal liabil-ity. So Alwyn was not immediately arrested. But he was bound to be put on trial with the public spitting at the Black Maria which carried him to court. The escape of Mornix was entirely due to the orders he had given, over-ruling Special Branch, and the evidence that he had prearranged the visit to What-combe Street was convincing.

You who knew him so well will always understand why he bolted while there was still time. Alwyn had the foolish pride of a man of honor which makes him retreat rather than fight when that honor is questioned. Whether he was right or wrong none of us can say. His behavior with his bank accounts was unbelievable for a responsible government servant. Officially unbelievable, I mean. Yet sheer, sober, human idiocy is the commonest thing in the world, and during the happy years I lived in England I was continually astounded by the serene eccentricities of my friends and neighbors. No doubt they said the same of me.

And here is something you don't know. I remember that when Alwyn was ten years old his mother insisted that he would be a poet — an opinion based on nothing at all but his obstinate belief in fairies. That imagination of his — the readiness to look beyond the factual — must have made him an outstanding security officer, but doesn't it also account for his refusal to face facts in private life? Money was just one of such facts. He treated it without respect because he loathed it.

I have of course an ulterior motive in allowing or persuading you to drag this unsavory business out into the light. You will have read the daily revelations of arrogance, dishonesty and contempt for Law in departments of our government, leaving us without even the illusion that there is honor among thieves. We in America are going through one of our periodical revolutions when we clean out the stables more thoroughly than any other country would ever dare. Because I know that, my pride in my country is unaffected. But now is the time to drive home the lesson that the end never justifies the means.

The Statement of Adrian Gurney

I

On that evening of July 1st which decided then and there the course of all my future life I was innocently waiting in my little box of an office for the arrival of my employer to sign the correspondence entrusted to me as personal assistant. There was one letter which I had typed and then signed with my own name, for the persistent exchanges of affection between Councillor Sokes and his latest immature tart were carried on through me. Herbert Sokes, I remember, was in his most poetical mood; he described in enthusiastic detail the charms and timidities which his little darling had artistically displayed during his last visit to London and his expectations for their next meeting. This remarkable correspondence which mixed depravity, fatherliness and even a dash of religion to taste suggested to me that he got as much pleasure from Miss Tacket's absence as he did from her presence.

Dangerous letters they would have been if Sokes had put his own name to them, but I willingly obliged him. I was a lost dog, accepting Sokes as my master and Caulby as my home.

It was a revolting town, developed by the railway in the eighteen seventies. Nine-tenths of it was composed of red brick houses, each with three front windows and a door. Gaiety was represented only in the frontage of the pubs, the most palatial being entirely faced by two different shades of mauve tiles; dignity, wherever required, was underlined by Gothic windows of stone or variegated brick. After so much solidity the mass Utopia of the High Street, lined by the glass and concrete of all the usual multiple stores, came as a relief.

Caulby was depressing but to be endured, for it meant to me a home and the possibility of a career. I gave it such affection as I could. A very different England it appeared from that which I had known up to the age of twelve, but I was obstinately determined to accept with open arms any and every aspect of my country.

My father farmed in Wiltshire. He was a man of dreams, almost a mystic in his feeling of union with the earth and with all the unknown cultivators of the past whose rolling green tombs and sacred stones littered parts of his land. They must always have felt their way by trial and error, and so very often did he. Long before maize was common in English gardens he took a chance with it, reckoning that it could be grown well enough in the soft valley of the Kennet and that he could not lose on an acre or two of his own chicken food with an expanding London market as a possible sideline. I never knew what report of miracle corn took him to Romania instead of the United States; it may have been the advice of the vicar whose brother imported caviar. At any rate, he returned home after eight weeks with a bushel of seed and a young Romanian wife as well. The maize showed a very small profit and the whirlwind marriage produced me.

Life, green and pleasant, might have so continued if my

13

adventurous father had not insisted on driving a tractor on too steep a slope where his neighbors would have been content to leave the tussocky grass alone or plough it up with horses. His widow tried to carry on alone. She was a merry, pretty woman, efficient too, and even in the market helped by everyone; but it was as if our too insular livestock would not respond to foreign care. Fowl pest and an outbreak of gid among the sheep finished her, and the sale of the farm hardly did more than pay the debts. She had no other profession and no way of providing for the pair of us, but in Romania there was still a resourceful family which appeared to be easily coping with communism.

In 1954 she returned home with me and soon married a consultant geologist, a jolly fellow who fully appreciated my difficulties and brought me up to get the best out of my adopted country: in fact to accept what must be accepted and enjoy whatever could be enjoyed. Having preserved with the utmost tact his reputation as a sound party member and being on excellent terms with Russian colleagues he got himself posted to Egypt to work on the Aswan Dam. Since my mother had recently died — a heart not equal to her gay vitality — he managed to take me with him. He had a theory that the dam was going to play merry hell with the Nile Delta and suggested that some young agronomists should take a look at the problem on the ground. As I was then at an admirable agricultural college — a keen student but in no way an expert — I was chosen to be one of the team. Family connections are as useful behind the Iron Curtain as anywhere else.

To me Egypt was the fabulous scene of British victories, wicked imperialists or not. But I found that I was not allowed to see much of the country or to mix freely with its people; the Russian colony was more closed and self-sufficient than the British had ever been. Boredom with the whole deadening system became intolerable. On an official visit to Cairo I

14

slipped away to the British Consulate where I presented my birth certificate.

Of course it was still far from plain sailing. Since I was close on nineteen I was entitled to my passport after details of my story had been confirmed, but I refused to have it sent to me for fear of compromising my sympathetic stepfather. So three months later I escaped — at least that was what I called my unauthorized dash to Cairo — and fortunately found my passport ready and waiting.

So there I was, unquestionably British but with no means of earning a living. The foreign merchants who would gladly have employed me had all been expelled; the native Egyptians had little use for a waif of dubious antecedents who could not speak Arabic. For two years I was a hanger-on of hotels and travel agencies, making just enough from small tips and split commissions to eat once a day and pay the rent on a bug-ridden room. There is no need to go into the shame and misery of it all. From this existence without a future or any chance of affording my passage to England I was rescued by the police who ran me in together with a few other forgotten, destitute British subjects. We were shipped home at our government's expense.

Due to my languages and do-anything appearance I landed a job as the lower sort of courier to a travel agency, which led me out of England almost as soon as I returned to it. For six months I stayed in Paris, attending incredulously to the stereotyped requirements of motor-coach tourists from the Midlands. In one such party was Herbert Sokes, demonstrating that he was just one of the boys though well able to afford greater comfort. I was useful to him — seeing to his personal tastes and, more important, ensuring his privacy — so he offered me a trial as personal assistant. The orphan from Egypt, who had the sense to say nothing of his embarrassing Romanian background, accepted gratefully. This was the stake in my own country which I wanted. Councillor Herbert Sokes, O.B.E, a small manufacturer of automobile accessories, seemed to me solid ground from which to climb the ladder of conventional living.

I spent two years in — or rather just outside — the factory of Sokes Ltd. Besides his managerial office Sokes had another, which he called the Parlor, where he received his private and political visitors. It was in a small cottage adjoining the factory with its own front door opening on to a quiet alley. I at first assumed that the most important piece of furniture in the Parlor was likely to be the comfortable couch. I was quite wrong. In his own community Herbert Sokes's private intrigues were all directed towards increasing his private capital.

This small-town boss is of no real importance to my story, but without him I cannot explain myself. He was a director of the local mortgage company and had a sleeping interest in an estate agency. As leader of the Conservative opposition on the Borough Council and a close friend — outside the council chamber — of the Labor chairman of the Housing Committee, he knew of all likely developments within the town. But his integrity was unquestionable. He always declared his interest, refusing to vote on any issue where private advantage might conflict with public service. Sokes was never corrupt and avoided any shadow of suspicion when he corrupted.

I thought I understood my employer and enjoyed our enigmatic relationship. He made a cheerful pretense of treating me as an unprincipled black sheep to whom anything might be confessed, and occasionally added to my small salary a cash bonus when I was bound to know a little — it was never everything — of the means by which a handsome profit had been secured. Sometimes I acted as runner between Councillor Sokes and his supposedly bitter opponent Alderman Gunsbotham. I was not shocked. My country-bred integrity had been overlaid by all I had observed since the age of twelve. What else could politicians be but crooks? Only newspapers

16

pretended to be horrified. For me the essential was that I had come home at last and that my affection for my employer was returned.

On that evening when he and I finally parted he did not follow his usual practice of approving or altering the private correspondence in my claustrophobic office but asked me to come into the Parlor. It was impossible to tell whether he was worried or not, for he kept up his Rotary and Committee manners with everyone except his wife — always jolly and never warm. His neat, oval face was a very clean-shaven mask, pale except where red and blue veins bore witness to the quantity of whisky and water which had to be consumed for the sake of good fellowship and which never noticeably affected him.

He waved me towards table and chair and poured me a drink. Himself sitting on the couch, he looked through the typed correspondence. His position somehow disassociated him from personal interest, as if he were running through family documents which only vaguely concerned him. He made no remark on three letters which I had been instructed to sign myself, one of which was the effusion to his washily depraved seventeen-year-old in Wandsworth.

"Good! Now there's one more little thing I want you to do for me, Mr. Gurney," he said.

He never addressed me as "Adrian." I approved, though observing that in other offices the use of Christian names was becoming common.

"All right, guv'nor! Let's have it!"

The office called him "Mr. Sokes" or "sir." "Guv'nor" was only used by the factory floor. I had picked it up before I was quite at home with all the subtleties of address and had then stuck to it. There seemed a slightly disreputable air about guv'nor which suited our intimate relationship.

"I need your receipt for that twelve hundred pounds. Just a formality. You'll never hear any more of it."

I was accustomed to handling cash for purchases or commitments in which the principal did not wish to appear. Another useful intermediary who could perform the most delicate disappearing tricks with bundles of notes was the local bookmaker. Len Shuffleton, Turf Accountant, fascinated me. In his own dealings with the public the man was scrupulously honest; otherwise he was a crook well up to Egyptian standards.

It was to him that I had paid, a month earlier, the sum of £1,200 in cash — an amount which suggested one thousand plus twenty percent commission. What Len had done with the thousand I strongly suspected. It had been paid to Alderman Gunsbotham for carrying his committee and party with him in an eloquent plea for the hard-won savings of the poor.

On the outskirts of Caulby were seventy acres of muddy land occupied by three struggling small-holders and their tumbledown cottages. Herbert Sokes and his dubious estate agency were after so promising a building site, but any move on their part to buy would have been instantly answered by a compulsory purchase order for Council housing at the low price of agricultural land, easily carried by the Labour majority.

To their astonishment Sokes himself proposed this compulsory purchase from the Conservative benches. The Labour councillors were disconcerted. They agreed with the motion; on the other hand it was their duty to vote against anything whatever proposed by Conservatives. Which way they would jump depended on their leader, Alderman Gunsbotham.

He spoke passionately against the hard-hearted motion of the Conservatives. Labour alone watched over the interests of the helpless. It was iniquitous to drive them out of their properties, bought with the miserable savings of workingmen, and force them to accept a price far too low to buy any other accommodation. So long as he and his great party were in control the land would never be bought compulsorily.

The result was that both parties emerged from the dispute

with honor and the plaudits of the local press. Gunsbotham had stood up nobly for the interests of the poor and secretly earned a thousand pounds for carrying his party with him. Sokes had reinforced his reputation for bluff honesty and — now that the Council had denied any intention of compulsory purchase — was free to buy the very contented small-holders out of their mud at the full market price and was holding the land for resale to the highest bidder.

Devoted servant though I was, I hesitated to give a receipt for money I had never had and I asked the guv'nor what he would do with it. Councillor Sokes laughed with his invariable geniality.

"Quite right to ask, Mr. Gurney! You're quite right! Well, it will go into the office safe and you can forget it."

"Not your personal safe?"

"The check you cashed for that twelve hundred was on the firm's account, not mine. So the firm must hold your receipt."

Something certainly had to be in the firm's safe for the auditors. I suggested charging it to advertising and said I thought I could fix the agent. He did not respond. He seemed to resent the hint of partnership.

"I understand that you wanted to buy a house. The firm is very generous to its employees."

"It would be like you, guv'nor," I said after thinking this over. "If I really needed the money, I believe you'd let me have it. But where's the house?"

"You are negotiating the down payment. I'll deal with that through our mortgage friends."

So he could probably; but it was the devil of a lot to ask. Affection insisted that Sokes would never let me down, while instinct was strongly against signing anything more than amorous correspondence.

"Well, if you are sure there's no other way out . . ." I began.

"It's the easiest — a straightforward receipt backdated.

Sign it and you won't be the loser. The last thing we want is any unpleasantness."

Unpleasantness. One could take that in several ways. I assumed my employer was referring to the fact that the political maneuvers had left a slight but increasing stink. Sokes urgently wanted that receipt so that he could challenge rumors by throwing open bank accounts to anyone who wished to inspect them.

"I've never been the loser yet, guv'nor," I answered gratefully, "and I know you well enough to be sure I won't lose any of your respect if I just want to give it some thought."

"My respect?" Sokes asked incredulously.

"Well, I mean — as a businessman would you do it yourself?"

His face slightly reddened. When he was annoyed, it was a reaction he could not control. Again I saw that he did not relish any parallel between himself and his personal assistant.

"Under the circumstances I should."

"Perhaps that is what I haven't understood, guv'nor — the circumstances."

"They could be, Mr. Gurney, that you forged my signature on a check for twelve hundred pounds. But we'll forget that. I want our relations to continue just as they are."

I replied that he couldn't be serious, that Len Shuffleton could witness I paid the money to him.

"You went straight from the bank to a bookmaker with twelve hundred pounds of the firm's money?"

I fully appreciated the threat. In Shuffleton's books were lost credit bets in the name of Adrian Gurney though they didn't amount to much more than thirty quid and Len had never yet pressed for settlement. That account could be altered to show that I had made a losing bet of twelve hundred on some favorite which was dead certain to win and had not. I doubted if Sokes when he instructed me to cash the check and take the money around to Shuffleton had ever intended an accusation of forgery; on the other hand he always left himself a way of retreat. I remembered noticing that Sokes's signature on the check had been in some way too careful, too deliberate. Suppose he had written it slowly over a tracing?

The right game was to calm him down. Anyone, after all, would try to avoid losing the good will of a useful, very confidential employee.

"In a hole, guv'nor?" I asked sympathetically. "But surely to God there's a way out without wanting to fix me?"

"Want it? Of course I don't! What I want is for you to do what you're told and forget about it."

"I'll forget about it all right. That's part of the job. No reason for any embarrassment between us."

"That is why I chose you, Mr. Gurney. I should have some trouble in finding anyone in this part of the world quite as obliging as you."

The implication was a savage shock. To Sokes, then, I was an unscrupulous, Anglicized wog. And wasn't it a fact? Like all cruel accusations which are ten percent true, it immediately became ninety percent true to the guilty conscience at the receiving end. My own picture of myself, when caught up in Sokes's deals and diversions, had been one of a loyal, cynically tolerant retainer. To a young man intimately acquainted with corruption — in Romania subtle and involving status rather than cash, in Egypt considered more entertaining than regrettable — there was nothing exceptional about Sokes either as a businessman or a local politician.

The bitterest disappointment of all was to find that Sokes had no affection for me. His lack of shame in my presence was because I didn't count. I was just a private pimp to be sacrificed when necessary in the certainty that I was too defenseless to do any damage and would not be believed if I tried.

I told him that he would not get his receipt.

"I shall, Mr. Gurney," he said, "when you think over the alternative."

21

I walked back to my depressing lodgings in a fury of agitation. I could not bring myself even to stop at my usual pub for a drink and a game of darts, feeling that the geniality of my acquaintances might be, like my employer's, a mere opening and shutting of the mouth. The sudden discovery that Sokes despised me shattered all self-confidence.

Unable to bear the prospect of my landlady's chops and tea, I bought a bottle of cheap red wine and plunged into a grubby little Italian restaurant off the High Street. The front of it was normally occupied by young criminals and their admiring friends; at the back was a room where the few foreign workers at Caulby were made welcome if they chose to drop in for a meal. I went there seldom, for my enjoyment of the place worried me, as if a disloyalty to my English birth.

I had dreaded the loneliness of my room, but loneliness at my table was that of the observer, alive and calculating. Veal and spaghetti, wine and harsh coffee helped to smooth out the two years of Caulby into some sort of perspective.

Would Sokes really go so far as to accuse me of forging that check and betting on a certainty with the money? Assuming that he had some very good reason to be alarmed, it looked as if he might. And then any magistrate would decide there was a case to be answered. What have you to say for yourself? Your Worship, he told me to pay that twelve hundred to the bookie and he made his signature on the check look as if it had been forged. But Mr. Sokes and Mr. Shuffleton deny anything so ridiculous. Mr. Sokes does not bet and you do. Moreover both these gentlemen, one a very prominent citizen of our town, have given evidence that their only contacts are on the management of the Old People's Home to which both have been good enough to give much of their valuable time.

Bail or remanded in custody for further inquiries? The inquiries when answered would not be helpful. No character reference from any employer. Earned a dubious living on the streets of Cairo and Paris. And then out would come my very private secret: that I had been brought up in Communist Romania. If I refused to give that receipt and Sokes carried out his threat I was going to be for all my life a suspect foreigner who had been in trouble with the law without a trade or any qualifications.

Right, then! Could I counterattack and put the screws on the guv'nor? Of all I suspected how much could be proved? Most of my knowledge of his dealings was composed of direction pointers, unmistakable to the personal assistant but pretty worthless to an outside investigator. The bribe to Alderman Gunsbotham was typical. I had no conclusive evidence. I could be indicted for criminal slander. No, I had nothing of genuine interest to the police, nothing even that the *Caulby Herald*, with the law of libel brooding over the editorial office, would dare to print.

Another thought leapt out of my bottle of wine. Sokes could have covered up that bribe to Gunsbotham in half a dozen different ways. The receipt he required me to sign was not essential. So his threat of prosecution was for general use against a potential blackmailer, intended to hang over my head if I opened my mouth about any dirty deals, past or future. It bound me into perpetual slavery — possibly quite profitable but leaving me always at the mercy of my employer. It was no wonder that he had resented any suggestion of partnership when he had all along considered his personal assistant on a par with a seller of filthy postcards.

So Caulby and Sokes were exploded, leaving me among the fall-out a free man without any ties of interest or affection. Suppose I just bolted and restarted a career somewhere else? But that would be most convenient for Sokes. A sudden disappearance was strong evidence, if it were needed, that the twelve hundred pounds had gone with me.

Suicide was another way out. I found the thought of poor Adrian stark and cold most touching. Also it would put Sokes and Len Shuffleton on the spot, for it would certainly occur to the police that one of the neatest ways to explain a shortage of cash was to blame someone who was no longer alive. A pity that one couldn't kill oneself without the inconvenience of dying!

Weary of me arguing with me — though the argument was becoming more genial — I finished the bottle and opened the evening paper. And there at the bottom of the front page was my answer! There, thanks to Uncle Vasile, was my pretended, pathetic, embarrassing suicide if only I had the impudence and could think quickly enough.

The front page before my eyes, short of a murder or some photogenic débutante in trouble with her parents, was playing up the mystery of one of the first Russian trawler fleets to pass through the English Channel. South Coast towns, wrote the reporter, would be able to see the lights of the fleet. What were the Russian intentions and was the Channel becoming a mere highway to the North Sea? He then quoted a Russian Embassy press handout which stated flatly that their intentions were to fish, that next day the fleet would be out of the Baltic on its way to the African grounds and that it would pass through the Straits of Dover between two and three A.M. the following night.

I was at once reminded of my mother's brother, Vasile. Social revolution, bribery and old friendship with the Port Captain of Sulina had made of him a trawler skipper in the Black Sea. He was quite content with his lot. Even when he had been a young man of fashion in pre-war Bucarest his chief interest — when not messing about with girls — had been messing about in boats. He was prepared to accept any political regime which actually paid him to do so.

On his rare visits to Bucarest he invariably called on us. My mother and stepfather welcomed him with fixed grins as the family curse, but I liked him. He would gather me into his arms, stinking of fish and vodka — the true breath, I thought, of ocean — and prophesy that he would see me through the storms of life. In a sense, by his mere existence, he did.

One of my duties in Paris was to use my languages in order to extract money for nothing from Communist tourists. While I was loosing off my spiel to a mixed bunch of them walking up the Rue Pigalle I was suddenly embraced with a roar of delight by Uncle Vasile. It turned out that he was something of a Stakhanovite; he had caught more Black Sea herrings in one season than any other skipper. Being a staunch and reliable party member he was rewarded by a free trip to Paris — ostensibly for an international conference on sizes of mesh. The Fishing Board offered to send his wife too. He had a job wriggling out of that. He said the hardest trial for the keen worker was not tough, daily routine but the irrational and inconvenient bursts of generosity.

For two weeks my uncle compelled me to spend all my free time with him, slipping his official guides who were only too glad to get rid of him. For once I was well fed, but he was far from the romantic figure of my boyhood. Sober, he could talk of nothing but fishing. Drunk, he had an engaging habit of putting on his navigation lights — red wine in the left hand, green chartreuse in the right — and proceeding around any restaurant under power. When I finally saw Uncle Vasile pushed into the train and said goodbye to the boot dangling from the window, I knew as much about the Romanian fishing industry as the Board which ran it — not enough, that is, to catch a fish, but quite enough to write a report.

Inspired by the evening paper which acted like a detonator on wine and thoughts of suicide, I reckoned that Ionel Petrescu, dockside clerk to the trawler base at Sulina, due for promotion and allowed a trip with the Russian Baltic fleet to see how they did things, was going to be a difficult character to unmask. Petrescu's education would be my own between 1954 and Egypt. Between 1961 and 1965 I would have to

uneventful career as a clerk, substantiated by plenty
~~of~~ details gathered from Uncle Vasile. If interrogated
~~by a~~ Romanian, I could pass with flying colors. A naval
~~petty~~ officer with some knowledge of trawling would be far
more dangerous. However, the impersonation of a refugee
could not be a serious criminal offense, and I could probably
carry it on for a month or two before I was exposed and
became a comedy pet of newspapers. By then Councillor
Bloody Sokes, O.B.E., would have run for cover.

The temptation to a desperate young man was irresistible.
But how to get rid of Adrian Gurney? Walking into the sea
was not very convincing since I had to reappear from the sea.
Yet the sea it had to be; nowhere else could one vanish without the police becoming suspicious about the absence of any
corpse. What of driving my old car over the edge of something? A cliff which I had seen on a short holiday in the Isle of
Purbeck might do. I remembered an approach over turf and
deep water a hundred feet below. But why isn't the driver
found drowned in his seat? Well, he was not killed by the
impact and found a little late that he wanted to live after all;
so he fought his way out of the car and was carried away by
the tide. Not bad, provided there was convincing evidence. If
that problem was worked out all the rest looked possible.

What sort of a letter to leave behind? It had to sound
lonely, frustrated and balmy enough to fool a psychiatrist. I
considered telling the truth about Sokes, Gunsbotham and
Len Shuffleton and raving, as neurotically as my pen could
manage, that I was revolted by a world in which a harmless,
young employee could be so betrayed. But that was a blunt,
provincial sort of revenge and it might fall flat. A subtler,
more Latin stab was needed which would fester in Sokes's
reputation for years and could never quite be scarred over.

With the last of the bottle genius for once sat on my shoulder. That, by God, would set the cat among the pigeons! Any
competent detective constable could get the truth out of

Sokes's detestable young floozy in ten minutes. And then Sokes would lie. The possible combinations of a puzzled police and a frantic Sokes were almost infinite.

I went home and composed my sad, last letter, to which I added a P.S.

Please break the news gently to Miss Julie Tacket, 3 Pokes Buildings, Wandsworth, and tell her I still love her.

My passport and a few private papers were packed into a knapsack together with a windbreaker and shorts for the hearty, nameless hiker I would be after the death of Adrian Gurney. At the bottom of the knapsack were Petrescu's clothes: a pair of trousers, a tattered shirt and a holed sweater which I had worn on the voyage home from Egypt; they had been bought secondhand in Bucarest and still had the labels of pre-war shops. Then, with that deadly farewell letter in my pocket, I filled up the tank of my car, leaving an impression of hopeless melancholy with the garage man, and drove off very cautiously through the night, taking six hours to cover a hundred and sixty miles. At three A.M. I turned off the Swanage-Kingston road and then lurched along a gated, rutted field track without lights. In a quarter of an hour I was on the headland, and a damned awful, Gadarene Swine sort of place it was, with a sharp slope of slippery turf running down to darkness and the crump of unseen breakers.

My next move was to smash the rear window from the inside to show the police that the missing driver, losing too late his taste for suicide, had escaped through it. Any of the side windows might be resting on the bottom but it seemed unlikely that the rear window would be, owing to the weight of the engine and air trapped in the car. I broke it with the starting handle, taking great care to see that none of the fragments fell on the turf, and made a hole big enough for a desperate, drowning man to get through — an improbable achievement but just possible if the window had already been damaged by the fall.

Taking off my coat, I sawed it back and forth over the jagged remains of the window. What microscopes could or couldn't reveal after a car had been under water I had not the faintest idea, but if they could detect threads and some blood I'd feed it to them with pleasure. I found myself incapable of making a shallow cut on my arm. Furious with this squeamishness I scraped too savagely on the glass and had to bandage myself quickly with a handkerchief.

All well so far. Knapsack out of the car. Starting handle on the back seat. Farewell letter in a cleft stick driven hard down into the turf. And now for the real job which I did not like at all. It would obviously be more convincing to send the car over the edge in gear than in neutral — proof that I had been inside it and had not merely taken off the brake and given it a shove from behind. I drove to the final slope in low, shifted up once and jumped out through the open door. I managed to slam it shut but at the cost of sliding down after the car, clutching frantically at turf too smooth to stop me, until a patch of wild thyme and a rabbit hole pulled me up. I heard the car hit the water and clung to solidity, amazed that people could ever find the courage to kill themselves.

Changing into the shorts and windbreaker, I strode off over the Purbeck Hills to Studland at a good four miles an hour. The light was growing and it was essential to get clear before dawn without attracting attention or allowing anyone to record a memory of me. After dozing for a few hours in the sand hills and shaving off a dark, furry moustache of which I had been youthfully proud I took a train from Bournemouth to London — and to a much-needed lunch — inconspicuous among other early holiday-makers.

A map of the Kent coast suggested that a very reasonable place for a refugee to swim ashore was the beach east of Folkestone below the railway line to Dover. It would have to be thoroughly reconnoitered but looked the sort of place where a few enthusiastic swimmers might appear early and not a soul would be wandering about in the small hours of the morning. I needed nothing else but darkness and a trowel.

The railway put me within walking distance of my objective — cautious walking, for there was always an outside chance of Ionel Petrescu being recognized by someone who had seen Adrian Gurney the evening before. By half past nine when dusk was falling I was among bushes and tumbled chalk above the beach. That was an unexpected bonus; the map had not indicated such very good cover where I could lie and watch. On the other hand the time of high water was as inconvenient as could be. No pretense of being stranded high and dry at the top of the tide was possible. I would have to keep moving up the beach with the waves until I was found.

After dark I changed into those old relics of Egypt and Bucarest and buried my passport with all other possessions, cutting out a square of turf, carefully replacing it, and scattering the surplus earth down a slope of rubble. I was oddly relieved by my new identity, accepting with surprise that the last two years in Caulby had been an utter waste — a planting of myself in soil where my roots could never take hold, where my pride of birth would have rotted away, and where a return to that agricultural life of which I dreamed would become less and less likely as time passed. Some day I hoped to come back as a self with an assured future and to recover that passport well wrapped in cellophane, its tomb marked by a seemingly casual pattern of lumps of chalk. Meanwhile Adrian Gurney must wait for the day of resurrection. I was well aware that I had condemned myself to a purgatory of self-discipline, but had not the sense to foresee what could be waiting for me.

A little before dawn I went down to the beach and walked along the water's edge, where my footprints would be washed out, until I came to a blackness between groyne and weed-covered rock. There I lay down on the sand, crawling up the empty beach just ahead of the tide. That became too risky in the growing light. I had to allow the arcs of foam to ripple over me and to endure the cold until somebody discovered the pitiable bit of flotsam.

"Oo, ma! 'Ere's a fella!"

Mr. Petrescu opened an eye under the lifeless hank of black hair which the Channel waves were washing back and forth across his forehead and thanked God that at last he had been noticed. He was as cold and miserable as if he had really swum to shore from outside the three-mile limit. He could only see a pair of unattractive shins patterned — for it was eight A.M. on a cold July morning — in red and blue belonging to some intrepid Britannia ready to rule the waves regardless of temperature or perhaps leaping at any respectable opportunity for taking off her clothes.

"You come away from there, Marlene!" an older voice screamed. "Don't yer touch it! 'Elp!"

Some more before-breakfast swimmers gathered around me. I did not dare raise my head to see how large my public was. They on their part were content to stare and shiver. The rising tide washed the weed of the groyne to and fro across my back, and I did not, I hoped, look as if artificial respiration would do much good. So long as no worthy citizen was tempted to try it, it was hard to see that my breathing was fairly normal.

All the same, I was near my limit of endurance. I reminded myself that if I had really swum in from the Russian fishing fleet I should be feeling a lot worse. But heroism is comparative. An office worker, far from fit after the sunless sky and fried chops of Caulby, was just as entitled to be sorry for himself after mild exposure and two nearly sleepless nights as the imaginary tough trawlerman who had fought the sea and dropped exhausted on that democratic sand.

At last a policeman appeared. The game was on.

I allowed myself to be pulled up the beach and turned over. My excited heart was beating far too strongly for me to sham unconsciousness, so I sat up with a jerk and squawked convincingly. The constable and the onlookers jumped back startled. I dragged myself limply to the policeman's sandy boots and kissed them.

The point which had most bothered me was how much English I should have. Fluent? That would take some explaining. None? But what a handicap during the months when I was supposed to be learning it. This first meeting with the Law instinctively settled the problem. Hardly any English had to be the answer. I hesitated between "I escape" and "Me escape" and chose the latter.

"That's all right, mate," the constable said. "You won't come to no harm here."

I felt my pulse pounding and the blood buzzing in my head. I did not try to control the faint. A bit of luck, I thought, as I passed out.

I was being wrapped in a blanket by two ambulance men. Some member of the obliging public was declaring:

"Saw him swim, I did! Saw his head out there like I see you!"

An independent witness to something which had not happened was too valuable to be lost.

"Why no fetch boat?" I demanded indignantly.

"Thought you was a Channel swimmer."

"In his clothes?" somebody asked.

"Couldn't see no more than his head."

The policeman, pulling out his notebook, asked what time that was.

"An hour ago, might be. Saw him from my bedroom window."

"It was my Marlene as found 'im," said the mother of the legs jealously.

Still dizzy though I was, I marked carefully that I had been seen swimming in broad daylight. My intended story was that I had swum ashore in darkness and collapsed on reaching the

31

beach, had collapsed in fact several times as I dragged myself higher up the sand with the advancing tide.

This suspiciously weak bit of fiction was no longer necessary. The irresistible desire of the anonymous public to become a named individual in the news had vastly improved it. Mr. John Fulton of 12 Reservoir Road, Heaton Mersey, Manchester — he had given his name aggressively to police and onlookers — had seen me off shore about seven A.M. I did not appear to be in difficulties and Mr. Fulton had thought no more about it. More accurate were two observers who claimed to have noticed me stuck between rock and groyne about seven-thirty but at the time had not recognized the washed-up lump as a body. That was much what I wanted. I had intended the pathetically draped seaweed to keep me on ice — and, by God it had! — until there were a few early risers around to witness the near tragedy.

As I was lifted into the ambulance I thought it had been a most convincing defection to the West, well worth being frozen and half drowned since first light. To be rescued by some knowledgeable local fisherman soon after I had dropped into position would not have been so satisfactory as my discovery by holiday-makers of such solid character that they were hopping around the beach before breakfast.

The ambulance decanted me into a comfortable hospital bed, where the house physician, speaking very slowly and clearly, told me that I was a brave fellow and that there seemed to be nothing wrong with me which a day's rest would not put right. He gave orders that I was to have all the breakfast I could eat and remain undisturbed till evening when the police would want to chat with me, but I should not be afraid of that. Relaxing with a cigarette after porridge, bacon and eggs I decided that I was not — not yet at any rate. Then gloriously warm I drifted into sleep and dreamed uneasily that I was winding an elongated Herbert Sokes into a forest of seaweed.

I woke up in the afternoon to find the doctor leaning over me.

"How are we feeling now?"

I opened my mouth, swallowed the perfect English which nearly came out, and instead pointed a finger down my gullet.

"Hongry!"

"What, again? Well, let's have a look at you."

Doctor and nurse spent half an hour on my lungs, heart and blood pressure. I was alarmed lest they might find something really wrong with me. I had quite enough to do watching the road without listening to the engine.

"We'll keep him here tonight, just in case," the doctor said. "But there's no reason why he should not get up and talk to the police."

In hospital dressing gown and pajamas I was escorted to a waiting room where I was handed over to a police inspector and a tall, worn, aggressive civilian who turned out to be a Russian interpreter and of a type to justify revolution. It seemed best to deflate the fellow, so I just smiled, nodded, and looked alternately obstinate and intelligent in the wrong places. After the Russian had worked himself into a temper with this illiterate peasant or probable spy he gave up.

"It r-r-refuses to say anything," he reported.

"You'll have to tell us all about it some time, you know," said the Inspector kindly.

"Me Romanian — spik — no — Rush," I brought out with an effort.

The interpreter looked a fool. The Inspector hid a grin. I burst into rapid French which I spoke with the lifeless accent of any middle-class, educated Romanian. No catching me out there. Any knowledgeable linguist would spot me at once as coming from somewhere at the eastern end of the Mediterranean.

I told my story: how, seeing the gay lights of Dover and Folkestone across the calm water, I had quietly and impulsively slipped into the sea from the *Nadezhda Krupskaya* and swum ashore. It was the only ship of which I knew the name. She was the mother ship, and there had been a photograph of her in the evening paper. The Inspector took it all down. Evidently he understood French, though he was unwilling to speak it. The Russian did the questioning. His manners did not improve. He made it clear that he despised all Romanians, white, red or indifferent.

The next day I went to jail pending further inquiries. It seemed to me no worse than a bad hotel on a wet day — always assuming that it could be treated as a temporary inconvenience. To be compelled to accept it as home for many months — which had been more than a possibility when dealing with a shameless Sokes — would have been an appalling fate. I wondered why punishment by boredom should be considered more humane than quicker tortures.

I was photographed and my fingerprints were taken. That could be the end of the game if Adrian Gurney's prints were also collected from any convenient surface in his Caulby lodgings; but the risk, I felt, was small. Caulby police were notable for the excellent organization of dances and frequent changes of Chief Constable. In a plain case of suicide they were not likely to sprinkle powder on toothglasses.

I was happier about the photograph in which I had managed to pose as proud, sullen and solid. This should be a fair picture of a foreign trawlerman with a nasty hangover, not very like a smiling youth with dark moustache and hair falling over one eyebrow — which was how I would appear if there were any snaps of me available. The only official photograph of Adrian Gurney would be the duplicate of his passport photo. That, if fished out from Foreign Office archives, showed an exhausted, undernourished outcast, all eyes, with the artificial smirk insisted upon by a cheap Cairo photographer.

My second interrogation was by a courteous Romanian

34

exile. Preliminary chatting showed that he was devoted to every stream and village of his own Wallachia. He said frankly that he could not see why a man who was neither rich nor in danger of arrest should want to leave it. This quite sincere approach had a cunning all of its own, for it forced the refugee to show how white-hot his indignation really was.

I decided against any indignation at all.

"If I didn't escape, I should have had to get married," I said.

"You had — well, anticipated matrimony?"

"Regularly on Tuesday evenings. And she was a very earnest, trusted party member."

"Flashing eyes and economics?"

"Exactly. So one longed to infect her with the taint of frivolity."

"You were successful?"

"Well, occasionally," I replied, grossly exaggerating a youthful affair in Aswan days. "But the trouble was that she was growing suspicious. And she wasn't a girl to scratch or throw things. I could see her slapping a report on her boss's desk and then I might find myself with a ten years' sentence merely because I'd enjoyed a charming Saturday between two Tuesdays."

"So you very wisely chose freedom," the Romanian agreed. "But why England?"

"France was too far to swim."

"I shouldn't say that to the Security Officer if I were you."

"Democracy, you think?"

"Democracy, certainly."

"Will he believe it?"

"No. But it's the right thing to say. Mention your perverse taste for political girlfriends of course!"

"It's very good of you to trust me."

"I trust the national character, my dear Mr. Petrescu. Communism will do very well for Bulgars, but for a Romanian it is inhuman. And now be good enough to tell me what a clerk from the Sulina fisheries was doing on a Russian trawler!"

I had my story ready for that question. I invented a cousin who was a marine biologist engaged in experimental fish farming. The cousin wanted to study Atlantic species and had no difficulty in getting permission to join the Russian fleet. At my urgent request, I had been taken along as interpreter.

"But you said you did not understand Russian."

"Well, what would you have said when faced with something like a Tsarist colonel with a knout? I am Romanian and proud of it."

"Where did you learn Russian?"

"In college."

I was on safe ground at last for I could talk of my education as it had been and as it would have continued if I had not gone to Egypt — which of course I never mentioned. The interview resolved itself into a pleasant chat that might — if there had been anything to drink — equally well have taken place in a Bucarest café.

His report released me from jail. I was put up at a hostel and provided with clothes at government expense. Two days later I was escorted to London and underwent a further and very lengthy interrogation, conducted this time partly in Russian and partly in French by a cordial Englishman who appeared satisfied, assured me that I would find nothing but good will, and wished me luck.

I was indeed impressed by the good will. A simple, furnished room was found me in the house of a French-speaking landlady and work which allowed me to keep my own hours and to feel of service to my true country. I was employed by the Institute of Foreign Affairs to translate magazine articles from Russian and Romanian into French. The librarian to whom I delivered my fair copies explained that they were required for educational departments of the EEC. That was the reason why the translations were not directly made into English. It seemed odd, but who was I to question it or have suspicions?

I joined an English class for immigrants to which I had been recommended by the police, but dropped the lessons as soon as I discovered that nobody was interested in my presence or absence; it was too much of a strain to keep up sham ignorance and a consistently bad accent. What I had not foreseen was my loneliness, except for casual contacts in restaurants or on the street. Patience, I told myself, was the only remedy. I had only to stick it out for a few more weeks and then I would be free to slide off into rural England and vanish.

Of Sokes and Caulby I knew nothing and was too cautious to make inquiries. There had been short paragraphs in one evening and two morning papers reporting the suicide of Adrian Gurney with a mention of the car but nothing about the motive. Evidently the suicide of an insignificant clerk was not news so long as the police kept the more puzzling features to themselves. My past must have come out as soon as Sokes stated that he had met his personal assistant in Paris. Therefore, I must have a passport, and reference to the Foreign Office would produce my history. But it seemed most unlikely that the routine answer to a police inquiry, perhaps dealt with by a clerk on a printed form, could lead to anyone spotting the possible connection between Gurney and Petrescu.

At any rate, all danger at Caulby would be over by now and Sokes's accounts in faultless order. The police, helped by some ingenious psychiatrist, might well decide that Adrian Gurney, frustrated outcast from Egypt and the streets of Paris, had been so upset by reading and signing his employer's love letters that he had suffered from the delusion that he himself was the lover and Sokes his powerful rival.

In spite of loneliness I was comforted by a feeling that I was never isolated from my fellows. Strangers in pubs would invite me to have a drink. Occasionally on the street people would ask me the time or — excusing themselves politely — the way to some street of which I had never heard. I put this down to something attractive about my face or perhaps an unaggressive bearing. After all, if you want to know the way or the time you have a choice of dozens of passersby and you choose unconsciously to appeal to the chap who looks least occupied and reasonably obliging. It seemed to my inexperienced mind a sort of compliment.

After six weeks the translation job dried up. I was told that for the present there were no suitable documents, that when there were any the library would get in touch with me and that meanwhile I should apply to my nearest Labour Exchange for work. The Exchange offered only manual labor but could not compel me to accept it; they advised me to take more trouble with my English if I wanted an office job. I was broke, worried and came to the conclusion that my face showed it, for the flattering casual contacts had become noticeably less.

I was wasting an afternoon — from the business point of view — in the National Portrait Gallery when I was joined by a well-dressed, obviously cultured citizen in his late forties. He remarked pleasantly that the typical English face had not changed much since the eighteenth century. I guessed that he himself was not English though his accent was perfect. After we had exchanged a few commonplaces he asked me what country I came from. When I replied that I was Romanian he broke enthusiastically into the language and we went at it like a couple of long-lost exiles. He was very free with information about himself, giving his name as Marghiloman of an old political family. He had escaped, he said, in the short interim between the liberation of the country by the Russians and the final takeover when the Iron Curtain came down; now that things were much easier, he had no trouble in corresponding with relations and was on friendly terms with the personnel of the London Embassy. He believed he could safely go back for a long stay whenever he liked.

On my part I did not tell the story of how I had arrived in England. Although Petrescu had only been news for a day, he might remember and draw me into difficult explanations. So I left my past vague, allowing him to think that my family lived in Paris and I had received special permission to join them there.

We got on splendidly and I was impressed by his general air of sophistication and his courtesy to the much younger man. In some ways I was still very simple. I had certainly shown a lot of panicky ingenuity in my own affairs but had rushed all my fences without stopping to think what might be on the other side. Looking back, I find my mixture of low cunning and overconfidence exactly like that of a growing boy.

We strolled across Trafalgar Square together and settled down at a quiet corner table in the saloon bar of a nearby pub. He appeared fascinated by the stories I could tell him, mostly humorous, of life under the present regime and relations with the Russians.

"It sounds as if you spoke Russian," he said.

"I do. Fluently but not very well."

He then hesitated as if thinking something over and deciding at last to take the plunge.

"Would you do something for me? Frankly, it is for them. But there's nothing whatever which need bother your conscience."

I asked him what it was. He replied that he wanted a message delivered. He could ask anybody to do it — or anybody who was not in an official position — but to carry conviction the messenger should be an obvious foreigner from Eastern Europe. A Romanian would do perfectly.

Carrying messages for Russians was too much even for my sweet innocence. I told him that I did not like it at all, but if he cared to give me the details I would at least listen.

"It's about that rat Alwyn Rory. He was clever enough to get clear and is safely in Moscow."

I had read of the escape of Lieutenant Mornix from 42 Whatcombe Street just before leaving Caulby. It must have increased the profits of the daily press to such an extent that they could afford to turn down advertisements. The story had everything — fornication in high places, spies a-spying, committees a-sitting, a minister resigning and the disappearance of Alwyn Rory, a civil servant belonging to MI5. Newspapers insisted that he had escaped to Russia, but the Russians had never claimed that he did.

"How do you know he's in Moscow?"

"Because I was at school with the First Secretary of the Romanian Embassy and we have kept up our friendship. On politics we agree to differ."

"It seems to me you'd be the perfect double agent," I said. He ignored the silly brashness of the remark.

"Yes, I am — if you mean just explaining one side to the other. So my friend entrusted to me a message for Rory's nearest relation — an aunt whom he is very fond of. He is anxious that she should know he is alive and that she should have his address. No harm in that, is there? The man can do no more damage to us."

I admitted rather reluctantly that it might be a kindly thing to do even if Rory did not deserve it.

"But naturally they don't want to risk sending it through the post or telephoning. They have to deny Rory's presence in Russia for the moment. Later on, of course, they'll let it leak through the correspondents of the London papers. Now, I wondered if you would go down and give her the address in person. You have enough English for that and you need say nothing at all about yourself. If a question of your bona fides comes up and she gets some Russian-speaking friend to test you, you'll pass."

"If the message is just an address and no more . . ." I began.

"I'll show it to you."

He pulled out an unsealed envelope and gave it to me. Inside was nothing but the name Alwyn Rory and a Moscow address.

"I shouldn't expect you to do it for nothing," he said.

I was a little unhappy about that; but his whole explanation sounded open and simple and I could see no way in which handing over the address might harm my country. In the very unlikely event of running into trouble I could always say I had been asked to deliver an envelope by a Romanian friend, a Mr. Marghiloman. That would only reinforce my identity as Ionel Petrescu. Besides, it seemed very possible that our own security people knew all about Marghiloman and were humane enough to allow a message to go through to the aunt. No doubt my reasoning was also affected by the fact that I was broke.

"I want you to establish good relations with Mrs. Hilliard," he went on. "To do that you might have to stay down there a day or two. So you had better take fifty pounds in case of unforeseen expenses. And when you come back you might tell me how you got on — whether she was ashamed or just maintaining Rory's innocence against the odds or perhaps pro-Russian. Suppose we meet here a week from today, same time?"

He gave me Mrs. Hilliard's address but said little more about her beyond the fact that she was a widow in her fifties and had had strong left-wing sympathies in her youth. She lived in South Devon at a house called Cleder's Priory in the village of Molesworthy.

I took his fifty and the envelope and went home. I must emphasize that I had nothing against Romania — except that it was not my country — and this very typical Romanian reminded me in some way of my stepfather, also a very pleasant, persuasive character ready to appreciate both sides of any intrigue. However, I have to admit a humiliating resemblance to the ingenuous American sitting alone in a foreign café and welcoming some highly respectable stranger of polished man-

41

ners who entertains him in his own language and offers to give him an option on the site of the Eiffel Tower.

Molesworthy was below the southern edge of Dartmoor. I took a train down to Totnes and then had a three-hour bus journey over a distance which a stout hearted walker could have covered in the same time. I had never realized that so many railways in Devon had been closed, thus returning country life, for those too old or too poor to drive, to the conditions of the eighteenth century.

I got off at Buckland and trailed along from signpost to signpost until I arrived at Molesworthy. I inspected three or four likely abodes for a widow, but none of them was called Cleder's Priory; so I went into the pub for a pint of bitter. It was just past opening time and the bar of the Crown and Thistle was empty. In reply to my inquiry the landlord said Cleder's Priory was lower down the valley, and added:

"You'll be the new Portuguese butler Mrs. Hilliard is expecting, I dare say?"

That seemed a handy excuse for my presence, so in my most grotesque English I allowed him to think that I had come down to be interviewed. Marghiloman had not given me the impression that Mrs. Hilliard was the sort of person to have butlers and I had expected that she lived quite modestly in some pretty village house.

"Is rich? True?" I asked.

"Well, not what you'd call stinking rich. Too well liked for that she is. She's got money all right, but she'll help anyone any time. Sporting old girl, too. Master of Hounds. It ain't what they call a fashionable pack, but we has our fun. And it's a damn shame that the married couple who worked for her left her like that."

"Zey 'ave a bust-up?"

"Dunno. But it was all along of her nephew. Well, you might as well know it now as later. He's that Rory which let the spy escape. I'd never have believed it of him and I don't. A real gentleman he was. I remember as once Mrs. Hilliard had just taken on my brother as whipper-in and I wanted to go out to see if he were any good, but I couldn't because the missus was away in Plymouth looking after her mother who was took ill as always when 'twas inconvenient. 'Don't you bother, Jack,' Mr. Rory says. 'I'll look after the bar and you can have my Sherry-and-Bitters' — lovely hunter he was! — 'so you don't break your bleeding neck trying to keep up with your brother on that damn screw of yours.' "

I had to look blank at all this rush of West Country talk, though God knows it was gloriously familiar, and got the conversation back to the vanished married couple.

"Worst snobs I ever knew! Always telling you how they'd worked for Lady Slingemup or some such name. And what do you suppose they did when the police and worse began snooping around here? They upped and cleared off! And if you get the job I hope you'll see that Mrs. Hilliard has the service she deserves. And you'll find we don't care whether a man's a Portugoose or a Chinaman so long as he's a sweet, easy bloke. You married?"

I said I wasn't but could do as much as any woman and better than most. That seemed to amuse him. He slapped me on the shoulder and assured me I'd get a good job easily in Kingsbridge or Salcombe if the old girl didn't like me.

Cleder's Priory was a gem of a seventeenth-century house, compact and ornate with parkland running up to the front door and a walled garden which looked as if it was all that remained of a much vaster one. I recognized that because our own farmhouse had stood in pasture. My father could not afford to keep up more than the kitchen garden and the fruit on its walls.

I rang the bell which Mrs. Hilliard answered herself. She was a very imposing personage in her middle fifties getting on for six feet tall, though some of that may have been made up by a mass of white hair almost as towering as in pictures of fashion two hundred years ago. She was dressed in a blue seaman's jersey, smart and expensive jodhpurs and a pair of carpet slippers.

She, too, asked if I was the Portuguese. I answered that I was Romanian and had been entrusted with a message for her. She took me into the entrance hall where I handed over the envelope while we both remained standing. She read the slip of paper. Eyes gave away nothing. Mouth was perhaps a little tighter than before.

"Your name?" she asked.

"My name it is Prefacutu."

"And who gave you this?"

"Anozzzer Romanian. In London."

"And where did he get it?"

"From zer Russian Embassy."

"I see. Well, thank you very much. You'll find it difficult to get back to London now, so you had better stay the night. That suits you?"

"Yes, Madame."

"Come along, and I'll show you your room. It's in the annex."

I picked up my bag and followed her through a fine, oak-paneled living room, furnished in half a dozen different and dignified styles so far as they could be seen under dogs and bits of saddlery. We went out through french windows into the walled garden closed on the far side by a two-story building like a range of stables — a blank face of ancient, rose-colored brick with magnificent pear trees espaliered over it.

She led me through a door into a sort of kitchen full of sacks and tubs with an immense, lidded boiler — a copper we used to call it — and a butcher's bloodstained slab; then up some stairs into a passage which looked as if it had once served as living quarters. She ushered me into a room which had indeed an old bed in it and a broken armchair. Before I could protest or even show surprise she had slammed the door and locked it.

44

"You can hear me all right?" she asked from outside.

"I just come bring letter," I said. "Know nozzing!"

"Well, what you do know you're going to spill. If you climb out of the window you'll land in the kennel yard. The hounds are all right if people come in through the gate, but one can't say what they might do to anyone who drops into the middle of them from the air. That boiler you passed is for cooking their meat, by the way. There's a pot under the bed. Empty it down the chute! Goodbye for the present, Mr. Prefacutu!"

I heard her footsteps go down the stairs and die away. She was quite right about the window. It was boarded up, but through the cracks I could see the hounds lazing in the yard below. Her suggestion that they might attack anyone who startled them by dropping from the sky was hardly believable, but might well alarm some city bred forcigner. However, it was not an experiment I was eager to try, though brought up among dogs including foxhound puppies. Every countryman has heard stories — usually myths — of babies and helpless old people who have fallen into pig sties or kennels.

The chute sounded hopeful, but it wasn't. Either it had been there since these outbuildings were first constructed or some groom had made it. It was a rusty iron pipe splayed out into a funnel at the top, and it led, my nose told me, directly down to the dung heap. Walls and doors were solid. So there I was.

Having satisfied myself that escape was going to be a hard night's work — assuming I could detach a leg of the iron bed to use as a lever — I sat down in the ruins of the chair and tried to make sense of my reception. It looked as if Mrs. Hilliard were about to hand me over to the police or — as the innkeeper put it — worse. If that was so, the sooner, the better. On the other hand she wanted a lengthy, personal chat with me first. She must also be reckoning that I had too guilty a conscience to yell for help. The old bitch, I said to myself, was wrong there. In the last of the light I saw through the boarded window someone attending to the hounds and shouted to him to let me out. He paid no attention whatever.

Nobody brought me anything to eat or drink. When night fell I wrenched off my bit of bed fairly easily and started to poke around in the pitch darkness for a bit of rotten flooring I had noticed earlier. I was making progress, or thought I was, when my improvised lever slipped on the smooth top of a beam and crushed my thumb against a sound plank. I called on God to damn and blast the thing to bloody hell and hopped around the room mouthing further comments on its birth and sexual practices.

"I'm afraid you must have injured yourself, Mr. Prefacutu," said a quiet voice outside the door. "And how very good your English is!"

My thumb hurt like the devil and I hadn't the heart to play the fool with broken English. Nothing gives away a man's true native language so absolutely as a fine string of idiomatic curses, especially if he reverts in agony to the barn-door dialect of his youth.

"Wiltshire, Mr. Prefacutu? Or is it Somerset?"

"I'm sorry. I couldn't know you were there."

"Oh, don't apologize! I've used much worse in the hunting field."

"Would you mind telling me why the hell you are keeping me here and spying on me?"

"Because I have had just about enough of slick young gentlemen from MI5 and their dumb agents."

"I am not a slick young gentleman from MI5. I could be one of their agents, but I don't think so."

"What'll you do if I let you out?"

"Dot you one and run."

"Why not have something to eat first?"

"I don't want anything to eat."

"Temper, temper! Come out of there, young man, and behave yourself!"

46

She unlocked the door and threw it back, standing on the far side of it.

"If there's any dotting to be done I'll do it. Go down the stairs in front of me and continue across the garden! You will see a rather larger man than you standing at the french window. Say good evening to him politely and sit down until I join you."

I did what she ordered, for there was no escape from the garden. I observed a burly man standing in the lit window and that he carried a hunting crop, so I greeted him as if all this was in the day's hospitable work. Mrs. Hilliard entered not far behind me.

"Thank you, John," she said to her retainer. "That will be all right now."

"I'll be over the way in the gun room, Master, if you should want me."

When he had gone out and closed the door, she offered me a cigarette and made herself comfortable between one very aged foxhound and an unmovable tom cat. I myself was more upright in a chair opposite to her. It was the proper position for interrogation though she had not obviously arranged it.

"Now, Mr. Prefacutu! Why did you come here speaking English like some sort of greaser just off the boat?"

I replied that I was told it might carry more conviction.

"Who told you? A Whitehall office boy?"

"I have nothing to do with Whitehall."

"Do you want to be fed to the hounds?"

"They might touch it boiled, Mrs. Hilliard, but not raw."

"I don't see why not. You won't taste of soot if you were brought up in Wiltshire."

"I can speak it."

"I'll say you can! Do you think the address you gave me is correct?"

"I don't see why it shouldn't be. The chap I got it from was really a Romanian and in touch with the Russian Embassy."

"What made him choose you?"

"Well, my mother was Romanian."

"Your father took your mother's name?"

"An old Romanian custom."

"Mr. Prefacutu, I guess that Women's Lib was not that popular in Romania when you were born."

I spotted for the first time that she was American or had lived long in America.

"Why do you find it inconvenient to use your real name?"

"That's no business of yours or theirs."

"By God, the boy has told me the truth for once!" she exclaimed. "What have they got on you?"

"Nothing at all."

"Well, they have now. You're a traitor and you'll fetch up in the Old Bailey."

"I don't see much harm in just giving you an address, Mrs. Hilliard. I haven't the least sympathy for your nephew. My opinion of him is just the same as that of the rest of my countrymen. He seems to have been a good fellow but lots of Communists are."

"What makes you think he was a nice guy?"

"Only something the landlord of your pub told me. I called in there to ask my way. He thought I was the Portuguese butler come down for an interview, just as you did."

"Boy, you've given me an idea. How about pretending to be just that for a day or two? I've a feeling that it's for your good and I can cancel the real interview. But you're perfectly free to have a meal and then go. John will drive you to Totnes. He'll say nothing of what happened and I shall tell Forrest at the pub that you didn't suit me."

I agreed to stay — an instant decision which needs a bit of explaining. In taking Mr. Marghiloman's money I had promised to observe her carefully and report on how she had reacted, but I don't think that counted for much. Curiosity decidedly did count. There were loose bits and pieces all over the place which might be picked up and used as they had been in the case of Uncle Vasile. And the lost dog was still in need of a leader in spite of the fact that its devotion to Councillor Sokes had been an unmitigated disaster. Mrs. Hilliard radiated leadership — the dominant female of a pack if ever I saw one. What she wanted of me or for me was beyond guessing, but my answer to her was certainly inspired by an instantaneous, improbable picture of a return to my own identity and my own West Country.

So I put on the black suit and black tie which she had rooted out from somewhere and next morning began my duties — or what resembled my duties near enough after a hint or two from her. She seemed to do very well without a resident married couple. Wives of the hunt servants came in for a few hours daily to clean up and accepted my presence quite naturally. Even John Penpole, the Huntsman, assumed that I had been mistaken on arrival for just another lousy snooper around the house and that I really was a Portuguese who had arrived unexpectedly.

All I knew was how to serve drinks and to make a variety of omelettes. That was enough to keep up appearances. When neighbors dropped in — which they did often for business or a chat — Mrs. Hilliard told them that I was only there for a day or two until a new couple turned up. She knew her village, she said, and she wasn't going to give them a juicy bit of scandal to enjoy about how the old girl had taken to good-looking young Latins in the flower of her age.

She was out to dinner, all dressed up, on the night after my arrival. The rest of the time she was at home and I saw a good deal of her, always speaking my broken English and taking orders respectfully. She called me "Willie," after asking me what my Christian name was and getting the answer that it was anything she liked.

The third day after my arrival gave us one of those glorious

English mornings when the scattered oaks and elms of the parkland around the house drooped in the green heat as if to protect the smaller life beneath them, Mrs. Hilliard told me that she was going out to sit on the Bank — a smooth turf rampart which must once have been an outer wall of the original priory — and at midday I was to bring her a well-iced Tom Collins in a pint glass.

When I arrived with the tray she was sitting among the armchair roots of an ancient mulberry — sprung as likely as not from a seed spat out by a passing monk. The aged foxhound, Bridget, was at her feet, and Sack-and-Sugar curled on top of her felt hat. Sack was a polecat ferret who plainly adored her and was treated with caution by everyone else. He was a melanistic sport, black with a yellowish-white belly, and had the air of a chattering familiar spirit — which she recognized by digging up the name of Sack-and-Sugar from the records of witch trials.

"Willie, we are now alone," she said. "I shall not have to endure your English and we can talk. By the way, did I see you from my window tickling Sack's tummy this morning?"

"Oughtn't I to?" I asked innocently.

"Well, anybody else who tried it would have had a hole in his thumb you could hang an earring from."

"I suppose he must have taken to me, Master."

There was a twinkle in her sea-blue eye, but I was not going to admit that I had four ferrets of my own as a boy, and the gaiety of them used to run back and forth between us.

"You don't trust me, do you?"

"I can see that everyone else does."

"Well, would you buy a secondhand car from me, as they say?"

"Not for a moment if it was a recent model."

"What the hell do you mean by that, Willie?"

"You wouldn't have had any respect for it. But I'd buy a thirty-year-old Rolls-Royce from you."

She threw up her head and bayed like a hound, upsetting Sack who had to scramble back by way of the white coiffure. It was the first time I had seen her laugh.

"Trust, Willie, is an instinct. You are a first-rate actor but a rather poor liar with no name and no past and only the vaguest indications that you were born an honest babe in Wiltshire. And yet I am sure that you are not working willingly for the Russians or for that whisky-sodden club of MI5. I stress *willingly*. Why do you think I asked you to stay on?"

"Because you couldn't make up your mind about me."

"Go up one, young Prefacutu! And I wanted time to ask a friend of mine for advice. That's where I went all dressed up to kill."

"What did he think?"

"That you don't know your ass from your elbow."

"'Ass, Mrs. Hilliard?"

"Willie, my upbringing as a young lady in Connecticut prevents me to this day from pronouncing that word as it should be. Ass it is and ass it will remain. And don't you talk to me about Chaucer!"

"Chaucer is the gardener?" I asked, for I didn't know his name.

"How far did your schooling go in Wiltshire?"

"A bit beyond the fox is in the box."

"Not in this hunting country, he isn't. But the cat is on the mat, and if we are to know why, you must decide that you don't like the job and return to London."

"I shall be sorry."

"So will Sack. He gets a mite bored with only me to talk to. And I shall give you a letter to my nephew — just a message saying that I have his address and could do with some caviar."

I agreed to deliver it, adding that if I ran into trouble she must promise to say exactly what happened.

"Word of honor. And now does your trust go far enough to give me your real name?"

I nearly did, but had to tell her that Willie would do very well for the time being.

I returned to London regretfully, well aware that I would gladly have stayed on as permanent butler if I knew anything about butling or a groom if I knew anything about horses. After two empty days I kept my appointment with Mr. Marghiloman and brightened up when I saw him already at the corner table in the pub.

After I had handed over Mrs. Hilliard's letter he led me on to talk about her. I kept quiet about her odd reception of me and told him that she seemed very calm and composed. I added, a bit romantically, that she had the air and finesse of a great lady. He ignored the vehement flow of my Romanian, saying with a smile that no doubt she could play the part if she wanted to.

This annoyed me. Mrs. Hilliard could doubtless play any part which suited her, and perhaps it was a part when first she arrived in Devon; but now it was an extension of her natural self and she belonged to her valley as if the steep, lush slopes of it had grown up around her. I stopped myself just in time from telling him so. Instead I remarked that I had too little experience of English and Americans to be able to see through them.

"She was a hell-cat in her youth, Mr. Prefacutu," he said. "Mixed up with all the revolutionaries of those days and ran guns for the Republicans in the Spanish Civil War."

"Well, she's a highly respectable Master of Hounds now."

"A pose! Engels rode to hounds. And her daughter is worse. Anarchist or Communist. She was mixed up in the escape of Mornix, too."

"I didn't know she had a daughter."

"You don't seem to have talked to her much."

"Not about her family."

"But according to you, you were four days in the house!"

Instinctively I decided to say nothing of being mistaken for a Portuguese manservant and being compelled to keep up the part, which accounted for the lack of any intimate conversation.

"Just waiting for her letter," I explained.

"And silent all the time?"

His pleasant voice had not altered, and the warning took a second to sink in. I began to suspect one of the reasons why he had asked me to go down with the Moscow address. There could be no better way of inserting myself into Mrs. Hilliard's life and any secrets she might have.

"Does Mrs. Hilliard go down to the sea much?"

"Not so far as I know."

"Or to the creeks of the Kingsbridge Estuary?"

"I don't think so. Kingsbridge is all of ten miles away."

"Did you ever see in the house a chart of the estuary?"

"Yes. There was one belonging to Alwyn Rory."

"Any marks on it?"

"Plenty. He must have done a lot of sailing there at one time."

"Did you ever see a chart of the estuary when you were on the *Nadezhda Krupskaya*, Ionel Petrescu?"

So he had known all along who I was. It didn't bother me, though I would have bolted straight out of the place if he had called me Adrian Gurney. I assumed of course that he was an agent of British security and that I had been framed. It stood to reason that there would be Romanian agents to keep an eye on dubious Romanians. I knew something — or thought I did — of the dirty tricks played by that sort of crook, bound to bring cases or be sacked. I decided to bluff it out.

"I'm in the clear with police and immigration authorities, and you can't send me back now," I said.

He must have picked up instantly what was in my mind.

"Oh, can't we?" he replied. "Not for carrying letters between a traitor in Moscow and his aunt?"

"I did it out of kindness, as you know. And Mrs. Hilliard will back me up."

"How did you hurt your thumb?"

"Squashed it in a door."

"What are you living on?"

"Savings."

"I think you had better have a steady job to keep you out of trouble."

"I'll take anything where they don't mind my bad English. I was doing all right with translations."

"Well, no time like the present!" he said, resuming his former cordiality. "I've got a publisher friend in Bloomsbury who might use you. He always works late and we can go up and see him now if you like. Are you prepared to tell all the truth about yourself?"

I said I was and went with him, babbling about the beauties of Romania as if I had no suspicions and meanwhile trying to think. Something in all this did not fit. I had been too long in England — let alone all that one unconsciously picks up in boyhood — to believe that British security would use so gross an *agent provocateur*. Any court would throw out the case against me at once.

But a genuine refugee from an East European country would not know that. I remembered Mrs. Hilliard's remark that the cat was on the mat and that delivery of her letter to her nephew would help us to know why. I hadn't time to puzzle over the why, but who was the cat? It sounded like MI5, suspecting that Rory, Mrs. Hilliard and her daughter had been up to something treasonable in the Kingsbridge estuary. On the other hand the blackmail smelt strongly of KGB, though it seemed highly improbable that the Russians believed I had really swum ashore from the fishing fleet.

Getting rid of Mr. Marghiloman and avoiding interrogation by his fictitious publisher friend turned out to be quite simple. We were strolling up the Charing Cross Road carrying northwards a roaring mass of impatient death. He was waiting meekly, like a disciplined foreigner, to cross Earlham Street when I saw a chance to dash over to the island in Cambridge Circus, and from there plunged across to the Palace Theatre a yard ahead of the thundering stream sweeping out of Shaftesbury Avenue. I don't know what happened to Marghiloman. I think he reached the island and had to stand there till the lights changed. Meanwhile I had half a dozen turnings to choose from. When I found a telephone box I decided to call Mrs. Hilliard who ought to be at home and sipping her outsize glass of sherry before dinner.

I got through to her at once and told her discreetly that the man who had been expecting me seemed likely to give trouble.

"You do surprise me, Willic," she said. "Where are you calling from?"

"A box in Soho."

"And you were wondering if there was still a job for a Portuguese till the sky clears?"

"As a matter of fact I was, Mrs. Hilliard."

"Were you thinking of going home before coming here?"

"Just to get my things."

"Well, if I were you I shouldn't. I suggest you take a train at once and then walk from wherever it lands you. And don't go through Molesworthy! You know the Penpoles' cottage in the wood — aim for that, preferably at night!"

"But it's not as serious as all that."

"Very likely it is not. But if Mr. Marghiloman is anxious for more conversation this is one of the places where he would look for you. Now, jump on the first bus you see, and do what I tell you!"

I decided that I had better obey, even if it blackened my character as a decent, docile refugee. Assuming Marghiloman did turn out to be a secret police agent after all, I could always plead that I escaped from him because I thought he was a Romanian spy out to kidnap or compromise me. So I took a bus to Paddington and found that in an hour there would be a fast train stopping at Swindon. This tempted me. Swindon was only twelve miles from my old home.

I had always been inhibited from any return — by shame, I think. My conscious mind had accepted Sokes and Caulby, the subconscious never. But the life of Cleder's Priory had cleansed me. I was destitute and an impostor, yet now I was utterly sure where I belonged. So why not have a look at my old home? So long as I did not stop and talk to anyone who had known my parents, nobody was likely to recognize the boy of twelve in a man of twenty-three whose hair had grown much darker, and complexion — Caulby after Cairo — an unhealthy yellow. There was no hurry to reach Molesworthy and I looked forward to covering much of the journey on foot.

It was nearly midnight when I got off at Swindon and I reckoned that it would be difficult to find a room for the night — especially since I had no baggage and did not look prosperous — so I might as well walk by well-remembered country roads till dawn and arrive at my home with the sun, if there was any. I sometimes think a small boy sees summer sunrise more often than others. I used to get out of bed when the dawn chorus of birds woke me and stand at the east window of my room feeling a content and sometimes a conscious joy at the miracle of another day. But then a window framed my whole world; now I myself was the outer world and that window only a point in time and space.

I had just started to climb the long, straight road on to the Marlborough Downs when I saw the blue light of a police car coming down the hill towards me. It must have been out to a remote farm on some scare of swine fever or anthrax, for all the roads come to a reverent standstill when they pass out of the Saxon lowland into the waving grass which washes the standing stones of our first ancestors and covers the Long Barrows of the dead.

I was self-conscious about my appearance — shabby town

suit, shoes too cheap for walking — so I lay down in tumbled ground where deerhorn picks had once created a field. The car passed me and pulled up lower down the slope. The night was still, so I could hear why the police had stopped. They were asking someone apparently walking to nowhere like myself:

"Anything wrong, sir?"

I could not hear his reply, but it satisfied them that his car had not broken down and that he was not in need of help. Evidently he did not belong on a lonely country road, for the police would not have stopped for a tramp or any obviously agricultural bloke strolling home after slap-and-tickle with his girl or a last inspection to see that some newly bought fatstock were settling down. He must be as out of place as I was.

I stayed in cover to take a look at him, more with the idea of having a companion on my walk than anything else. When he came abreast of me, stepping out smartly and silently, I saw even by starlight what was wrong. He gave an impression of having abandoned his car somewhere or just jumped off a train. And so, by God, he had! I had paid no particular attention to the other passengers who had left the train at Swindon and passed the ticket collector in front of me, but there had been only one man among several women, wearing a dark suit and a dark, unbuttoned raincoat. Build right. Raincoat right. He was undoubtedly the same man.

It did not make sense. How the hell could anyone guess that Adrian Gurney, alias Ionel Petrescu, was going to look at his old home? The only solution was that Marghiloman had telephoned his headquarters as soon as he lost me. Watch his home, he would say, and try Paddington Station in case he's off to warn Mrs. Hilliard of — well, whatever she ought to be warned about. But how does the Paddington man know me? Answer disconcerting. I must have been pointed out to him some time and he must have been close behind me when I bought a ticket to Swindon.

He could have stayed right on my heels if I had taken the

expected train to Totnes and even sat next to me on the bus next morning. But by going to Swindon and plunging straight into my mysterious homeland I had completely sunk him. I wondered where the devil he thought I was aiming for in the dark and why — and what he would report back when his wanderings took him to a telephone. He had hopelessly lost me now, for there were cross lanes ahead and one of them was the prehistoric Ridge Way which he would never recognize as a road at all.

When the sun rose I looked down again on my village and the square, stone house to the west of it where I was born. The walled garden had gone and in its place was a range of batteries for laying hens. The forest of hawthorn above the upper ley, into which I would vanish when deservedly unpopular at home, had been grubbed up and was now good grass with bullocks on it of a crossbreed I did not know. The barns were of concrete, white-roofed, instead of a mess of ancient timber where the calves could snuggle down between warm walls of baled straw, and I with them. That farmer must have been making twice as much as my father, even allowing for inflation.

I did not go down for a closer look. I was not in the least depressed by the changes, which represented the style in which I should have farmed myself with perhaps a bit more tolerance for old ways; but I saw little hope of such peace for Ionel Petrescu, and it was that thought which made me turn away.

I slept through the morning sheltered from the wind by the kindly grave of some neolithic ancestor, and then struck south enjoying every moment of the walk and free to speak normal English since I had no pretense to keep up. I covered the twenty-odd miles to Westbury, too exhilarated to feel more than healthy tiredness, and got on a train to Tiverton — a part of Devon where no one could conceivably expect me. On arrival I had to take stock of myself. I needed new shoes, toilet

58

necessaries, a knapsack and some sort of cheap windbreaker instead of coat and tie. When I had bought them and paid for a night's lodging, there was little left of Marghiloman's fifty pounds.

Next day there was a steady drizzle from the Atlantic. I started off stiff, with a blister on my heel and feeling that I had been far too hasty in bolting from London. I did not want to sponge on Mrs. Hilliard and was depressed at the thought of my future when she had given me her advice and I had sneaked out by the back door. Perhaps I could get a job on a remote farm and drop the identity of Ionel Petrescu, pretending that I had just come out of prison. No farmer would mind that so long as I proved myself a willing worker.

Speculations on the crime I might have committed cheered me up, and soon afterwards a kindly truck driver picked me out of the rain and gave me a lift. He was bound for Plymouth and dropped me off on the way with only some ten miles to walk to Molesworthy. Eventually I settled down on a dry bank from which I could see the chimneys of Cleder's Priory and nothing at all of the village.

I had long hours of the evening to wait there. Mrs. Hilliard's instructions began to seem unnecessarily dramatic. All this stuff about making my way to the Huntsman's cottage after dark sounded as if coverts and parkland were full of spies and fieldglasses. When I had been playing the Portuguese a week earlier she never bothered about where I went or who saw me. However, I supposed I had better behave as if the man in the raincoat were waiting for me in Molesworthy.

John Penpole's cottage was somewhere in the woodland between me and the house, exactly where I did not know. I had been there once by a metaled track from the Priory, but never from this side. In the dusk I saw a girl on a horse cantering easily through tall bracken which proved that she must be on a path. She rode as far as a knoll further along the ridge where I was, searched for something that was not there and with very obvious annoyance cantered back again, disappearing into the wood.

In the last of the light I went up to the point where the girl had halted and found the path without difficulty. The narrow strip of turf between tall bracken could not be missed even in the dark. It led me into the wood and soon I saw ahead of me the lit curtains of John's fairy-tale cottage.

As soon as I entered the clearing, his hunt terriers started to yap. John came to the door, beckoning me in with a cordial nod. Mrs. Hilliard and Mrs. Penpole were sitting in the living room. A jug of cider with the remains of a large pollock and a raspberry pie suggested that she had had supper there. When I addressed her respectfully in my broken English, she said:

"We're all friends here, Willie. Wiltshire or plain English as you like, but not that bloody awful noise."

John's red face split with a grin. Unless one knew him well the sudden gash joining together his set of horseman's wrinkles on both sides of the mouth was hard to interpret. It could be a tightening of thin lips or a genial smile.

"We'll leave you alone with him, Master," he said.

"No, you won't. You stay here and Willie and I will use the kitchen. If we hear anyone come to the front door we'll slip out at the back. I'll cut him a sandwich or two if you don't mind, Amy, and we'll take the cider."

When we were settled on hard chairs with the kitchen table between us, I asked her if she had been waiting for me.

"I was so. And I sent my daughter up to the top of the hill to look for a leash I hadn't left there. It occurred to me a bit late that if you had avoided Molesworthy you could be stumbling around half the night before you found the private path. Now, what sort of trouble do you think you're in, Willie?"

I told her all that happened after I delivered her letter and of the attempt to keep track of my movements.

"So your name is not Prefacoot or whatever, but Petrescu

60

— which doesn't make things any easier when I've been taking it all along that you were born and bred in this country."

"I said Marghiloman thought my name was Petrescu, Mrs. Hilliard."

"And you thought he wasn't an agent of MI5?"

"I don't really know what that is. Just security police?"

"It sits in an office swapping files about suspects and working out the wrong line for hounds to follow. The hounds are called Special Branch and are not pleased when people like you talk of Security Police. We've had the whole pack of 'em here searching the house from top to bottom. Knew all about little Eudora's politics when she was twenty. There are two sets of jerks, Willie, who never forget the Spanish Civil War — left-wing socialists and right-wing dicks. They gave my married couple polite hell which is why they left and I wasn't that sorry. Dragged up more dirt about my crazy daughter than I knew myself. Had a go at John and Amy. Tapped all the telephones — or so the village postmistress said, though I guess she'd never notice it if they did. I'd had about enough of it when you blew in."

I said I hoped that I had not started up her troubles all over again.

"What do you think the man in the raincoat was up to?"

"Ordered to find out what I was doing in Swindon and stuck to the trail."

"We'll hope that's all. What *were* you doing in Swindon?"

"Well, you warned me not to go through Molesworthy, so I thought I'd make a job of it and not risk traveling down to Devon. I got off at Swindon because the train was going to Bristol."

"O.K. But when you had dished this guy in the raincoat why did you carry on over the Marlborough Downs?"

"It seemed easier than turning back."

"Did you live near Swindon in happier days?" she asked acutely.

"It's got all Wiltshire to the south, Mrs. Hilliard."

"See here, Willie — why should I shop you when you can chop me? What have you done and why did you do it?"

She was irresistible, and I gave her my whole life story. When I had finished, she said:

"Adrian — no, we'll keep it Willie — you thought the Russian trawler fleet was out just to catch fish?"

"Yes, of course."

Voice must have carried conviction, for it was what I did think. My naïveté was not all that astonishing. Brought up in a Communist country, I had been brainwashed by steady propaganda that Russian intentions were always peaceful and always misunderstood. None of us wholly believed it, but there was no reason to suspect that very necessary fishing could be cover for active espionage. And provincial Caulby had not enlightened me. Ten years ago the trawler fleets and their objectives were not so widely publicized as now.

"God Almighty, boy, you must have set everyone a puzzle! It's you they are after. I don't see how Alwyn's letter comes in, but it's you."

"Who's they?"

"That's what I'm going to ask a friend of mine — the same I went to see the day after your arrival when you saw me all dressed up for dinner. He won't split on you nor will I."

The hunt terriers started to yap. John immediately came through the kitchen and out by the back door into darkness. He returned almost at once to say that it was only Miss Tessa.

"Thank you, John. You and I will be going out later."

"Very good, Master. Tide's dead low about two."

We followed him back to the living room and were all sitting there innocently when Tessa Hilliard came in.

"Not another of them!" she exclaimed, looking at me with utter contempt.

"No, dear, that's the Portuguese who was here."

"Why has he come back?"

"Just to return some money that John lent him. You know how it is. Nobody ever trusts the post in foreign countries."

"Mrs 'Illiard, I go now," I said, taking my cue. "I 'ave not notice zer time."

"Nonsense, boy! Stay the night with the Penpoles and the baker will give you a lift to the main road in the morning. What is it, Tessa?"

I gathered that she had arrived from London earlier in the day and after her ride had spent the evening with friends in the village, dropping in to the Crown and Thistle. She was a tall, slim girl with a calmly determined air which did not quite fit her bitten nails and the angry impatience which I had noticed when she thought she was alone. Her face was triangular and resembled her mother's, opening up like a tulip from delicate chin to a broad, high brow. I found her intensely attractive, and wondered if the left-wing opinions which Marghiloman had mentioned were sufficiently far-out to give a shabby Portuguese half a chance.

"Forrest gave me a message for you. I was to tell you the two Americans had gone off in their car after a meal and weren't back yet. What Americans?"

"Oh, they came down yesterday and are staying with him. Slung with cameras. Very humble and very persistent. You know the type. They were taking shots of the house from all angles yesterday. Perhaps Forrest was warning me that they might turn up to look at the chimneys by moonlight. If they do, darling, give 'em a nightcap and tell them I've gone to bed."

"What the hell are they doing here anyway?"

"They are either carrying the benefits of civilization into Devon or bringing back the peace of Devon to America. It depends on how some earnest professor of sociology taught them to view thatched cottages with no drains."

Tessa hung around a bit talking to the Penpoles and then, as her mother showed no sign of moving, went back to the house. Mrs. Hilliard must have noticed a faint atmosphere of disapproval in the room, but she addressed herself to me rather than the Penpoles.

"I'm sorry, Willie, but one can always read in Tessa's face whatever she doesn't want to think."

Possibly — for a mother. The girl's mouth was sensitive and uncertain at the corners, which could set nearly as hard as John's or slightly quiver. The quiver, it's true, was liable to give her away in any situation which demanded a convincing mask.

"You haven't been fishing in American waters, have you, Willie?"

It was a remark which meant nothing to John, but had definite implications for me now that she had opened my eyes to all the interest there might be in a refugee swimming ashore from a Russian trawler fleet. I replied that she was the only American I had ever met and I could not believe she was typical.

"I became what I wanted to become, Willie. And I tried to bring up Alwyn just as my two men would have wished."

I could only look my sympathy. Words were inadequate — and anyway an impertinence — when I thought of the traitor and what the disgrace must have meant to her. She let it go at that, and shortly afterwards went back to the house with John.

Mrs. Penpole left me alone while she made up a bed for me and then took me upstairs to a pleasant little attic, so near to the trees that it would have tempted a squirrel. After saying good night she turned in the doorway, her round, rosy face peering at me with rather the expression of my mother when she was pretending to be stern.

"What I want to know, young man, is be 'ee on our side or bain't 'ee."

I replied that Mrs. Hilliard seemed to think I was.

"And I 'ope her's right with 'ee actin' as a Portugal and all.

And if it be Mr. Alwyn 'ee wants to know more about, 'e's bin under my veet like a fourpenny rabbit since 'e were that 'igh, and I tell 'ee Mr. Alwyn couldn't 'ave done what they'm sayin' no more than I can stand on me 'ead no more. The only fault 'e 'ad was to see the best in everyone."

I led her on to talk of her employer, asking what Mrs. Hilliard meant by her two men. Had she married twice?

Indeed not, Mrs. Penpole said as if it were quite unthinkable. She had meant Alwyn's father, Major Rory. Filling up the doorway, she gave me then and there a sketch of the family history. The Hilliards had been prosperous farmers at Cleder's Priory, father to son for eight generations until the last Hilliard who had become a man of mark in South Devon — partly due to a university education, partly to his interest in all the classless sports of horsemen. And gloriously classless he seems to have been, equally at home with laborers, the neighboring farmers and the county magnates.

" 'Ee could meet anyone at his table, me dear," she said. "And them as was mazed by it, well, they doan't come again and good riddance. Too good for this world 'e was and the Lord took 'im early."

So much for Hilliard — and as fair a time as another to fill in the youth of Eudora though from later knowledge. She had been as much in revolt against wealthy, stockbroking parents as any hippies of today, and with more reason considering all the economic miseries of America in the nineteen thirties. She met the brothers-in-law, Hilliard and Major Rory, when they were running a refugee camp for Spanish Republican children on the Devon coast and were both desolated by the loss of Hilliard's sister who had broken her neck in the hunting field. Eudora was weary, I think, of protests and marchings, of anarchist sacrifice and Communist treachery; she was ready to see that integrity and deep love of fellow men were not the exclusive possessions of the left. So she married Hilliard and

65

surrendered herself to the simplicity of his country life. When Major Rory was killed at Dunkirk, his thirteen-year-old son, Alwyn, made his home with the Hilliards.

"Mrs. Hilliard seems to have fallen in love with England," I said.

"That's as may be, Mr. Willie, but us zurely fell in love with she."

I slept soundly, though not quite off guard since I heard John creep into the cottage just before dawn and wondered why he and Mrs. Hilliard had stayed up so very late. I was woken up by Amy Penpole with a breakfast tray. When I apologized for not being up and about already, she reminded me that I was supposed to have gone off with the baker's van and so I should stay where I was and not come downstairs.

I sat there trying to plan what I ought to do and how I could disentangle Eudora Hilliard from all the embarrassment I had caused her and myself from whatever mess I was in. I was not supposed to show myself in Molesworthy or at the house or even at the Penpoles' cottage. Tessa was being deliberately deceived about me. The pretense of being a Portuguese was finished. Obviously Ionel Petrescu must be removed as far as possible from everyone who wanted a serious talk with him. If Mrs. Hilliard was right and he was believed to have secrets of Russian trawlers, it was surprising that he had been put through such a perfunctory interrogation in London.

She turned up in the middle of the morning looking worn and old, and bringing Sack-and-Sugar with her for comfort. He was annoyed at not being allowed to walk and wriggled furiously in the poacher's pocket of her tweed coat.

She asked me if Amy was looking after me all right and agreed that I had better stay up in the attic for the time being.

"Are you sure you have told me everything?"

I said that I had told her everything I knew and it would all be clearer if we knew who "they" were. When could she ask her friend?

66

"I asked him last night. He said he would have to think it over but meanwhile you had better get out of here. What do you yourself feel you ought to do?"

"Leave tonight. No one saw me arrive and no one will see me go."

"If you don't lose your way in the dark. Let's see what Sack has to say."

She put him down on the floor of the attic. He humped himself round the angle between floor and wall examining everything and then climbed to my shoulder, opening with his claws a shallow scratch on my neck which he proceeded to lick with enjoyment. Ferrets can't help it. The long, non-retractable claws can be the devil wherever one's skin is too tight or too thin. It is then their habit to kiss the wound better and get a snack at the same time.

"He says it's good, tasty Wiltshire, but that blood may be about when ferrets and others are trusted too easily."

"I trusted him because I know him. Like trusting you," I answered, burying my hand in the shapeless bunch of fine fur and getting very gently nipped in acknowledgment.

"Well, isn't that nice! But I'm not sure you should, Willie — not all the way. Now, follow the path you know until you come to the ford and then don't go too far south or you'll get tied up among the creeks of the Kingsbridge Estuary. And of course keep clear of Totnes! Once you're well inland, you'll take some finding. And I'm going to give you some money to carry you over and you have to accept it. What will you do?"

"Get taken on wherever I see them starting the potato harvest."

She collected Sack who had burrowed under the carpet and become a wave instead of a particle. We decided that I should never risk sending her an address, but I promised an anonymous picture postcard to let her know that all was well with me.

The long day passed with the aid of a dog-eared volume

called *Everyman's Farriery* which was as depressing as a medical dictionary and made me wonder how anybody managed to get a horse on the road at all. When it was full dark I shouldered my knapsack with enough food and drink in it to last me a day and thanked John and Amy. Mrs. Hilliard must have given me a good character reference for they treated me as if I were their personal agent about to set off into enemy territory.

I knew the path as far as the top of the ridge. The narrow ribbon of turf, pitted by hooves, was unmistakable even at night; but when I reached the bare knoll where Tessa had failed to find the leash I was not sure of the way — what with the sheep tracks and the dead-end alleys into the surrounding bracken where a cow might have calved or hounds crashed in after a hare till John called them off. The ridge was so familiar to Mrs. Hilliard that I doubt if she realized how it would appear to a stranger in starlight.

Eventually I found the right opening and started downhill. There was not a sound, and I could not hear my own footsteps on the short turf until I was walking through a mush of last year's brown stems which had fallen across the path. The swishing disturbed some creature so close that I could just make out the waving tops of the fern as it pushed through the stems. I stood still, instinctively alarmed, for the hillside was as lonely as any in England and the forest of waist-high bracken, an intangible surface stretching away like the top of a cloud, could hide anything. Having dismissed tigers as highly improbable — I used to frighten myself deliciously with them as a boy — I was left with badger or rabbit, both too small for such a marked swaying of the tops, or deer or sheep which would plunge noisily away. The only common animal I could think of, too bulky to slip between stems but able to wriggle away at ground level, was man. So I did the same on the opposite side of the path, hoping that the other fellow had only heard my approach and had not caught sight of me.

Again there was absolute silence for what seemed a very long time. It confirmed my guess that it was not an animal, but a man who was trying to avoid me or lying in wait for me. I ventured to stick up my head. Nothing to be seen. A light breeze had sprung up from the south which was rustling the fronds. I was impatient to get past him and away, so I pushed very slowly through the stems causing, I hoped, so delicate a movement above me that it would not be distinguishable in the dark from the effect of the wind. Once on the soundless turf of the path and in the black shadow of the wall of bracken I started to crawl downhill, paying close attention to fallen fronds and deep hoofmarks with standing water. After a minute or two of this concentration on the ground I looked up, and there bang opposite me was a bearded man on hands and knees playing exactly the same game.

We stared at each other with, as it were, one paw raised. If we had been animals, one would have eventually snarled and displayed and the other — unless equally dominant — slid off into cover. As it was, we had equally guilty consciences, which comes to the same thing. It's also possible that the human sense of the comic had some influence, for there could hardly be a more preposterous situation than two grown men very cautiously crawling towards each other on hands and knees. So far as I remember, the complete banality of our greeting went something like this:

"Adrian Gurney, of course!"

"Then you must be Mrs. Hilliard's friend."

"Yes," he said. "Yes, that's right."

"We both had the same idea when the breeze blew up."

"Obvious, when you come to think of it."

It was perplexing why Mrs. Hilliard's friend — so respectable that she put on smart clothes to dine with him — should be as anxious not to be spotted as I myself. When he stood up, muddy to the knees and with an untidy beard going gray, I could smell him.

"I suppose we ought to have fired simultaneously," I said with the hearty inanity of youth.

"Ever handled an automatic?"

"No."

"The chances are you'd have been high and right. And I'm out of practice. So neither would have scored."

"Well, perhaps I'd better be on my way."

"You couldn't run back and give a message to John Penpole, could you? Then I wouldn't have to go down to the house."

"Of course. I've plenty of time."

"Just say that their friend has gone away. But before you go, Mr. Gurney, tell me one thing — when you were interrogated what ship did you say you escaped from?"

"*Nadezhda Krupskaya.* There was a photograph of her in the paper."

"I see. That clarifies matters a lot."

"Then can't you tell me who's after me and why. According to Mrs. Hilliard, you said I didn't know my arse from my elbow."

Pushing halfway into the bracken he made himself comfortable, leaning on one arm.

"Sit down," he said, "and I'll do my best. Where you slipped up, Mr. Gurney, was in your superb contempt for Caulby police. And you might have got away with it if it hadn't been for Miss What's-It of Wandsworth. But when you committed suicide and compelled your employer to tie himself into knots it was certain they would send your fingerprints to Scotland Yard.

"Now then! What happens when this very dubious character, Ionel Petrescu, swims ashore? He may be a crook or a spy or very useful indeed. His prints go automatically to the Yard, but it is unnecessary for the moment to put a name to them. Back comes the reply to MI5 that the prints are those of the late Adrian Gurney.

"Within a week they have the whole of your history. Then let us imagine a small conference of these whisky-sodden louts, as Eudora calls them, at which some bright spark asks why the police should be allowed to run you in as a pretended suicide and public nuisance when you have propaganda value as Ionel Petrescu besides other likely values.

"That brings us to what you really want to know. First of all a fake job was found for you and you were left quite free to live as you liked. They wanted to see who your contacts were, who tried to contact you and if you would be any use as an agent. How long were you on your own?"

"About five weeks."

"Well, that must have been enough to convince them that your life was exceptionally dull and that you were of no interest to anyone. But patience pays off. Other people were watching them and you and waiting till they were sure you had no protection. When the lion has finished his meal, the jackals come around."

"Mrs. Hilliard thought I must have been a puzzle."

"Considering that the *Nadezhda Krupskaya* is stuffed so full of aerials and electronics that she must blow out her fish through the bottom as soon as the trawl starts spilling them in over the top, it's not surprising. So we will try to follow Russian reasoning when they learn of your well-publicized landing. (1) Nobody was missing from that or any other ship; therefore this Ionel Petrescu was a British agent who somehow managed to hide on board till there was a chance of getting home with his information. (2) But their security makes this so unlikely that it can be dismissed; therefore you were probably slung out of, say, a midget submarine and swam ashore. (3) But if that is so, why was your arrival publicized? Answer — a very weak one — to persuade them that we know a lot more about their trawlers than we really do."

He turned to the subject of Marghiloman, still speaking as if he was well accustomed to the concise summary of reports.

"Marghiloman has found out (a) that apparently you are a genuine Romanian and not under orders to pretend to be one; (b) that since you gave a false name there is something fishy about you although your life in London has been an open book — perhaps too open; (c) that you were prepared to do a very questionable job for another Romanian, so that you are or soon can be made wide open to blackmail, and you will then confess the truth about yourself or else."

"But why tail me?"

"I have several answers to that, Mr. Gurney, none of them sure. But I am glad to see you take care in lonely places."

"You think I may be in danger?"

"Of kidnapping, very possibly. You are a refugee, known to be without protection and without family or intimate friends. Who is going to know if you disappear?"

That was unquestionably true. After all, I was counting on it myself that I could disappear. I said that he seemed to be very familiar with the ways of MI5 and asked him if he had ever known Alwyn Rory.

"Quite well."

"Around here no one can believe he was guilty. What do you think?"

"He was guilty of folly, overconfidence and perhaps cowardice. But he was not a traitor."

"If only he had not defected one could believe it. I'd like to believe it."

"He did not defect."

"How do you know?"

"I am Rory. The letter you brought to Eudora was a rather crude attempt to find out whether she believed I had escaped to Russia."

I did not know what I ought to say. Absurdly the "ought" seemed more important than anything I wanted to say. All the inexplicable behavior of Mrs. Hilliard and the Penpoles, prepared to defend their fugitive even to the extent of imprisoning a suspicious stranger till he talked, at once fell into place. It was hard to make a complete about-turn and accept all the blast of newspaper indignation as mistaken. On the other hand the only clear realities among all these drifting phantoms of cold war at sea were my trust in Eudora Hilliard, the waving bracken which was so kindly a shelter both to this fugitive and myself, and his personality with its incisive intelligence and direct, well-calculated, take-it-or-leave-it attack. So I gave to the shock and simply carried on from his last remark.

"But the Russians must know you are not in Moscow," I said.

"Mr. Gurney, I have spent fifteen years trying to follow Russian reasoning, and I haven't succeeded yet."

"Hadn't you better call me Willie? Your aunt does."

Consciously I only meant that if we were ever in the presense of a third party I'd like the name of Gurney to be avoided. But how much more the simple remark implied: that I had no intention of giving him away and that there might even be some mutual activity.

"You're quite right. I will get used to Willie."

"Why on earth did you let people think you were in Moscow? And how did you do it?"

"Never mind the how! Why? Well, for two reasons. One was to throw off the hunt until I had a chance of getting clear away to some country where I could not be extradited. I was almost certain to be convicted and even if I got off my career was over and my name would stink. The other reason was to find out who shopped me before I left."

I asked him where he had been hiding. He would not tell me in case I ever found myself in a position where I might be forced to give it away.

"But I'll put you in the picture and you can pass it on to Eudora," he said. "Last night, after I had heard your story from her, I was making my way back to my health resort — let's say it was at the edge of a river — when I spotted two

73

men on the opposite bank. They were nowhere near the right place or our rendezvous, and I satisfied myself that they were just waiting, not searching. But obviously I was in danger. So I lay up during the day and when we met I was taking the deadly risk of visiting the house to tell her I had to clear out."

"I hope it had nothing to do with me."

"I think now that it may have done."

"But what a coincidence that we ran into each other!"

"Not altogether. Both of us had to move tonight, me to the house, you from it. Both in danger, possibly from the same quarter. And only one path which avoids the village."

I wished him luck, expecting that he would be gone when I returned, and trotted back over the knoll down to the Penpoles' cottage. When I was near the edge of the wood I heard the terriers yapping. Then they stopped. There was no light behind the curtains. Like the trees around it, the cottage was alive but impassive. I did not want to break the silence, so I threw several handfuls of gravel at the Penpoles' bedroom window.

"What are you doing here? I thought you had left."

It was Tessa, standing stiffly a few yards behind me, wide eyes luminous in the dark. That was why the terriers had stopped barking.

My mind was running over and over the conversation with Alwyn Rory and tuned to straight English. Startled and with no time to think, I carried on with it, forgetting that the last time I saw her I was the Portuguese servant.

"I left something behind," I said.

"You're always coming back for something. What is it this time?"

"My watch."

"Where would it be? In your room? I'll get it."

"John might have it in his pocket. Where are they?"

"At the Cricket Club dance, and so is my mother. Why are

74

you pretending to be a Portuguese? Does she know what you are?"

She sounded ready to burst, and I could understand Mrs. Hilliard's distrust. Judging by her voice the girl seemed a reckless liability, likely to be indiscreet; yet I was impressed by her air of determination and her confident challenge to the stranger.

I said that Mrs. Hilliard did know, feeling that if I said she didn't young Tessa might go screaming for the police or dash into that Cricket Club dance with the news of her discovery. Her reaction was quite unexpected.

"My mother tells me nothing!" she exclaimed, and I heard a sob in her voice. "It isn't fair! What are you doing? What had you got to say to John? Is it about Alwyn?"

"Rory? No, I have nothing to do with him."

"Of course you have! What are you up to? I took the trouble to ask the baker if he had picked anyone up this morning. That's why I am here while they're all out — to see and listen and to hell with you!"

"It paid off, Tessa," said Alwyn's voice from the darkness.

She was in his arms in an instant, stroking his hair and crying her eyes out with the sudden relief. At first I thought they were lovers and moved tactfully away into the night. But it was not that at all. They considered themselves brother and sister rather than cousins, with perhaps a bit of father and daughter in it since he was seventeen when she was born. He had been around for Tessa to worship ever since her cradle.

He came over to me with his arm round her shoulders.

"I'm sorry, Willie," he said. "As soon as I was alone — well, you may learn how it is. One begins to distrust logic and instinct. So I followed you."

I told him there was no need to apologize, that I would have done the same.

"And you'd be right, and don't forget it! But at my age I should be sure."

75

When he gave Tessa the message for Eudora, she exclaimed that she couldn't possibly talk to her mother without reproaching her for her unfair silence and having a row. Alwyn told her that was silly. Eudora was forced to trust the Penpoles but had no right to compromise anyone else. He added:

"There would never be any reason for rows, Tessa, if you remembered that she is you, only thirty years older. Eudora — I can see her as a girl carted off by a policeman and slapping his face. She doesn't mistrust you. She mistrusts herself in you, and you can tell her so with my love. Did anybody see you come here?"

"No. I left by the garden and through the stables."

He put on a pair of owlish, thick-rimmed glasses and patted his wavy, graying hair further down on his forehead, asking if she would recognize him. She peered closely into his face studying it from all angles, partly to be sure of his safety and partly, I think, because she wanted to store his features away in memory.

"I probably would if I was looking for you," she said, "but never if I wasn't. And you have gone a little gray. Where have you been?"

He refused to tell her, giving the same reason he had given to me, and then asked her if she knew what had happened to Rachel Iwyrne.*

"I still see her sometimes. She gave up the flat at Whatcombe Street and is writing a book. Your beastly people gave her hell."

"They had to."

"When shall I see you again?"

"When you get a letter from a foreign country with an invitation to come out and visit someone you've never heard of."

"You're sure it wouldn't be better to face it out?"

---

* The Miss X of the Prologue. Her name at this time meant nothing to me. A. G.

"Tessa dear, I hardly know which would be worse — to be found guilty when all of you down here believe I couldn't be, or to be acquitted when all England took it for granted I was guilty. To disappear and be forgotten — that's all I want."

They said goodbye, and Alwyn and I started back together — not with any intention of remaining together but because the path was the only safe route and we had to be well away from the district before dawn.

He knew his country inside out, having wandered all through it during his school holidays and hunted over it in more recent years whenever he could come down from London for a winter weekend. He led me across the Dartmouth road and after that by deep Devon lanes, windless and lightless as mine shafts, which climbed to bridle paths where the southwest wind ruffled the grass and one knew that in daylight would be somewhere a glimpse of the sea. When the sun came up we were resting in a combe not far from Harberton, clear of all those who might be curious about us, with a stream at our feet and a crumbly, red bank which fitted our backs — a pair of unwashed hikers, just possibly father and son, with nothing to single us out from other innocents.

Casually, talking for himself as much as for me, he reviewed the unsatisfactory situation we had left behind and followed in imagination his cousin's movements as she passed cautiously back from the Penpoles' cottage to the walled garden, miserably aware that she might have compromised his safety and shying at any vertical blackness which could be an observer creeping through the trees on a parallel course. But it was not that which disturbed him. He seemed to anticipate some conflict of emotions when she met her mother.

Seeing that I was puzzled by Tessa's character, he explained a little of her, love and amusement at her absurdities in his voice. She supported herself and earned her living as simply as any middle-class working girl. It was Eudora's conviction — inspired by the gin-swilling, privileged youngsters who infested wealthy New England society in her youth — that Tessa had to make her way in the world without a private income. The same, years earlier, had applied to him. Both of them accepted this nonintervention — more than accepted it. They couldn't imagine anything else. When Tessa married or if she needed capital to buy a business she would get it, but meanwhile she must be the co-equal of her contemporaries.

Far from resenting this discipline, she gloried in it. Nothing would have induced her to become a conventional county débutante exploiting hereditary wealth. She saw herself as a white-collar worker with a right to pursue her ideal visions of what society ought to be and to ignore what it actually was. Her two-room flat was shared with a young zoologist, a year or two older; that was an economy, she insisted, though in fact it was an airy gesture meant to prove that to civilized human beings sex was irrelevant. Naturally this infuriated her mother who at that age — I suspect, though Alwyn didn't say so — had shared bedrooms, sleeping bags and hillsides with the opposite sex, but not for a ridiculous principle.

After a sleep in the morning we set off on a long march which landed us near sunset on the slope below Powderham Castle overlooking the River Exe. Alwyn was exhausted. Wherever he had been, it was somewhere with no opportunity for exercise. Myself I thought we had now lost all interested parties, if there ever were any, and could safely treat ourselves to a bed and a good cleanup; but Alwyn wanted to lie another night close to his own earth.

During the day I had come to know him as well as I had ever known any man. He may well have puzzled his colleagues at MI5, for he was no townsman and no sort of policeman. I think he may have been brilliant in dealing with foreign agents and less sure with his own folk. He was too fond of them. As Amy Penpole had said, his only fault was to see the best in everyone — not perhaps a desirable quality in a security officer.

The silver estuary of the Exe spread out beneath us, all the way from the unspectacular, very English river to the golden shoals where curlews called and the half ebb streamed fast out of the narrows with the sand on one side and the red cliffs on the other. I felt that the river presented itself to him as a boundary between his home and the wide world which he proposed to re-enter, as if once across the Exe he would never return. He was wrong in that. He did return. It had been a brilliant move to hole up in Devon until his escape to Moscow was accepted and he could slide out unnoticed into exile; but I doubt if he ever realized how strong was his reluctance to leave the deep green womb of his birth.

His physical weariness emphasized melancholy. He needed me, young as I was, for we shared the same sort of upbringing — mine interrupted at the age of twelve, his not until the disaster. The long shadows of elms on the evening grass were to him sheer poetry, while for me they included the comfort of the cattle beneath them; but our love of country had the same quality. A peasant love.

He told me something of the Mornix case, perhaps to dispel any lingering doubts that I might have. When he came to the question of his overdraft I nearly asked him why he had not appealed to Eudora, but kept my mouth shut on the impertinence. Remembering how she had brought up the pair of cousins, I saw that it would never even have occurred to him. His career, his debts, his future were profoundly his own.

"Can't you think of anybody who knew your habit of shoving bank accounts away when you didn't want to look at them?" I asked.

He replied somewhat haughtily that for six weeks he had thought of little else.

"Not Tessa? She might have let it slip somewhere."

"Certainly not Tessa. I've never shown her the defenseless side of me."

"She seems to think all police are an outrage on humanity."

79

"She's a sweet joke. Special Branch had to put her through the hoops since she had often visited Whatcombe Street. But they would have got in a couple of interviews all she could tell them and are unlikely to have bothered her afterwards."

"And you're sure of this Rachel Iwyrne?"

"Quite sure. She couldn't possibly know of the bank statements. Tessa was more intimate with her than I ever was. I liked her well enough to recommend her to the Minister when he wanted to know about communes — and only God Almighty could have foreseen that he would fall in love with her and that Mornix would escape through Whatcombe Street."

"From what you tell me about her she sounds unreliable."

He took up my remark so sharply that I suspected he was not quite so sure of her political sympathies as he had been. He said that it depended what I meant by unreliable, that Cromwell's Puritans were unreliable but patriots more flaming in foreign war than the royalist Establishment. Rachel's passion for turning society scientifically upside-down meant more love of country, not less.

"Of course she is wide open to libel and misrepresentation," he went on. "So was Eudora in her youth. So is Tessa. The CIA blew their tops when Rachel took up with her Minister. But there was nothing treasonable about her. We told them that what was good enough for half a dozen distinguished dons, the London School of Economics and MI5 ought to be good enough for them. But they suspected the Old Boy Network of stalling them. That was why they went behind our backs to their tame M.P. and leaked the Mornix escape when we were trying to keep it quiet. I don't know how the Russians framed me or why. Dog doesn't normally eat dog. But my duty is to find out. And alone."

I asked him if he really believed it was worth the risk. After all, with his experience, he could reach Brazil or some other convenient country, and if he had to exchange elms for palms it was better than the streets of London and getting caught.

"I won't be caught by MI5 if I am careful. By the Russians I might be, and that's good night. It's safe, you see, because I don't exist. Not a question from anybody if I disappear completely and for ever as if I were picked off the face of the earth by little green men."

"Did they nearly get you the night before last?"

"I don't think so. All that is certain is that the two men I saw had tried to follow Eudora and John and lost them in the dark. Now that you've given me more details than she could, I see that it was you they expected Eudora to meet, not me. Whoever wants to talk to you had no idea he was near an unexpected prize."

"So you are going back again?"

"No. That's over. I'm going first to Forty-two Whatcombe Street if it isn't watched."

He described the commune and its youthful inhabitants.

"With gray hair?" I asked. "You'll never pass."

"I'm not going to open my shirt down to the navel with a medallion of Hitler hanging on it. I have other ideas, Willie."

I did not at all want to be picked off the face of the earth by little men, red or green. On the other hand, Eudora, Alwyn and the impetuous Tessa — they had become in their way such a definite, tangible part of all I had longed for in Bucarest and Cairo and Caulby. I was committed to them and nothing else. So I asked:

"Could I go to Whatcombe Street for you?"

When he refused to allow it, I reminded him that after living at the bottom of society in Cairo and not far off it in Paris I ought to be able to play the part and get away with it. And if Mornix could make himself unrecognizable, so could I — given a bit of help. But of course I would not know what questions to ask.

He looked at me and through me as if I were a complete stranger who had to be summed up instantly and conclusively. After all, to him I was no more than a companion on a cross-country walk who, according to his dubious account of himself, had shown some enterprise and ingenuity in the past.

"Why do you want to mix yourself up in this?" he asked.

I made a very immature, rambling attempt to explain my motives — a medley of self-interest and liking for them all, together with an incoherent statement of faith which nobody but Alwyn would have come near to understanding. It boiled down to saying that all this — by which I vaguely meant the tumbled valleys of the Exe and the Otter and the blue, smooth hills of Dorset on the horizon — would not taste so good if it wasn't served.

"You sound like Tessa," he said, smiling. "You want an earthly paradise."

"Tessa hasn't got it and thinks she knows how to make it. But if you had lived my life, you'd see that now in a way, for me, I *have* got it. And if I feel that to me it is worth it, that's my business and I can't express it any better."

"You've expressed it well enough for both of us. Now, questions are easy. If you are accepted, you might get some new angle of the story from them without trying. All I want is a picture of who were the suspects at the end of it all and what 42 Whatcombe Street knew but wasn't saying."

"How shall I find you?"

"Don't bother about that! I shall find you. Now, Tessa could help with your appearance. Don't go near her digs, but telephone her to meet you somewhere" — he gave me her home and business numbers — "and tell her what you are doing for me, but not a word more than you must."

"As Ionel Petrescu?"

"Not on any account. Just as Willie. Dig up that passport of yours sometime and keep it in your pocket as a last resort in any emergency. Are you sure you can find it?"

I explained that since I had hidden it at night it should not be too difficult to pick up the markers at night, and I described the overgrown chalk slope where it was.

I left him tucked in between bales of barley straw with the bats of early dusk for company. I had no anxiety about him in his present circumstances. As he said, he did not exist. Nor, for that matter, did I. There appeared to be some disadvantages about nonexistence, but so long as neither of us ran into someone who was actually looking for us — an unlikely accident — we were safe.

I crossed the river below Exeter and spent a long, comfortable night in the usual cottage with the usual motherly woman, kindly to youth in spite of the fact that it had a three-day beard and was a menace to the daintiness of the bathroom. In the morning I took a bus to London, getting off in the outer suburbs. It was a bit of a puzzle where to live until I was ready to tackle Whatcombe Street, for I had little experience of my own country between the extremes of rural village and respectable lodgings in a provincial town. Eventually I ran across two young men and a girl with bedrolls on their backs and sandals on their feet who directed me to a cheap and cheerful house in Greenwich, frequented by foreign students who wanted to see the historic river. There I met contemporaries, not much younger than myself, from very conventional backgrounds compared to my own yet expressing protest in their style of dress and speech. I liked them, and had little doubt that I could make myself acceptable at Whatcombe Street.

Alwyn had advised me to call Tessa at her office since she shared a downstairs telephone with other young women who were always fluttering to and from it making privacy difficult. She was secretary to one of the partners in a vast firm of chartered accountants, and one would normally get her at the extension number. The first time I got her boss, so I started a sales patter until he cut me off. The second time I got Tessa.

I said shortly that I was Willie and would wait in any public place she suggested with news for her. The reply — Temple

Gardens at a quarter to six — was immediate and businesslike with none of the agitation I expected.

I did not expect either that she would look as she did when she walked towards me between the lawns of the Gardens. Evidently social revolution was kept for evenings and weekends. She had caught from Eudora the upright, debonair way of holding herself, more common among American women than English. She was also very charmingly dressed in the kind of tunicky thing which had just become fashionable. With her fair hair shoulder length she looked at a little distance like a picture of some Anglo-Saxon boy in a history of costume, and close to was all the more feminine by contrast.

I explained to her that I wanted the right clothes in which to idle up to 42 Whatcombe Street and ask if I could have a pad for the night.

"Don't ask for anything," she said. "Just wander in and sit down. If somebody offers you pot, take it. But perhaps you like the stuff?"

"I've smoked hashish in Egypt and much prefer alcohol."

"You'll find they don't use it much. What were you doing in Egypt?"

I pulled myself up. That had been a quite unnecessary remark.

"On my way to Portugal."

"Thank you. I won't ask any more questions."

"That takes a weight off my mind. Your mother said I was a very poor liar."

"I had a hell of a row with her. Why do you all distrust me?"

"Because you are utterly honest, Miss Hilliard. And so the less you know, the better."

"Oh, I see! You mean I'm a poor liar too."

She cheered up a lot. That was not at all the same thing as being accused of indiscretion.

"You'll need jeans instead of trousers, and that windbreaker is too square," she said. "I think you'd be all right with an Afghan coat and some beads. And if anyone asks you who recommended Whatcombe Street, say it was Rupert and you met him in Cornwall."

After giving me a good description of the young man, his normal wanderings and his opinions, she promised to buy me a proper outfit in the King's Road and leave it in a suitcase at Charing Cross Station. If I turned up next day at the same time she would give me the ticket and I could collect it.

"May I ask just one question? It might be useful to Alwyn when you see him."

"Provided you don't go off the deep end when I refuse to answer."

"Have you met anyone called Ionel Petrescu?"

"No," I replied truthfully. "Why?"

She then told me all that had happened after we said good-bye to her. Alwyn's premonition of trouble had been right.

When Eudora returned from the Cricket Club dance, she was intercepted on her way to bed by her excitedly whispering daughter. Tessa delivered Alwyn's message and was bitterly hurt when her mother, too, refused to tell her where he had been hidden or to give any clear account of what I was doing in his company. The fact was, of course, that she did not know and must have been anxious lest I should turn out, after all, to be an incredibly clever security agent.

"I was so proud of her and eager to help," Tessa said, "and then she accused me of coming down to the Priory to poke about in the middle of the night instead of staying in London with my half-baked friends like Rachel Iwyrne to whom I'd introduced Alwyn."

I am sure the insinuation was not anything like as strong as that, even allowing for her mother's anxiety, but it was strong enough for an oversensitive Tessa who night after night had accused herself of being indirectly responsible for the whole disaster at Whatcombe Street. The result was that she swore she would never again come down to Cleder's Priory so long as she lived, jumped straight into her car, and started back to London.

She was belting along between Bovey Tracy and Exeter, probably driving as dangerously as any twenty-year-old in a filthy temper, when a car passed her and waved her down. Two men got out, shoved official-looking identity cards at her, and claimed to be police officers. Having searched the back of the car and the trunk, they flashed lights on the nearside hedge as if thinking it possible that a passenger had jumped out. They asked her why she was in such a hurry and if she did not realize that she was endangering other lives besides her own. When they had reduced her to pulp by their air of authority they invited her to help police with their inquiries.

They were, they said, Special Branch officers on the lookout for a certain Ionel Petrescu and had reason to believe she might be giving him a lift. She angrily denied any knowledge of Petrescu and asked what he looked like. The description seemed vague, as all police descriptions are except to policemen, and she was too impatient to listen carefully. She never spotted that it fitted me and assumed that they were really on the trail of Alwyn after she had aroused suspicion by her fast, sudden departure from Molesworthy.

"Had the car followed you all the way from there?" I asked.

"No, only for some miles. But I'll bet there were pigs of some sort on the road keeping track of me by radio."

For Tessa it was the last straw that Special Branch, after torturing her mother and herself for weeks — she had almost persuaded herself that it was physical torture — should still be at it. She arrived back in her Fulham flat at nine in the morning bursting to tell someone about the latest police atrocity, but found that all her friends in the building had left for their offices; and so, trapped between anxiety for Alwyn and fury with her mother, she called up Rachel Iwyrne — to her the other innocent and persecuted victim of the Mornix case.

I looked sympathetic and said nothing. It was alarming to imagine the girl nobly reminding herself that she must never neglect dear Rachel merely because she had ruined the career of a Minister by living at an address from which a spy had escaped. Tessa saw right through my tactful silence and said fiercely that I must not be prejudiced; that sort of thing could happen to any woman who had the courage to reject bourgeois values.

Well, perhaps it could; so I reserved judgment. Later on this Rachel became a far-too-close acquaintance of mine and I could then understand that to ruthlessly idealistic youth she might be irresistible.

Rachel had come around to Tessa's flat at once and calmed her down. Tessa did not mention the reasons for her sudden departure from Molesworthy — that was too delicate ground — but let go all her resentment at high-handed police action and demanded why she should be suspected of giving lifts to an unknown Ionel Petrescu. Rachel answered that of course there must be some connection with Alwyn, wherever he was hiding, that the investigation must be still going on, and that they should both always be prepared for more questioning. Eventually Rachel helped her to pack a bag and charitably insisted on putting her up and protecting her for at least a few days.

What, Tessa asked me, did I think of it all? I played it down, saying that probably it had nothing at all to do with Alwyn and that the police might have been looking for some prisoner escaped from Dartmoor. Anyway I could not understand why Special Branch should have taken an interest in Ionel Petrescu. But one thing in her story had particularly aroused my curiosity: that Rachel, speaking of Alwyn, should have used the phrase "wherever he was hiding." Tessa was sure of her words. It sounded as if the woman knew or suspected that he was not in Russia.

However, I was not going to emphasize that and start off my alliance with Alwyn's difficult cousin on the wrong foot. I found myself fascinated by her as well as respecting her, and I tried to lead the conversation to Molesworthy and more personal ground.

"Do you always call your mother Eudora?"

"Yes. She wouldn't let Alwyn call her Aunt Eudora because she said it sounded like the family terror. And I picked it up from him."

"Where did she get Sack?"

"Bought the little freak half-grown off a gamekeeper! Her precious Sack! She's a ridiculous old bag."

"But there's no one who doesn't love her."

Tessa growled like an offended cat and did not deny it.

"Sometime you must tell me all the truth. Will you?" she asked.

"When there is no more danger, yes."

"I think you'll be bored when there isn't."

"God forbid! I just want to be a simple farmer if there's ever a chance of it."

"You?"

"I thought you said you weren't going to ask any questions."

"But surely you can tell me about yourself. Why are you doing this for Alwyn?"

"I don't know. Because I'm sorry for him. Because we have the same values. It isn't that I resent injustice. I've learned to live with that."

"But such a risk for a stranger!"

"None of you three could ever be a stranger to me."

"Or you to us, Farmer Willie," she answered.

Her steady eyes held a comradeship which I had never known from any woman of my own age, so I felt I could ignore the plural "us."

The following day I took over the luggage ticket. Tessa

hardly stopped. Whatever I was, she had realized that we should be seen together as little as possible. I had the impression that she had been thinking over her mother's courage and continual anxiety and at last appreciated Eudora's determination that no one should end up in jail but herself.

I recovered the suitcase and changed in the station lavatory, blushing for myself. Tessa's choice for me was far worse than the Afghan garment. She had bought what appeared to be a Hussar's frockcoat, dark blue with decaying frogs. A florid label from a Youth Boutique had been loosely sewn over the discreet original of Savile Row. There were also jeans and sandals to which a note was attached: *Take off your socks.* When I emerged from the lavatory, a passing porter remarked:

"Lost the band, squire?"

Probably I should not have laughed, only proceeded on my way in unshaven dignity. But my amusement did a lot for morale, getting me contentedly into my part as the first burst of applause must do for an actor.

The scene at 42 Whatcombe Street was much as Alwyn had described it. There was a girl in the porch dressed in plastic deerskin and an old curtain with an enormous sphere of frizzy blonde hair. She was thoughtfully scratching it while talking to a bloke whose merry eyes were just visible and dominated a splendid set of dark whiskers. I passed them with a hello, went in boldly, sat down on the floor with my back against the wall, and began to eat some stale food in my knapsack. My uniform coat and sandals seemed to be a passport, but hair and beard were hopelessly insufficient. I decided that my two elder brothers — stockbrokers both of them — had held me down and cut it all off.

Nobody paid more than passing attention to me. I was there, and since a roof over his head was every man's right I could stay there. Having finished my stale bread and jam, I asked where the tap was. Whiskers had dropped his girl and come in to inspect me. He tossed me a can of beer and asked

89

me where the hell I got that coat. I said it was my grand-father's and he hadn't missed it yet.

There were three large rooms in the flat with a kitchen and bathroom at the end of a passage. Eight occupants were visible when I arrived. After dark there were thirteen. How many were visitors and how many permanent lodgers, and of the lot how many slept there on any given night it was difficult to establish. Special Branch would certainly have had a job to sort them out. They looked damned odd, but the communal living was a successful fact and would have suited me fine if I had had the enterprise to discover a similar joint in Paris instead of struggling on my own. Furniture was common property, mostly broken but serviceable, bought for a song and left be-hind when a member cleared out. If you hadn't got a bed you used a sleeping bag or — in my case — the floor, frockcoat and a borrowed pillow. Yet things were comparatively orderly as I found when I slipped out to buy some chops and asked Whiskers and his girl to join me. We waited patiently for our turn at the kitchen, and I was not popular when I wiped the grease off used plates with a banana skin instead of washing them. I had thought it was a nice touch and in character.

In the course of the evening questions about my life were perfunctory, but about my opinions they went fairly deep. The members of the commune were consumed by curiosity about a very unsatisfactory world and I sympathized with their en-thusiasm for change, futile though it was. I tended towards a Maoist position, with which I was familiar from lectures at school on Marxist heresies and from reading the Little Red Book which always seemed to me an admirable manual for Boy Scouts, easily defensible and possibly what China needed.

Nobody bothered about where I came from or what my surname was. Willie was enough. They did ask me who had told me I could find friends there, and I produced Rupert. Oh, yes, he had been very much one of them in the spring before the fuzz turned the place inside out. I pretended alarm and asked what the fuzz had been after. And so that first night I got an outline of the story from their point of view.

The house belonged to Rachel Iwyrne who had let the ground-floor flat to the commune and herself lived above. Lieutenant Mornix had walked in with a nod and a smile past a group of four who were sitting on the porch enjoying the sun. They thought he was going upstairs to see Rachel, but instead he entered the flat, the door of which was always open. There he was ignored; they supposed he was an architect or builder come to see about some promised alterations.

He went down the passage and out of the back door into a little yard containing only the dustbins and a plane tree. Most of the space was occupied by a chap called Bob who was mending a sofa and half blocking the door. No one actually saw Mornix's movements; he must have come back, nipped into the bathroom which was just inside the back door, changed there, and jumped out of the window into the yard. The next thing was that Bob and a stranger looking like an extra-hairy apostle walked out of the front door, said they had some money and why not all go around to the boozer? So a few of them did. Bob set up the drinks, left the bar with his friend to telephone, and was never seen again.

All the next day I stayed on, establishing my bona fides by carrying a banner in a minor demo against the borough council — for what cause I never knew — and cultivating Whiskers's friendship. When we went out together in the evening he became very frank over his red wine. His name was Ciampra and he was a Maltese whose parents had sent him to England to complete his education, enrolling him in a college which advertised extensively in the hope of catching innocents abroad and specialized in fake degrees.

Ciampra discovered the swindle in a matter of weeks but had not enlightened his parents. He had reverted to the normal interests of Mediterranean youth and by means of passing from one opinionated girl to another had eventually arrived at the haven of 42 Whatcombe Street. He had no moral sense whatever, but instead of living off the vices of society, like so many of his London compatriots, he had decided to exploit the virtues. His ambition was to buy a degree in theology from his college and start up a new religion — likely to be more profitable in the long run than a new brothel with the advantage that the police could not demand a cut. He had seen through me, he told me. I'd got too much sense of humor and was overacting. That frockcoat had shown him that I was out for an easy pad and girlfriends just as he was.

I said that after the story I had heard about a spy escaping I'd have thought they would all be more suspicious of strangers.

"We are, Willie," he replied. "Two narks we've thrown out already. They made the mistake of never washing. Overacting, like you. But I could see they weren't enjoying it. Too serious. Too many questions."

"Did they find out any more, do you think?"

"They can't have done, because I hear Miss Rachel is still around. She used to come downstairs and look us over like a bloody anthropologist. Influence of Premarital Sex on Political Concepts. Title of Thesis! Saw it on her notebook!"

"Wouldn't you expect her to be still around?"

He reminded me that everyone assumed Mornix had changed in the bathroom. The door was locked; his clothes were found inside; and he had got out through the window, which was open, to join Bob in the yard.

"Anything wrong with that?" he asked.

One had to have lived in the place to find anything wrong with it. I said that what with girls washing their hair or their panties, blokes outside yammering for a pee, somebody having a bath, somebody else wanting the soap so he could wash at the kitchen sink, it seemed to me difficult for this Bob to have made sure that the bathroom was free when Mornix needed it.

"And you can't do a job of that sort without split timing," he pointed out. "I know."

He didn't say how he knew. It was unnecessary. I think it likely that his quick intelligence had been recognized in a less high-minded world than that of Whatcombe Street and that he had sat in on the neat plotting of crime.

"Notice the plane tree and the high wall around the yard?" he asked. "There's one of Miss Rachel's windows which can't be seen at all from over the way. Suppose she drops a knotted rope or something? Mornix is up there in three seconds flat. Changes. Drops down. And there he is helping Bob to knock tacks in the sofa.

"Bob waits till he can make a jump for the bathroom. Throws down Mornix's clothes on the floor, locks the door, gets out of the window, and off they go. That puts Miss Rachel in the clear. She swore to Jesus that she'd been up in her flat typing out notes on the sleeping arrangements of the natives down below and had never seen or heard a thing. And there wasn't a scrap of evidence against her."

The following morning before I left I went with him to have a look at the yard, the window and the plane tree. His theory held up. Mornix's quick change could very well have been managed that way, taking the risk of someone leaning out of a window in the adjoining houses at the wrong moment.

I asked him why he had not put it to the police who might have been able to find some trace of the rope on the window-sill or in Rachel's flat. He was shocked that I should think he could be that sort of bloke. Some of those innocents in the commune might be capable of it, he said, but not he.

"I'm a good citizen," he added. "And you know what that means — keep clear of the fuzz!"

"But if you believe the woman was an agent of the KGB?"

"So what? Start mucking about with her and they'd whip her off to Russia like Rory. And I'll tell you another of them

— Rory's sister Tessa. Friend of Rachel's she was and belongs to the IMG."

"What's that?"

"International Marxist Group. That old billy-goat Trotsky."

"Then she wouldn't be mixed up with the Communist party."

"Well up on it all, aren't you? I heard you carrying on about Mao as if you believed it. Now, how do you think we could make a bit out of what we know?"

Being a young fraud himself, he could spot another on sight as his more earnest companions could not. My impression was that he was getting bored with living from hand to mouth and could possibly be useful. I gave nothing away beyond an understanding grin, telling him that I would keep in touch with him. I agreed to take his greasy, black sweatshirt in exchange for my military frock which he thought would add to his reputation as a harmless clown.

The next step was to report to Alwyn what I had learned of Rachel both from Tessa and at Whatcombe Street. Whatever he made of it, his blind confidence in her was bound to be shaken. But how to get in touch with him? He had said that I should leave that to him, though unless he was watching the street — which must be too big a risk to take — he could not know what my movements had been.

I telephoned Tessa's office to see if she could give me any discreet hint and was told she was up in Glasgow with her boss; so I waited till evening and called her home. It was a pleasant male voice which eventually came to the telephone and answered me.

"Tommy Bostock. Tessa is away. Can I give her a message?"

"Would you tell her that Willie called?"

"Willie? There's a telegram here which may be a message for you."

"What does it say?"

"Willie's passport ready for collection Tuesday night. No signature. Are you a friend of hers? Have we met? I'm the chap who shares the flat with her."

Though I had heard of this arrangement, I felt now an unreasonable touch of jealousy. I said coldly that we had not met and that I knew her in Devon.

"Oh, good! Well, look here, I'm worried about her. You might be able to give me some advice. Could you come around?"

The last thing I wanted was to call at Tessa's flat. It was one of the very few places which Marghiloman & Co. might consider worth watching. Tommy Bostock must have noticed my hesitation, for he added at once:

"Or I'll meet you wherever you are. My car's outside."

There was a pub down the street from the box where I was telephoning, and I suggested it. He was there in ten minutes. Neither of us recognized the other, for each was expecting the opposite of what he saw. Tessa's flatmate would be, I reckoned, something of a Whatcombe Street type; he on his part assumed that a friend from Devon would be tweedy and respectable. What he saw was sandaled, scruffy, with a beard at its most squalid week-old stage, and what I saw was a young Londoner very informally but elegantly dressed.

We were staring at each other doubtfully for a full minute before he made the first move, and I admitted I was Willie.

"When in Rome, do as the Romans?" he asked with a smile.

"Exactly."

"I imagine you know all about us from Eudora Hilliard?"

"Well, no."

"I suppose it's not the sort of thing she'd talk about. But there's nothing in it. Tessa goes her way and I go mine."

He seemed a very sensible chap and I asked him what made him agree to the joint flat.

"I'm very fond of her and I wanted to see if it could possi-

95

bly work. Her territory, you see, not mine. There's no real parallel in other mammals. Occasionally she makes a display of hostility and I at once respond with the correct gestures of submission. That inhibits her very proper instinct to eat me or throw me out. Well, but I'm boring you. The fact is that she's gone to stay with that awful woman, Rachel Iwyrne."

"Good God! What made her do that?"

"Protest, I think. She had a row with her mother and then got stopped on the road by police. I gather it was Special Branch after her again. Lucky she doesn't know how to make a bomb!"

"Do they think she might?"

"No, of course not. What I meant was that she's in the mood to blow something up in aid of the Anarchists' Annual Dinner and Dance. I wanted to ask you whether you think I should ring her mother and tell her Tessa is with this Rachel."

It was plain that whatever I answered would make up his mind. I wished I could consult Alwyn, but that could not be before the next day, Tuesday. His telegram was as clear as it was ingenious. If I went to pick up my passport he would be there or thereabouts, and our meeting could not be traced.

I advised Tommy to call Eudora at once. After all, she was headquarters with a clearer picture of the whole threatening setup than I had.

"I'd better say it was you who told me to ring. Eudora thinks I'm a bloody fool. So I am probably. But I cherish our golden girl and I know I'm good for her. What's your name besides Willie?"

That was a nasty one. I did not want the name of Adrian Gurney or the Portuguese being bandied about in Molesworthy, but I had to answer.

"Willie Yonell," I said. That would alert Eudora and no one else.

I collected my own clothes at Charing Cross Station and changed back to the comfort of my windbreaker. I had been continually shivering since parting from the uniform coat. A hardy lot, the inhabitants of Whatcombe Street, male and female! By rights they should all have died of pneumonia After spending the night in the Greenwich house, I approached Folkestone much as I had done before, getting off the train at a silent, country station and walking the last part of the journey after dark in case I should be seen and recognized by any of the police who had received Ionel Petrescu. Over the Channel was a brighter moon than on my first visit and different patterns of black and white, so I ran into more trouble finding my markers than I expected. I might have lost patience and tried again some other night if I had not had time to waste waiting for Alwyn to turn up.

When at last I had recovered the passport and replaced all other personal papers I settled down nearby. About two in the morning I saw the quick flash of a torch on the opposite slope which showed me in what direction to look so that I soon picked up a bush which moved among the others. We sat down in a hollow and I measured out my news, starting with Tessa's adventure when returning from Molesworthy.

"Too clumsy for our people," he said, "and if I am right they know all about Ionel Petrescu. It sounds to me like your Mr. Marghiloman's work and the same two men who followed Eudora and John. Was Tessa frightened?"

"No, but blazing angry and in tears. She is being comforted by Rachel who took her home and is looking after her."

"Rachel protective? That's very unlike her. Emphatically heterosexual and not a bit maternal."

"She was fishing for information. She told Tessa that there must be some connection between Ionel Petrescu and Alwyn Rory, wherever he is. Tessa was sure of her words. Wherever he is. What reason has Rachel got to suppose you are not in Moscow and who told her?"

"Anything else?"

I could see that I had him worried and that it would now be

safe to open up Ciampra's theory without being told it was ridiculous.

To my surprise he accepted it and blasted himself for appalling misjudgment, for being as guilty professionally as it he had taken the bribe.

"I was never happy about that bathroom," he said. "When I had all the reports on my desk I was sure Mornix had changed under cover of the sofa Bob was mending, though if he did — unless he was lying down — he would have been in full view of the houses opposite. That would not have mattered provided his getaway was quick enough. But in fact not a soul in those houses at the back saw him. Yet they did see Bob."

"Doesn't it clear you?"

"No. Makes it worse. If Rachel was involved the evidence against me is stronger, not weaker."

Then he started thinking aloud:

"She knows I am not in Moscow. She does not know who Petrescu is. Well, that's quite likely. The KGB is very departmentalized. No reason why she should understand what they are up to. Nor do I, damn it! They could have picked you up any time after they were satisfied that you had no protection. Marghiloman nearly did it for them. Are you sure he was Romanian?"

"Well, if he wasn't he had been born and bred there."

"He doesn't quite fit. The only certainty is that it's you and the fishing fleet which interest him."

Myself, I had found him a typical KGB man, but I could not argue with such an expert as Alwyn. I asked him where he had been for the last week.

"In London. Always on the move. Testing my nerves. I cannot get accustomed to seeing people I used to know. I daren't pass them in case they sense my fear."

"You're still after Mornix?"

"Mornix, my dear Willie, is certainly dead. Why should the KGB hide him and take the risk of running him out of the country when he is no use to them any more? Their only problem is disposal and a few deep-frozen packages will take care of that. No, what I want is to clear myself before I go."

He repeated that in London he was helpless — a badly wanted man without a base or friends. He could not pick up the trail again. He could not make contact and attack.

"By God!" he exclaimed. "I've a mind to go back to Devon and make them come to me!"

"How?"

"Through Rachel. I think I might appeal to her for help. She is an old acquaintance, so it will seem natural to her. Then, when she betrays me to the KGB, the game between me and them is on."

We saw the sun rise over the North Sea, diminishing the Channel to a blue and silver stream between white cliffs till cloud came up with the tide and turned the river of Europe to ocean with no near neighbor beyond the mist. I wanted a good insular breakfast and suggested that there was no risk if we went back a mile or two to some inland village. Alwyn allowed himself to be persuaded, but I could see what he meant when he said his nerves were none too solid. He was confident enough in the open, but the close presence of other human beings made him look undefinably guilty. I ought to have shown the same uneasiness, yet I doubt if I ever did. Lack of imagination and the conceit of youth.

I told him of my first reception at Cleder's Priory. He laughed and said that Eudora had given him much the same account of it.

"She really should have known better. What infuriated her was the childishness of MI5, as she thought, sending down a little foreign agent with a transparent trick to catch her out. Willie, I think it is time you broke loose from the whole affair and started on your way to becoming Adrian Gurney again."

His advice on how to do it was alarming. He said that the KGB had obviously been ordered to find out who I was and where the devil I came from. I was of no interest to them, but they had to be sure of it.

"So, if I were you, I should tell them the whole truth, backed by your passport, and get clear," he went on. "If they threatened to inform the police, call their bluff! I don't see your Councillor Sokes or the police taking any very serious action."

I was not on any account going to show the Russians my passport. My stepfather would have the blackest of black marks against him though all he had done was to take me to Egypt. However, I saw no reason why I should not insist that my name was really Ioncl Petrescu and let them hunt for my relations till they gave up.

"Suppose they know of the connection between you and me?" I asked.

"They can't. There isn't any beyond the letter which they themselves made you take down to Eudora. And why they did that God knows! All one can ever count on is that most governments would rather tell the truth if it is possible while the Russians on principle would rather tell a lie even if it isn't possible."

He gave me precise instructions how to get in touch with them. I was not to write or telephone or call at any of the East European embassies; if I did, I risked coming to the notice of MI5. I must use some harmless agent— for example, Ciampra — to deliver a message to the Russian Naval Attaché and I should arrange for the meeting with their emissary to be in a public place just to keep him out of any temptation to be awkward.

"But I am sure you will have no trouble at all at a first meeting. Probably a second meeting will be suggested at which you will be questioned by someone tougher. If you then see trouble threatening, go at once to the police and ask for Special Branch! Tell them your whole story, leaving me right out of it—which is dead easy since they believe I am in Moscow."

The more I thought of his advice, the wiser it seemed. All I regretted was that I might never see him or the Hilliards again unless it was from the public gallery in the Law Courts. He guessed what I was thinking and put his hand on my shoulder, saying that I should never lose Eudora and Tessa and that if all went well and Adrian Gurney could take time off from his sheep to go abroad there was no one he would more gladly see.

I returned to London a little apprehensive but on the whole with a sense of relief, for there seemed to be an end in sight to all the unexpected trouble which Petrescu's defection had caused me. Alwyn was undoubtedly right in insisting that MI5 knew all about me and that Sokes would never open his mouth. The only crime I had ever committed was faking a suicide, and that was unlikely to carry any penalty worse than a fine and a long lecture from the magistrate on wasting the time of the police.

After checking in at the Greenwich hostel — since it still seemed a reasonable precaution to have an address where I was lost among other drifting youth — I telephoned Ciampra to meet me at a Chelsea pub where his style of dressing would not be remarkable and we were unlikely to meet any of his companions. He turned up wearing my full-dress military frock. Whatcombe Street had done more damage to it than sixty years and any minor imperial campaign, for it now had a deep purple wine stain under the left breast. After the fourth beer he admitted that he had put it there as a conversation piece.

"A bloke thought I'd nicked it and stopped me in the street," he said.

"What kind of a bloke?"

"Military Club sort of bloke. Too young to be the grandpa

you said you'd got it off. So I let him see the label and all. 'Most sorry to have troubled you,' he said, 'and perhaps you will allow me to buy you a drink.' "

Clamun gave a wild imitation of a real haw-haw English accent, straight from St. James's Palace.

"You told him where you did get it?"

"No. Off a mate in a pub, I said. But he knew I lived at Whatcombe Street."

That rang a faint alarm bell. However, no harm seemed to have been done.

I explained that I had been looking into the best way to make a bit for us both out of the Mornix escape as he had suggested, and that I had had a talk with a crook newspaperman who was interested in a big story and would split with us. First he wanted to contact the Press Officer of the Russian Embassy and had given me a fiver to deliver a note to him. I didn't want to risk that myself. I'd had a bit of an argument with the police already and was afraid I might be recognized. The fiver was his if he would hand the note in and hop it quick.

"Want me to go like this?" he asked.

That was what I had intended. He could well be delivering a protest from some Marxist society on the lunatic fringe.

"It might put them on to Whatcombe Street, and we don't want that yet," he warned me.

I most surely did not. But one can't keep everything in mind all the time. Only then did I remember that the KGB knew nothing of my visit to Whatcombe Street and that any association with the place could be deadly.

"Have you got any other clothes?"

"Bottom of my bag, friend Willie! Any time I get nicked, it's collar and tie for me. And I'll never do it again, Your Worship, and God bless the kind British police!"

He looked crumpled but almost respectable — say, a science student meeting his aunt for lunch — when I picked him up again outside Chelsea Town Hall. I gave him his fiver and the letter and — unknown to him — watched him deliver it from a safe distance. I had written in Russian:

I understand that you wish to talk to the Romanian, Ionel Petrescu, who came ashore at Folkestone on the morning of July 3rd. He is very willing to be questioned and will be in the small mammal house of the London Zoo at 4:30 on Wednesday next.

When Wednesday came I shaved off my sprouting whiskers and dressed as befitted a poor refugee trying to earn a decent living. At four-thirty I was in the small mammal house wishing I could free the little creatures nervously trotting up and down their cages much as I was — all so easily to be tamed, but heaven help the neighbors' chickens!

The public passed quickly through the house on the way to more spectacular exhibits. Only a father with two young children loitered by the cages, appearing fascinated by mink and sable. I ruled him out at once, expecting some heavily built, round-headed Slav in a suit too tight for him. It was not until I heard him speaking Russian to his sons that I realized this slim, distinguished, dark-haired father was my man.

I murmured "Ionel Petrescu" as the family passed me, and he responded with a splendid act in excellent English as if I were an old friend whom he had inexcusably failed to recognize. He even introduced me to his children.

We strolled outside where with complete naturalness he sent his boys off to line up for elephant and camel rides while we sat down on a bench in the main avenue and watched them. I stuck carefully to my thick English accent until he switched the language to Russian and remarked politely that I spoke it well for a Romanian.

"Now, what was it you wished to tell me, Mr. Petrescu?"

"Only this — that the KGB is following me about and that there's no reason for it."

"The KGB? There is no such thing in England."

"Well, whatever they call themselves."

"I think you are mistaken. From our files we know you are a Romanian who wished to desert your country and for reasons of your own — to get a pension of some sort? — invented this story of escape from a fishing fleet. I presume the British know it too, and only pretended to accept your story since all defections to the West are valuable propaganda. We have no interest in you whatever."

"Then why did your agent Marghiloman persuade me to take that letter down to Mrs. Hilliard?"

"Who is Mrs. Hilliard?"

"The aunt of Alwyn Rory."

The name of Rory made him sit up at once. He asked me to describe Marghiloman, which I did. I then gave him the whole story so far as it concerned myself — how Marghiloman had tried to detain me on my return from Molesworthy and had me followed at Swindon, and how I had returned to Mrs. Hilliard as my one friend in a foreign country to ask what I ought to do. I said that I did not wish to spend my whole life in hiding and that I had decided to put my head into the wolf's den and see if it really wanted to eat me.

He heard me out in silence and asked if Ionel Petrescu was my true name. I pulled out the documents which the police had given me and showed them in the hope of impressing him though they proved nothing. I was very conscious of Adrian Gurney's passport in another pocket, separated from him only by a bit of cloth.

"You have no reason to be afraid, Ionel Petrescu," he said. "If a man is fool enough to leave his country and there is nothing else against him, we don't let him waste our time. Few of them are any better off. You yourself don't look very prosperous."

"I could be if your people would leave me alone."

"Would you object to being questioned by someone who knows more of the background than I do?"

"Not at all. I'd be glad. But where?"

"Oh, not in the Lubianka prison! You are too nervous, Petrescu. Wherever you like."

"I don't want to get into trouble with the British."

"Privacy? I'll guarantee that. Can you row a boat?"

"As a trawlerman I ought to be able to."

That made him laugh. I have never associated laughter with the KGB. I think this chap must have been an assistant Naval Attaché. He said that I should take a boat on the river at Richmond Bridge and row upstream until someone hailed me from the left bank. I was then to take him on board and cross to the other bank. I should wear something bright yellow — scarf or shirt — so that I could be recognized.

"Recognized?"

"My dear Ionel Petrescu, you are consumed by a sense of self-importance. I doubt if any of our people in London could recognize you."

I found this hard to believe and assumed that it was one of those attempts at lying even when it wasn't possible of which Alwyn had spoken. However, there was no doubt that if I wanted to be left alone once and for all I had better go boating and see what I picked up. My contact told me to start from Richmond Bridge at eleven the next morning. If it was raining and thus an unlikely time for anyone to be enjoying the river I should come the following day.

It turned out to be warm, blue river and green banks full of activity for a weekday. So, with a yellow scarf round my neck, I started off up the stately Richmond reach between the meadows and the leafy towpath. I had never rowed, and anyone who watched the skiff rolling and splashing would have known at once that I was no fisherman. Just short of Eel Pie Island a woman gave me a comradely wave from the towpath. I had noticed the gay summer frock while still some distance away and thought how pleasant it would be to have such a companion sitting on the stern cushion. But no luck with beautiful spies! Her face was round and competent — she might have been a District Nurse on her day off — and the rest of her rather indefinite. When she came aboard I crossed to the other bank as instructed, and appreciated how simple and sensible the move was. If anyone was interested in her movements he would have to go around by one of the distant bridges before he could catch up with us.

She told me to pull in under cover of Eel Pie Island and to take the stern seat while she rested on the sculls. Finding that my English was barely comprehensible, she started to speak Russian and asked me how I had really left Romania. I refused to tell her on the grounds that I did not wish innocent persons to get into trouble, but otherwise gave her a coherent story which would be hard to check. I said that I had tried to make a living in Paris, had been suspected by French police of embezzlement — details founded on Caulby here — and paid a seaman to smuggle me into England. A few days after I had landed, sleeping rough and not knowing in the least what to do, I heard of the trawler fleet and put on my act of having swum ashore from it in the hope of regularizing my position and getting some sort of charitable handout. The facts of what happened when I was found were convincing, for I related them exactly as they were.

"Typically Romanian!" she said rudely. "And the immigration officers believed you?"

"I don't know whether they did at first, but afterwards, yes."

And I continued with the story of my quiet life, translations and all, up to the meeting with Marghiloman.

She questioned me at length about him and then turned to Eudora, asking if she believed her nephew was in Moscow. No doubt about that, I said.

"Did she ever say why he should have escaped to Russia, if he did?"

"No. She assumed you had arranged it."

"Did she tell you on what evidence the British Tribunal decided that he must be guilty?"

"No."

"She believed him innocent?"

"She would have liked to, but how could she after he had defected?"

"Mr. Petrescu, you are clearly on quite intimate terms with her. Can you find out what was the evidence against Rory?"

I knew very well what the damning evidence was: the bank accounts. But if I said so it would be plain that I had heard it directly from Alwyn or that Alwyn had been able to tell his aunt. Very deep waters, and all the deeper because there was no clue to what she wanted. It might be that the KGB did not know what the effect of their fake bribe had been or that they wondered how far Rachel's cover as a harmless intellectual was blown.

"Mrs. Hilliard must know or suspect what it was. You will ask her."

"I do not want to be involved."

"It could mean a useful sum of money for you if you found out the truth."

"Not me! I'm not clever enough."

"You are quite as intelligent as most agents, Mr. Petrescu. Have you family in Romania?"

"Find out!"

"We shall, whether your name is Petrescu or not."

She gave two hearty pulls on the sculls which would have taken us out into the middle of the Volga, let alone the Thames.

"There are two of my companions idling suspiciously at Richmond Bridge, and I am sure that they have been followed by British security police. If you do not agree to do what you are told I shall row you back and both of them will receive us cordially at the landing stage. Instead of dreaming that you are under surveillance by us, you will be suspect to the British from then on."

I told her that I would jump overboard and that she could go to hell and pay the hire of the boat as well.

"If you do, it will be in full view of all the people on both banks. However you explain your extraordinary action, the police will be interested and you will be exposed."

"I shall not be. Escape from the KGB!"

"What were you doing with them in the first place? Difficult to explain, Mr. Petrescu, especially if we pass the word to the police that you are a criminal and a fraud and that they should find out how you really entered England."

It was in my mind to tell her straight out that I was not Petrescu but Adrian Gurney, British subject. It may be that I should have done so; but it must be remembered that I was muddled by these persistent questions which made no sense. I also foresaw that if MI5 were to learn that Adrian Gurney — that impostor whom they had allowed to stew in his own juice — was suspiciously involved in the affair of Alwyn Rory, their interrogators would be much too good for me.

So could I risk going down to Molesworthy as an agent of the KGB? It was tempting, and one could almost say it was a patriotic duty. If I could find Alwyn, I could let him know that the Russians were willing to pay to find out what the damning evidence against him was, so that either they didn't frame him or didn't know that it had worked.

"Suppose I agree and disappear?"

"You could try, Petrescu, but eventually we should catch up with you. Didn't you want to be free of all surveillance? Refuse to work for us and you will never feel secure. Agree, and I promise you will be left alone. You have only to report to me that you cannot get the information we need and to tell me what you did get. But if you can find out what the evidence was which broke Alwyn Rory and if your report is confirmed — shall we say five hundred pounds?"

I pretended to be surprised and delighted. She then said that I should always keep an eye open for any stranger who wanted to talk to me. He would introduce himself by: *Good morning, I mean, good afternoon* or *Good afternoon, I mean, good evening* or whatever was appropriate to the time of day. I was to reply: *It's all this summer time.* Most ingenious! It was a typically eccentric English reply which would not attract the attention of any third party — or, if it did, the attention would be laughing and sympathetic.

I dropped her off on the towpath, paddling around for an hour before returning to Richmond Bridge. Now that I had the KGB off my back I was ready to visit Molesworthy without any precautions. But there remained the enigmatic Marghiloman. Father at the zoo had obviously never heard of him. However, that meant nothing; a diplomat might well be unfamiliar with the dirtier activities of his staff. My boatwoman had neither admitted that he was working for the Russians, nor said that he was not. On the whole I was inclined to think that he was an agent of MI5 after all, or perhaps an overzealous private eye. There were probably such chaps gathering information in hope of profit like free-lance journalists.

Puzzling over Marghiloman it suddenly occurred to me that I myself was now a double agent — for Alwyn and the KGB. The realization startled me. One doesn't easily recognize oneself under a formal label of that sort. When I considered that in the matter of Mornix's escape from Whatcombe Street I was also doing a job for MI5 — though quite without their knowledge — I could call myself a triple agent, which must be a rarity. I found that comic, while well aware that the joke was in the same class of sick humor as coffins and feet set in concrete.

So the triple agent was professionally cautious and left Greenwich on foot, which experience showed to be far the best way of avoiding persons who might wish to trace his movements. No ticket collectors. No bus conductors. No police checks on motor vehicles. I was now splendidly fit after so much open air and exercise, all the yellow of my complexion having turned to a weatherbeaten rural tan. I reached Basingstoke in two days which was good going. A train to Exeter and two more days' walking landed me in the morning on the slope of the knoll above Cleder's Priory.

II

I had lost all sense of urgency, that artificial urgency of London where women chattered their way from one shop window to another and men hurried to earn a living by selling unnecessary objects or to spend money on acquiring them. Febrile activity is not so apparent in Eastern Europe. One would have more sympathy for communism if only its chief ambition was not to catch up in the race after futility.

Below me deep Devon spread over combes and hillocks without a human being in sight unless one counted two splashes of color on the seats of distant tractors. Yet every acre of the scene — woodland, pasture, corn ready for harvest — was the result of unremitting work, unremitting love. Urgency? There was never anything else in the life of the land, but no sign of it and certainly no pretense of it.

In the valley behind me I caught a glimpse of Eudora, John Penpole and the pack returning from exercising the hounds. I had never seen her on a horse before. That straight pillar of devotion and integrity was a formidable sight when mounted on a dapple gray which must have been all of seventeen hands. In a narrow lane they came on Tessa, whose lower half at once vanished in the flood of adoring hounds. I had no idea that she had left London. She had evidently made up the quarrel with Eudora, for I could just hear the ring of their voices and it was happy.

Eudora and John rode on with the pack, intending to skirt the high ground and return to the kennels by way of Molesworthy. Tessa climbed directly up the path through the bracken. She looked in her natural environment, exposing my dream of romantically rescuing her from London as the nonsense it was. I don't know why the fact that she was walking alone and using her eyes should have revealed to me another Tessa. If she had been riding I might have felt that she was merely forcing herself into some resentful pleasure; but as it was I could understand why her Tommy Bostock had accepted me so easily when I claimed to be a friend of hers from Devon. He had been aware of this other Tessa, as I was not.

At the top of the ridge her eyes were following a pair of sailing buzzards and she did not see me until I said good morning.

"You turn up like a bad penny, Adrian," she said.

"I see you've been talking to Eudora. About time for both of you!"

"Yes. She couldn't understand what you were doing with Alwyn."

"And what have you told her?"

"Everything."

After talking to Tommy Bostock, Eudora had driven straight to London and sailed like a battleship into Rachel's flat, guns hooded and the pennants of England, Old and New, streaming behind. She and Tessa had fallen into each other's arms and at once returned to Molesworthy. Thereafter there was little point in either keeping secrets from the other when Alwyn had trusted Tessa to groom me for the Whatcombe Street caper.

"What about Rachel?"

She did not answer, but asked me if I had seen Alwyn recently.

"Over a week ago. He is still in England."

"Are they on his trail? Is he in danger?"

"He doesn't think so."

"Adrian, tell me if I've done the right thing! Look at this!"

She pulled out an envelope from her shirt pocket and handed it to me; it contained two sheets of paper — one, she said, in Rachel's writing, the other in Alwyn's, both unsigned.

Alwyn's to Rachel read:

"We are both in danger. Can I talk to you? T knows where I am. She was there on her tenth birthday."

Rachel's note to Tessa was:

"Greatly surprised to get this. I thought he was away."

Alwyn must have dropped his message at Rachel's flat before leaving London, for he would not have trusted post or telephone. It was cleverly worded — merely a warning that the investigation of both was far from over and without any hint of innocence or guilt.

"How did you get it?" I asked.

"It was given to Amy Penpole by a young man she didn't know."

Tessa said that she had not yet consulted Eudora whose prejudice against Rachel was too strong.

"She would not have let me answer. She would have said it was a trap."

"So it is. But for Rachel."

I had always been apprehensive of what the effect on Tessa might be when she learned the truth about her patronizing friend, and hoped that it would be someone else who had to disillusion her. Now I had to do it myself, and just at the moment when I felt that confidence was growing.

"What do you mean?"

"I found out at Whatcombe Street that Rachel helped Mornix to escape. It could not have been done without her."

"Did Alwyn believe it when you told him?"

"He did. It fitted."

She was silent too long, and I said inanely that it must be a shock.

"Yes. But once one knows it, no. It's always been in the back of my mind, Adrian. It wasn't that I couldn't believe it. It's that I wouldn't."

She saw how uneasy I was at her silence and put her hand over mine.

"I was trying to remember what I could have given away. Nothing, I think. I have never even hinted that he wasn't in Moscow. And of course she must have known all along. But I'm glad you never told me who Ionel Petrescu was."

"That doesn't matter anymore. Nobody is looking for him."

"And nobody is looking for Adrian Gurney either?"

"Adrian Gurney is in suspended animation. I am just Willie, and I have news for Alwyn which he ought to know. Where is he and what did you do?"

She had acted as soon as she received the message and telephoned Rachel to meet her at the village of Frogmore. Then she had guided her as far as the entrance to a track which led up to the patch of neglected woodland where Alwyn was.

"He used to have a hide there for watching a buzzard's nest. He wanted to make notes of everything the pair caught and brought back. It was the day after my tenth birthday and he said that now he had a treat of our own for me. A gypsy picnic. I'll never forget it. Grilled young rabbit and sorrel salad and fat wild strawberries and cream. From the edge of the wood you could see for miles around. The hide was made of hazel wands and turf. There wouldn't be much of it left, but he could repair it in a day and it was quite comfortable and rainproof."

"You didn't go up yourself with Rachel?"

"No. Lots of reasons. I didn't want to intrude. So I just asked her to give Alwyn my love and picked her up later. I can take you there now if you like."

But I did not wish to intrude either. The unexpected situation was very tricky. It was impossible to guess what Alwyn was up to or who might be with him, and there was the added difficulty that the KGB might after all be keeping an eye on their new agent.

"I suppose he can reach us if he needs us?"

"Easily. Does he know you are here?"

"No. He told me to stay right out of it. I meant to, but now I can't."

She asked why I couldn't, saying that he was right and that I ought to consider the risk of assisting a trusted government servant believed to have taken a bribe from the KGB and defected to Moscow. God knows I had considered it, but the thing had happened and the risk was irrelevant.

"Because Alwyn has taken me back into my world."

"The land? You really want to make your life on it?"

I was amazed that she had remembered a single remark of mine in Temple Gardens and had spotted what I vaguely meant by my world. On the face of it love of the land hardly explained a half-British exile up to the eyes in essentially urban intrigue.

"Don't you, Tessa?"

"It's opting out. It's an escape."

"What's wrong with an escape? Nothing is worth serving except what one loves. And who can love forms of government?"

"Democrats pretend they do."

"Well, let 'em!"

I told her something of my conversations with Alwyn, though they had not been conversations so much as silences.

"We don't love England for what it makes or votes or thinks," I explained, "but for what it is — for the sake of the eyes one was born with, if you like."

"Just the peace and the green?"

"Oh, much more than that! I can't analyze it. The fields have their own honor and everywhere else it's only a funny word. Values — I found that yours were mine."

"Eudora's and Alwyn's?"

"And yours — the other Tessa."

"You can't cut me in half like a piece of cheese. Are you coming down to the house with me?"

I had to refuse though I wanted hours more of her. It would be too difficult to explain to any women working in the house the reappearance of a Willie who could no longer pretend to be a Portuguese.

"Where will you be if Alwyn needs you?" she asked.

"Is there a pub where no one is likely to recognize me, but not too far away?"

"Amy's sister at South Pool can give you a room. You can trust her not to talk, and John can visit you there."

South Pool was at the end of a creek running east from the Kingsbridge Estuary. A boat could come alongside the road at half tide, but anyone who had run up against the ebb had not time for more than one drink at the pub before he'd find his dinghy hard aground on the mud. So it was not much of a place for the holiday-maker unless he liked messing about in boats with the accent on the mess. The cottage where I stayed suited me well and was typical of South Devon — fuchsia hedge, valerian growing out of the garden wall, a room to let and a notice of Cream Teas.

On the third day, which was August twenty-ninth, I came back from exploring the creeks in which Marghiloman had been so interested, and was told by Amy's sister in a confidential whisper that if I took the footpath up the valley I would find Mrs. Hilliard who wanted to talk to me. I followed the stream but saw no sign of her until a piercing whistle came from behind a hedge. She was too downright for patient hide-and-seek. The whistle could have been heard quarter of a mile off.

When I joined her I recognized her veiled, firm expression as that which I had seen on the day I delivered Alwyn's Moscow address.

"We're in trouble, Willie," she said.

Alwyn had turned up at John's cottage the previous night and sent for her and Tessa. He said that his plans had gone wrong and he was about to be taken off by boat. He had brought it on himself and there was no way of getting out of it. As he did not know when he would see them again he had come down to say goodbye.

Eudora was now in the picture, aware of Rachel's visit to him and of my conversation with Tessa, but she could not get all the complicated details out of him for he would not stop more than ten minutes, insisting that he had to be back before dawn in case of early visitors. She told him that I had come down to give him some vital message and that she was sure I would help. He replied that I was a bloody young fool and was to obey him and keep out. On no account was anyone to visit his hide.

It all sounded to me like Alwyn at the end of his tether with no fight left in him. I was having none of that. I told her that if she could show me from a distance exactly where he was holed up I would act the part of a busy agricultural laborer, passing directly below the birthday wood so that he could see me. I would not disobey and call on him, but would let him know unmistakably that I was there if it was safe to talk and I was needed.

We went separately to her car which was higher up the valley, and drove off at once by a roundabout route. So far away from Alwyn's retreat such precautions were probably unnecessary but we were taking no chances. As soon as the wood was in sight on the ragged Devon skyline, so tumbled compared to the clean sweep of my own downland, Eudora pointed out the landmarks and where I could strike a footpath. She then drove down into a deep lane where the car was safe from observation.

I could see why buzzards and Alwyn had chosen the place to nest in undisturbed. The long strip of pasture below the wood was shamefully neglected. My guess was that it belonged to some farmer who could not get labor and was himself too old to bother with an outlying patch of poor land. There were thistles, clumps of bramble and a few sheep competing with rabbits for the grass. I could think of no way of making my presence convincing. There was nothing that a farmhand could usefully do.

However, the Lord managed it for me as for Abraham — providing not a ram caught in a thicket but a ewe stuck fast in a bramble bush. Alwyn must have spotted her and would be cursing himself because he could not take the risk of being asked by a grateful farmer — who might turn up at any time — where he had come from and where he was going.

It took a full ten minutes to cut her free with a pocket knife and without gloves. In the course of the operation he was bound to see and recognize me. I came out bleeding, and the ewe, as always, thought it was all my fault and didn't stop to say thank you. But still there was no Alwyn and I continued to circle the hill.

A tongue of the copse straggled down thinly to the lower ground, and there I came on him. He was standing against a tree and beckoned me to him.

"What are you doing here?" he asked in an army voice. "I told you to confess who you are and get on with your life."

"It wasn't very good advice. Thanks to you, I am now in the pay of the KGB."

He asked me what the hell I meant and I told him they wanted me to find out from Eudora what the evidence was which sunk him.

"As if they didn't know!"

"Well, it's worth five hundred pounds to them."

"Then I should tell them and take it and give your Mr. Marghiloman a case of champagne."

"They don't know who Marghiloman is."

"Willie, you are being led up the garden path again. Of course they do! Now go!"

"Are you expecting anyone?"

"That's not your business."

"It is and I won't go. It's not fair to leave Eudora and Tessa without a proper explanation. All they know is that you were trying to clear yourself through Rachel and it's gone wrong."

"Come on up!"

I don't know what the hide looked like when it was first built; since only buzzards had to be deceived, it was probably little more than a screen. The improved model was a low turf-and-hazel beehive in the hollow torn out by a fallen elm, using the great slab of earth and roots as a back wall. A casual passerby would never have noticed it, for the outline was broken by a branch of the elm trailing dead ivy. The earth floor was dry and the roof rainproof. He had been living on oatmeal biscuits, tins of beef and water from a seepage — hardly big enough to call a spring — which was depressing fare for a civil servant who had notably enjoyed his food and wine.

I managed to make him laugh with an account of my KGB interrogations, and that broke the spell. Discomfort and the intensity with which he plotted and re-plotted his schemes in his own lonely head had kept him for some time without laughter.

He told me that when Rachel came up to see him he had expanded his SOS message, pretending that MI5 now suspected that he was in Devon. If he was caught and brought to trial, Rachel would inevitably be days in the witness box, and defending counsel was bound to leave a large question mark over her activities even though she was completely innocent. He would prefer, he said to her, to escape abroad and leave things as they were rather than engage in a hopeless fight. So was there anything that Rachel could do to help him and herself? He never let her suspect that he knew she was guilty.

Rachel agreed to try. Of course she did. She could hand him over to her Russian masters before MI5 could get at him. And she must have foreseen as clearly as Judas what was likely to happen to him. She spoke of a friend with a van who might be persuaded to pick him up so long as she only said that he was in political trouble without giving away his identity. Two days later she returned with the friend.

"Not the kind of man I expected," Alwyn said. "Not a tough. Not a fiery Communist from the Clyde. I'd have taken him for a university lecturer. Possibly he is. Just the sort of chap to have far-out, left-wing opinions with a tendency to anarchism, and reasonably likely, given a good sob story, to help anyone in trouble for direct action. In old days I would have put him down as a harmless nuisance and never suspected that the KGB had got him by the short hairs. Their penetration is deadly clever."

So it was arranged that on the afternoon of August thirtieth Rachel and friend were to drive slowly along a by-road easily reached by Alwyn across country. Yes, he knew that his game was far too dangerous to be played in this way by ear, but there was no other procedure open to him. He foresaw that the KGB would have difficulty in disposing of him immediately. There must be some delay, some sort of cat-and-mouse act which would give him a chance of unexpectedly bringing in the police and putting his finger on evidence which would stand up in court.

On the twenty-eighth the lecturer fellow turned up alone, approaching the copse as I had done, but from the other side, and waiting to be signaled on. He told Alwyn very reasonably that he didn't like a long journey with a wanted man inside his van and that it would be best to run him straight down to some safe spot on the Kingsbridge Estuary where he could be taken off by boat. That had been arranged. A friend with a motor cruiser was willing to pick him up on the evening of the twenty-ninth, a day earlier than had been agreed. Quarter of an hour later he would be out of Salcombe Harbor and could be landed wherever he wished in England or France. Alwyn had to admit that it was a much more satisfactory solution and showed enthusiastic gratitude.

He asked why his rescue could not be at night. Because somebody in the scattered cottages or from the deck of a moored yacht might notice suspicious movement and possibly warn the Customs. At the end of the day, however, there was nothing remarkable in a cruiser sending the dinghy ashore to pick up a guest or a crewman, and a credible answer to any question could be invented.

Alwyn was invited to choose the spot and mark it on the map. Somewhere remote but as near as possible to the harbor entrance. He had suggested the foreshore below the woods near the junction of the South Pool and Goodshelter creeks. The van could get fairly close and there was a rough path down to the water. The beach was hard shale and a cruiser of normal shallow draft could come within five hundred yards at half tide.

"So there it is. At eight-thirty tonight," he said. "Rachel and her friend genuinely believe that I trust them to help me to escape. If I back out now, I gain nothing."

"You're not going to run for it? You're giving up?"

"No, Willie, not quite. There's a slim chance for me to get clear without arousing suspicion — if it works."

I did not see why the boat was worse for him than the van and said that if the KGB wanted to get rid of him they could close up and bury him where he was.

"They could indeed. But KGB 13 like to avoid burial. It's never safe. The deep sea is."

"What's KGB 13?"

"The assassination squad."

"But in God's name why?"

"I told you long ago. While at liberty I am a continual

embarrassment. But as soon as I am dead they can safely say that I defected. Invaluable propaganda! All over Europe and America our security is discredited."

"Then you have to live!"

"No, I don't have to. I have only to make it impossible for them to claim that I am alive and in Russia."

"Get the police and catch the lot on the foreshore!"

"And tell the police what? That I am Alwyn Rory and being rescued by KGB agents?"

"We ought to be able to identify the cruiser."

"She won't have arrived yet. If I were doing this, I should come in casually as if looking for an anchorage, turn to starboard just past the harbor, pick up my passenger, decide that none of the creeks had enough water at low tide, and run straight out again."

"Does John Penpole know all these creeks?"

"I have ordered you to keep out!"

"But you can't stop me. And if I'm not to make matters worse . . ."

"Then just watch if you must! Your evidence might be of use sometime or other. Don't be seen and for God's sake don't attempt any violence! You could only lose."

I asked him if he expected Rachel to be there. He replied that she was not that kind of agent.

"Propaganda, fishing for information, possibly recruiting — that would be her line. I should guess that the escape of Mornix was the only time they ever used her for rough stuff. That house of hers with all the fancy dress tenants underneath was a gift."

He was in no mood to answer more questions, so I wished him luck and slid away. It was already after five when I reached Eudora and the car. Her only comment when she heard my story was that she'd welcome a chance to boil Rachel for the hounds but guessed they'd throw up. There was no time to lose. She drove straight back through Molesworthy to the house and on to the Penpole cottage, with me on the floor of the car.

While I was wondering how much John should be told, Eudora went straight to the point.

"John, Mr. Alwyn is being taken off by boat tonight at eight-thirty and he doesn't want to go. You and Willie here will watch what happens. That should be easy from the woods on the point. Don't mix it with them, but get him back here if you see half a chance!"

"Very good, Master. The captain will have to keep an eye on his chart."

"Of course he will, John. He's probably a bloody admiral in Willie's trawler fleet."

"Is there any objection to my taking Mr. Alwyn's ten-bore?"

I think she was about to say that he could take a punt and loaded punt gun if he liked, but I reminded them that Alwyn had strictly forbidden all violence. I had a feeling that his very exact choice of the rendezvous was not calculated to help his gallant rescuers and that we should not interfere. If police were alerted by shots and he was caught, there was not a scrap of believable evidence in his favor.

"Where shall we put him if we get him, Master?" John asked.

"In the car. I'll be parked off the lane down from Cousin's Cross. And then in the kennel room until he tells us whether he wants to go back to the old place or not."

To avoid too much coming and going of Eudora and curiosity among the villagers of Molesworthy, John and I walked over the ridge by the path through the bracken and were picked up by Tessa's car. She let us out a couple of miles to the east of the point and by half past seven we were lying down among tall tussocky grass well back from the water and close to the path by which Alwyn and his supposed lecturer were almost certain to come.

He had chosen the spot well — trees and brown water and a gentle current as if we were at the junction of two rivers far from the sea. A solitary fishing boat was chugging up the creek against the ebb. Three or four small craft were moored to the opposite shore; further out, towards the main channel, was a converted ship's lifeboat anchored bow and stern, appearing derelict though she had a canvas cover, shabby and streaked with gull droppings, to keep out the rain. In the South Pool creek was nothing. Half of Salcombe was in sight over a mile away — another world occupied with the business of its waterfront.

The evening was overcast with only a ribbon of clear sky, hardly wider than the setting sun, between cloud and the western hills. We heard feet stumbling down the stony path to our left, but nobody came as far as the beach. Soon afterwards a white motor cruiser appeared end on, feeling her way up from the main harbor against the tide. There was nothing about her to attract attention. The distant hum of the diesels promised plenty of power when it was needed. She might have come around from Plymouth on one side or Dartmouth on the other, and I have little doubt that her papers were in perfect order and her owner as British as I was — or rather more so. But no mere victim of blackmail could have been trusted not to mess up essential details; secret and enthusiastic sympathy with the Communist State must have been responsible for the exactitude with which he had obeyed orders.

She did not anchor but remained in the channel stemming the tide while the pram she towed was pulled alongside. A solitary oarsman dropped into it and began to row towards the point. At the same time Alwyn, his postgraduate protester and a woman who had to be Rachel stepped out of cover on to the beach. I was surprised to see her. Either she was mistrusted or had been brought along to give Alwyn confidence.

As the pram's keel grated on the muddy shale I had a job keeping John Penpole quiet. He wanted to burst on to the beach and start a free-for-all. I put an arm across his shoulders — gesture rather than compulsion — and whispered that it would do no good as the rower was armed. But I am sure he was not. He was just a deckhand with no suspicions. My experience of secret agents, friendly, enemy or what you will, suggests that nine times out of ten cunning and smooth operation are the only weapons ever needed. The tenth time is rare and likely to be more embarrassing than useful.

Alwyn said effusive goodbyes to his kindly helpers and sat down in the stern of the pram. The other fellow pushed it off and began to pull for the cruiser. When they were about two hundred yards out, I heard Alwyn yell:

"Look out, man! Pull with your right! You'll be aground!"

The startled oarsman obeyed and dipped his sculls for one more hearty pull to get clear. I could see the discolored water as the pram glided over a mudbank and stopped. Alwyn appeared to be cursing either his luck or the rower's carelessness, probably both. The other fellow tried to push the pram off. That was no use, for if he succeeded in moving the pram he pulled it straight back again trying to withdraw the scull. Awful stuff that mud was — a gray, sandy color above and jet black underneath.

I could not hear details of the conversation, just low and intense voices. Alwyn must have used his most military and cocksure manner. He stood up as if to get out and push. The rower wouldn't let him and lowered himself cautiously over the bow. A circular black pool spread around him as he sank to his waist, frantically trying to get back into the pram which heeled over and must have shipped a bucketful. As soon as it righted, Alwyn stood up at the stern, bent his knees, and hurled himself as far as he could with a resounding belly flop. Frog kicks in the black porridge took him off the shoal and he settled down to a steady stroke for our shore. I thought he would never make it, for the current threatened to carry him down beyond the point; but twice I saw him treading water as if feeling for the hard bottom where fresh water scoured the channel at low tide. He walked towards us nearly up to his shoulders and must have then hit mud again for he struck out boldly and managed to land on the point before the brown ebb could sweep him past it.

Meanwhile the pair of fellow travelers had prudently retired to the woods. Alwyn walked back along the shale, dripping a trail of black behind him. They came out to meet him, Rachel fluttering and asking if the rower could swim.

"I don't know and I don't care!" Alwyn stormed. "The damned fool! He'll never get back into the pram. His only chance is to hang on to it and yell for help. And as they can't reach him he'll be there till dawn."

No word betrayed the fact that he knew they were both working for the KGB. He sounded appalled at what they had let themselves in for just to do a kindness and at the carelessness of idiots who didn't look behind them when they were rowing on a falling tide.

"We'd better take him back to where he was," Rachel said to her companion.

At the moment I could see nothing attractive in her, strung tight with nerves as she was. She might be devastating in argument and a dark-eyed bit of excitement in bed: but if one did not particularly want either, all that remained was a little woman like a tense wire rope.

Still, she merits a fairer description, though I do not much wish to recall her to mind. I must allow her an ivory skin, severe but delicate features, a perfect figure and lustrous hair drawn back into a coil of black snakes. Her large eyes disturbed me. Sometimes they were quite expressionless; sometimes they emanated a glow of passion in reserve, no doubt as serviceable in politics as in sex. Alwyn had admired her intellect and fiery honesty. Her Minister, fascinated by the other promise of the eyes, went hell-bent for that.

She was oddly insistent on taking Alwyn back to his hide. It seemed to me the last place he ought to be. He too knew that but agreed, saying that he could not swim as far as the cruiser which appeared to have no other boat. So the three started up the path as dusk closed in.

At this point I determined to take a hand. Alwyn's original plan was to trap at least Rachel, and that now could be done. The lecturer fellow was scrambling up at a panicky speed and making so much noise that none of them could hear me moving silently along behind them. Near the top I caught up, signing to John to show himself but to stay well behind.

"I am a Customs Officer and I have reason to believe . . ."

That was enough for higher education. I thought it would be. He had a fairly level stretch of grass ahead of him and showed a turn of speed straight from the university playing fields before vanishing into a farther belt of trees.

Rachel was too intelligent to be bluffed and required me to identify myself. The difficulty, as I saw it, was to keep her quiet. I thought she might scream for help or force Alwyn to take some thoroughly awkward action which he could not refuse. Wild inspiration came to me.

"My name is Ionel Petrescu. After this man was safely on board, the boat was to come back for me."

"Is your car still here, Ionel?" Alwyn asked.

Rachel was then completely muddled. Ionel Petrescu, she remembered, was an unknown wanted by the police. That much was in his favor. But apparently Petrescu knew who had organized this rescue which Alwyn was not supposed to know. Yet Alwyn and Petrescu were acquainted.

I replied that my car was up the lane and broke off to have a word with John further down the path, telling him not to recognize Alwyn and to escort the pair to the car. Then I went on ahead to warn Eudora to keep out of the way until we had Rachel safely stowed away in the trunk.

Eudora showed her intense relief by remarking sharply that Alwyn seemed more efficient when using boyhood experience of huts and mudbanks than when trying to run security single-handed. She nipped into the bushes with a flurry of long American legs and vanished like an elderly wood nymph.

As soon as the others arrived I told Rachel that the driver and I had perfect cover for our activities but that she herself would have to travel in the trunk for a few miles. When she protested and Alwyn made a pretense of backing her up I threatened to leave the pair of them unless they obeyed me. So we curled her up into the boot; Eudora silently got into the car; and John drove us as far as the ford below the bracken path where Eudora hid again while Rachel, Alwyn and I got out.

It was now dark. Rachel had never visited Cleder's Priory and was inclined to start at rabbits as we walked over the ridge and down. We took her through the back part of the house, across the walled garden and up to the room over the kennels where I had been temporarily imprisoned. I noticed that the meat for the hounds had been very bloodily butchered and that the boiler was alight. Rachel averted her eyes. The sight was far from reassuring for a woman whose knowledge of the country was limited to conference hotels and discreet weekends at more romantic inns.

When we entered the kennel room we found Eudora perched on the table like a white-crested vulture. Sack-and-Sugar had come with her and was on his hind legs busily investigating the only hole in the room — that which led down to the manure heap — and chattering with annoyance because the pipe was too steep and slippery to be explored. Eudora greeted Rachel with every appearance of gratitude and friendship and waved her into the broken armchair. I squatted on the floor, a tired but very sinister Petrescu.

Rachel said she was so relieved to find herself among friends and waited for us to explain where she was and why — a point which Eudora cordially ignored as if the woman had dropped in unexpectedly after her car had broken down in the district. As Rachel's responses were a little forced Eudora carried on a monologue first about Tessa, then about Sack whom she pretended to have caught wild and tamed. She added a few amusing stories of how he fussed over his meat which had to be fresh so that he could lick up the blood.

Meanwhile Alwyn had slipped off to reassure Tessa and warn her to keep out of the kennel room. After taking a shower and changing he joined us — the first time I had ever seen him decently dressed as a country gentleman. He started on Rachel with every sign of sympathy.

"How on earth did you get dragged into this? You had done enough. I wasn't expecting you."

"I thought we were going to pick you up tomorrow in your wood," she said. "I didn't know anything about a boat being arranged for today."

"Well, what happened?"

"I had just gone out after breakfast to post a letter and he drove alongside me in the van and said I had to come with him then and there."

Myself I did not spot any special implication in the "had to" but Alwyn was on it at once.

"I thought he was a pal of yours from the libertarian left."

"He is. That's why I couldn't let him down."

Alwyn congratulated her on her courage, saying that he himself would have been alarmed at being picked up so early in the day and told he had to go straight down to Devon.

"After all, nobody knows where you are," he added.

"It doesn't matter. The only thing that bothers me is how to get back now that he has bolted with the van. What made you tell him you were a Customs Officer, Mr. Petrescu?"

"Oh, I just wanted to get rid of him," I said. "I don't like amateurs."

"He's no amateur with those useful connections. Could he possibly have fooled you, Rachel?" Alwyn asked.

She laughed at this, saying that she had known him for

years, but Alwyn pretended nervousness. It covered his interrogation of her so that she thought he only wanted to be reassured.

"When did he tell you about the boat?"

"Not until we were nearly there."

"It looks as if he didn't trust you."

"Perhaps he didn't. I don't know. I hadn't thought of that."

Then she herself started to put questions and he very cleverly allowed it.

"Where were you going to ask the captain to put you ashore?"

"Brittany, if he could make it."

"You were a bit trustful yourself, weren't you, Alwyn?"

"It was a chance and I had to take it."

"What I have never understood is why the security people believed you were in Moscow. How did you do it?"

"Very easy for anyone in my position. I flew to Berlin and called on a colleague who did not yet know I was suspect. I booked a seat on the Moscow plane and another — secretly — on the Paris plane leaving at nearly the same time. When the Moscow flight was called my friend saw me go to it. He did not see me switch to the line of passengers for the Paris flight, where I landed an hour and a half later. France to England clandestinely — which was not difficult for someone who earned his living trying to prevent any such thing. So there you are! The flight to Moscow was easy as pie for our people to trace except that I was never on the plane — and the Russians, if I know them, would never say whether I was or was not until they saw what was to be gained."

I imagine that all this was true, though at some time he must have used a second passport with a false name. His object was plain: to give Rachel confidence and put her off her guard.

"Where did you mean us to take you in the van tomorrow?" Rachel asked.

Alwyn continued to let her think she was in command and replied nervously that he preferred not to say.

"This friend of yours might give me away to the police. I have to know who he was and why you chose him when I asked you to help."

"Well, he seemed just the right person."

"Is he your boss or are you his?"

"Neither of us of course."

"You said you *had* to go with him."

"For your sake, Alwyn."

"Then why did he come to see me alone yesterday?"

"I didn't know he had. Perhaps he did not quite trust me, as you said."

"Or perhaps he wanted you on the shore to give me confidence. I might have refused to go at the last moment."

"Yes, it must have been that."

"I wonder why he only told you when you were nearly here. Unknown plan, unknown risks — I suppose you might have refused to take part."

"There was nothing I could do."

"So he was your boss?"

"No! I've told you he wasn't!"

"But since you went with him without arguing he must have been able to give orders."

"He couldn't give orders to anyone," she snapped.

"Weak?"

"Yes."

"Then who sent him to me yesterday and told you nothing about it?"

"He won't give you away," she said, avoiding an answer.

"What is there to give away if he did not know who I was?"

She tried hard to stumble her way out of that one but could not. Eventually she admitted:

"Well, yes. He did know you were Alwyn Rory."

"And he dealt with that hot potato all by himself?"

130

"He has a brilliant brain."

"Not much use in this sort of thing unless directed. What has the KGB got on him?"

"The KGB? I don't understand."

"Rachel, your first act after I asked you to help me was to report to the KGB and take their orders."

"How can you think such a thing? There were no orders."

"Was the rope quickly tacked down inside the sofa?" Alwyn asked.

That shot went right home. She was silent far too long before demanding with a smile what on earth he was talking about.

"Ionel, tell her how Mornix escaped!"

I gave her the story which lost nothing in the telling. She continued to smile and said it was nonsense. There had never been any rope and Special Branch had cleared her.

Eudora slid off the table and recovered Sack who was burrowing into the aged mattress on the bed and throwing out the stuffing behind him.

"So it was you who entered Alwyn's flat and looked at his bank accounts and faked the evidence!"

"What have bank accounts to do with it?"

Eudora dropped Sack on the floor close to the chair on which Rachel was lounging, insolently relaxed. His eternal curiosity was aroused. A ferret does not sit erect on his tail like a stoat, but will stretch up with forepaws against anything perpendicular such as a post, a box or a human leg to have a good look around. He found the edge of Rachel's chair very satisfactory — good grip for the claws, pleasant darkness beyond. She stiffened, not daring to move until he disappeared up her skirt. Then she shrieked and tried to grab him. Sack, who preferred to be removed gently from such intimate exploration, chattered, twisted, and bit.

Eudora gathered him up while Rachel stood against the wall, mouthing words which would not quite come out and paddling her hands in the air. It was the rapport between Eudora and her savage, serpentine bundle of twisting fur which terrified her as much as the bite. She may have shared the uneasiness with which our ancestors observed the relationship between a sinister woman and her too familiar pet. In fact the conversation going on between Eudora and the indignant Sack was no more mysterious than between a little girl and a puppy.

"When did you enter Alwyn's flat?" Eudora asked.

"I never did. I don't know what the evidence against him was. They wanted me to find out."

"Then you do work for the KGB?"

"Take it away! I don't know anything about bank accounts."

I reminded Alwyn that I had good reason to believe she was telling the truth. He made no comment but took over the interrogation again.

"No one knows where you are, Rachel. You said that did not matter."

"I'll be found. They'll soon find me."

"The KGB will be very glad if you can't be found."

"The police will find me. Take it away! You'll all be caught."

"The police? I don't believe it."

"You'll see! You daren't touch me!"

"What was that letter you put in the post this morning?"

"To a friend. I swear it."

It was an obvious lie. Her voice gave it away.

"Willie, hold her down!" Eudora ordered.

I had some faint stirrings of chivalry. One cannot help feeling it even if a woman tells you to use violence on a woman. Rachel was a pitiable sight, nerve gone and always dabbing at her upper thigh from which a thread of blood was showing below the knee. It was only a tiny trickle from the inner skin of the thigh, but I can see that it did suggest to an excitable character that Sack would be very careless where he bit.

It was not necessary to hold her down. She was shivering against the wall when Eudora pinned her there and set down Sack close to her feet. He promptly stood up against her leg. She was not to know that he could not climb tights and she had no idea what the beast was — mink, wolverine or she might have imagined some little horror specially bred for MI5. He could just reach the bottom of the thread of blood and his little rose-pink tongue licked it up without malice.

"Well, would you believe he could touch it?" Eudora exclaimed in a full American accent, and then burst into good Devon:

"Doan 'ee frit yerself, Za-ack! Zuck, Za-ack! Rabbits, Za-ack!"

Rachel backed away, remorselessly followed by Eudora with her familiar wriggling in her hand. He had caught the atmosphere as animals always do, and I would not have cared to play with him. Rachel broke down completely.

Yes, the letter had been addressed to Scotland Yard. She described the wood where Alwyn was and gave the time when the van would arrive to rescue him. She had hoped to restore her reputation and to avert all suspicion against her by standing up in court and giving evidence for the prosecution. She had sent her letter EXPRESS so that if the Post Office for once paid some attention to the label it should already have reached Scotland Yard.

"So that is why you were so anxious that I should go back to the hide. How were you going to tell them that you found out where I was?" Alwyn asked.

"The truth — that you wanted me to help you to escape abroad."

"But that is evidence that if I was involved in the escape of Mornix, so were you."

"I couldn't help that."

"Leave her to me, Alwyn!" Eudora hissed — it was the sort

of hiss you might expect from a dinosaur. "She was going to tell the police that she found it out from Tessa."

"No!"

Eudora slung her across the bed and set Sack down on it.

"Yes, Tessa! Silly little Tessa!" Rachel screamed

"Well, we don't need to hear any more, Sack," Eudora remarked. "What will the police do when they get her letter, Alwyn?"

"Collect Rachel from her flat. Not there. Vanished without trace unless they have the luck to find someone who saw her picked up on the street. Strong suspicion that the KGB have pulled a fast one. They will have already cordoned my wood at a distance. At first light they may go straight in or they may wait for the van to arrive. When they find evidence that I was there very recently and have cleared out just in time, probably a helicopter, road blocks and dogs. Then inquiries here. Stick to your story that I am in Russia. You have the letter to show with my address."

Eudora at once insisted that he and Rachel must go to earth in the old place until the hunt was called off.

"And you, Willie, bolt for it now!"

I had to think that out quickly. If Alwyn were caught, he still could not prove his innocence. He could say how the Whatcombe Street escape was done and that Rachel was the agent who did it. But that did not help. There was a strong presumption that the pair had collaborated and that each was now trying to throw the blame on the other.

Ciampra — it seemed very probable that he would be brought into the case with his story of the mysterious Willie and the letter dropped at the Russian Embassy. No difficulty in establishing that a person known as Willie and pretending to be a Portuguese had visited Cleder's Priory. Rachel, if discovered and interrogated, could identify Willie as Ionel Petrescu, and a cheerful interview he would have with MI5 after that.

"How safe is your old hideout?" I asked Alwyn.

"It has never been searched or even noticed. Your two Marghiloman agents looked right at it."

Marghiloman. I had almost forgotten him. That was another complication, whether he was KGB or MI5. I didn't care for my chances at all. Probably I exaggerated the strength of that police cordon — now in position for it was two A.M. — but it seemed to me that if I bolted as Eudora wanted me to and if I were caught and held for further inquiries, my scent or my footprints could show that I had visited Alwyn in the birthday hut. Mr. Petrescu, whether Adrian Gurney or not, would go inside for conspiracy, let alone any other unanticipated charges.

"I think I'd better come with you," I said.

Alwyn agreed. He apologized for it afterwards, saying that he doubted if he was right but that he would almost rather give himself up than be confined alone with Rachel. There was also the question of keeping an eye on her. He had to sleep sometime.

We left immediately by the bracken path with Rachel between us. Eudora picked us up at the ford and again we folded Rachel in the boot while Alwyn and I lay under a rug on the floor of the car. It was a nerve-racking drive, for if police were watching the lanes south of Molesworthy they had us cold; but the only alternative was to walk twelve miles at top speed — impossible for a limp Rachel. We were not stopped, and Eudora parked off the track down from Cousin's Cross fairly close to the spot where she had picked us up five hours earlier.

There were no sounds from the mudbank and no lights where the cruiser had been. Alwyn reckoned that she must have crept as close to the shoal as she could get, sounding all the way, and then thrown a rope or perhaps launched a life raft. At any rate she had pulled off her pram and her man and would now be well out to sea. There was little chance that her movements could have been singled out among the clumsy comings and goings of holiday yachtsmen.

The tide was now rising, but the water was much lower than before, looking like a stagnant pond at the bottom of the deep, still valley. On the opposite shore the half-derelict converted lifeboat was lying over on the mud. I could just make out the dark shape against all the other darknesses.

"That's it," Alwyn said. "We have to wait another hour before I can get at her."

Earlier in the evening light she had appeared quite uninhabitable in spite of the old canvas cover. Nobody but a very patient fugitive could have stayed in her without fire or lamp, only moving out on the darkest nights to meet Eudora and John and take in supplies. I couldn't imagine how three of us were going to live in her undetected.

"Can you swim, Rachel?"

"No."

"You must have been bored in the Aegean with your Minister. He's like a fish in the water."

"I watched him," she answered sullenly.

Eudora and Alwyn returned to the car and came back to the foreshore carrying a child's inflatable canoe, a case of tinned food and a demijohn of water.

"That will have to do us for a couple of days. Then Eudora will drop more supplies if it's safe."

"Who does the boat belong to?"

"Nobody knows exactly. She drowned her owner and was found and towed in. He used to come down from London. Somebody — his heir we supposed — had the cover fitted to her many years ago and just left her on the moorings. I had a look over her once to see if she was worth repairing. She was, but I couldn't track down the owner. She's a melancholy fixture now. Nobody notices her any longer."

When she was afloat, Alwyn stripped and swam off to her, returning in a few minutes. He loaded the canoe with food and water, put his clothes on top and told us to do the same. Rachel began to yap protests. When the volume increased, Eudora slammed a hand over her mouth.

"You are going with them now. You can do what you like when they are safe."

"I want to go in the canoe."

"It's full."

"I can't swim. Really."

"Then I will tow you," said Alwyn. "One yell and you go under!"

When she was down to bra and panties he made her slide into the water and swam on his back with his hands under her shoulders. She made no fuss, probably glad that she was in his hands, not the questionable Ionel Petrescu's. I followed, pushing the canoe which trailed a line behind it, the other end of which was in Eudora's hand. Wind rustled the leaves of the trees on both banks with a continuous hiss, but there was none on the black water which rose without sound or ripple. When I was halfway across a pair of widgeon got up with squawk and clatter. That was the only disturbance of solitude.

As I came up to the derelict I saw that the canvas cover had been loosened a little aft of the counter. Alwyn's head was sticking out above a hanging rope with loops in it for feet and hands. I passed clothes and supplies up to him.

"Give a couple of sharp tugs on the line and Eudora will pull the canoe back," he whispered.

All was pitch dark inside. We sat on the cockpit grating since the canvas cover came down too low to use the seats. Rachel was in the cabin, an old fur coat keeping her warm in the cold, damp air. He had told her that if she yelled or started hammering on the sides I should be ordered to deal with her. A good touch, that was. She had known Alwyn long enough to be pretty sure he was incapable of brutality, but I might well be an experienced thug.

At dawn a dull light came through the canvas and I could

see where I was. Forward of the cockpit the deck was flush except for the low curve of the cabin roof. Under the canvas, supported by a spar running fore and aft, there was just room to crawl past the roof up to the bows.

He had cut some small, irregular slits in the canvas which gave a complete view of the creek. If all was silent the gulls settled on the derelict. The white streaks of their droppings and the sides green with weed prohibited any thought that the interior of the boat could be habitable. As Alwyn said, she was a part of the landscape, a fixture which belonged to the mud.

"What about sanitary arrangements?"

"Difficult. Buckets. She's got one in there. The only solution is to empty over the side on the ebb."

It was the devil to keep quiet such a highly strung character as Rachel. She was always making little nervous movements and noises and frightening off the gulls. Fortunately there were enough small craft about at the top of the tide to account for our best camouflage taking flight.

Alwyn spent some time in the cabin with her, leaving half open the moldering mahogany doors. Instead of dressing, she remained in the comfort of the fur coat very casually fastened if at all, determined to arouse our interest. I don't think she meant to oblige us both in quick succession. Possibly she hoped to arouse jealousy and a desert island sort of row. If I had been alone with her I should have had to keep myself firmly under control. I could now at last understand that unfortunate Minister of the Crown who had merely wanted to be briefed on the ideals and policies of the commune downstairs and had found an irresistible itch for the more fascinating occupation upstairs.

She was eager to talk about and excuse herself, managing to skate over the treachery to Alwyn while demanding pity. It was not the usual blackmail by which the KGB had caught her, nothing to do with compromising photographs or perversities in some establishment too swell and silver-plated to be vulgarly called a whorehouse. In Rachel's highly intellectual and fairly permissive society she would have to have had the depravity of a Messalina for any of that to tempt her. Political perversities had been her downfall. Having toyed with communism, rejected Trotskyism, and decided that Europe had not enough patriotic peasants to put up with Mao's Boy-Scoutism, she had reached a blind alley of hopelessness in which she had decided that before society could be remade it must suffer — not exactly revolution, but a complete breakdown of law and order. I put this Pilgrim's Progress of hers with a crudity which would have earned her utter contempt. It was in fact complex, genuine and far too erudite for me.

She never realized any more than the other savage innocents that her group was a sitting duck for infiltration by the KGB. They got hold of papers and letters in which she had considered targets for the single-handed bomber which would cause maximum disruption at a small cost in lives. Two of her proposals had actually been carried out.

The KGB had used no coarse threats. Their agent remained courteously respectful of her beliefs, merely suggesting what she might do to help the International Left, whether strictly Communist or not, whom she should meet and what political information it would be useful to have. It was not until the Mornix escape that she was left in no doubt at all about who was secretly employing her and that she must obey or be exposed.

She insisted that when she reported to her contact Alwyn's cry for help she was sure they would get him out of the country.

"Why should they?" he asked.

"Well, you were a nuisance. It would be far better for them if you were safely out of England."

"Leaving me free to say they helped me, and how?"

"But they want to avoid all the embarrassment of your arrest and trial."

"They also want to use my supposed flight to Moscow as propaganda. But if they are to do that, I have to be dead."

"It never occurred to me, Alwyn," she said.

"No? Yet you have a reputation for clear thinking."

The day passed in utter boredom, one of us often asleep while the other kept watch on Rachel. In the early evening at slack water a rowboat came around the corner from South Pool. As it approached we saw that it was John Penpole at the oars with one of his terriers sitting up on the prow like a little figurehead. He drifted alongside and stood up to throw a stick as far as he could, steadying himself with one hand on the derelict. The terrier plunged in. John let go and pulled clear of us with the dog following. It was beautifully done. Nobody could have guessed that the steadying hand had inserted a note under the canvas.

"We have had polite hell from your former office," Eudora wrote. "Police dogs everywhere. John and I exercised the hounds early this morning, passing wherever you had walked including garden, house and kennel room plus half the pack in the bathroom. So they had no luck. One Alsatian bitten on the nose by Sack. They know you left the wood in a small van, and nothing more. Search is concentrated away to the east. So far as I know, Rachel's disappearance still not reported."

Alwyn whispered this out to both of us with the exception of the last sentence. Without any change of voice he substituted:

"They have been asking what we know of Rachel and I think have connected her with the van or with her earlier visit to you."

He then continued with the last lines of the note before putting a match to it:

"In case my movements are watched I am staying at home, properly indignant. Nobody is interested in Willie. Send him ashore at bottom of tide."

Rachel was very quiet. Three years in Holloway was what

she foresaw, police informant or not. I was quiet too. Having seen what happened to the yachthand when he stepped out of his dinghy I felt that Eudora had overlooked the mud. Nobody could go ashore or visit us while the boat lay over on God knows what depth of black slime.

When the sun had set and we could hear the ebb gurgling under the bows, Alwyn bolted Rachel in the cabin along with her fears and whatever conscience she had. She was now very amenable. Having realized that she was helpless, she played her dependence on him for all it was worth.

"She wouldn't understand, but it's better if she doesn't see what we do," he explained.

I pointed out that I didn't understand either.

"You will. When you first met me, did I look as if I had swum ashore?"

He wriggled up to the bows, cast off the mooring chain, and silently let it out inch by inch before making fast again. When the boat settled on the mud she had been carried four or five yards downstream by the ebb. It was highly unlikely that anyone on the bank would notice in gathering darkness that the movement was more than the usual slackening and tightening of the chains according to the tide.

At low water Alwyn gave a very nervous Petrescu his navigation orders. I was to slip out under the canvas, hang on by one hand, reach for the stern chain with the other and drop into the mud which would only come up to my knees; then I was to walk straight down to the main channel which had only a foot of water over a hard bottom and follow the channel up until it appeared to divide; if I went boldly into the mud of the left-hand branch I could walk ashore. I must not stay more than an hour or I should have difficulty in returning on board.

I did what I was told. When I dropped into the mud, indistinguishable from night, it seemed to me that there was a lot more than two feet of it, but I did hit bottom and could move. On the extended mooring the counter was nearly overhanging a gully in the mudbank worn by a trickle of fresh water. When I had sploshed down this gully into the channel I might have been walking in any inland stream, out of sight at the bottom of a black valley. Alwyn's knowledge of the creek was amazingly exact. I had never understood how during his long stay on board he had been able to meet Eudora and take on supplies without swimming or risking a boat. He was only stranded when both periods of low water happened to be in daylight or clear moonlight.

I advanced cautiously up the left-hand branch — or what I hoped was the branch for it was not at all obvious — a mere depression in the mud and in places over my knees. It led me safely to shore and I sat down on the bank of the creek, noticing for the first time the curious nature of the night. There was a diaphanous mist in the valley, showing a faint sheet of silver where the moon ought to be. All sound was deadened and I had the impression that in this unworldly luminescence the land like myself was expectant.

I heard something moving behind me and slid quietly down on to the shale where I was invisible. Then Tessa appeared — a very anxious Tessa putting a finger to her lips when I showed myself and beckoning to me to follow her. She moved fast and silently over the shale until we came to the head of the creek where the stream poured down through beds of rushes. She crossed the dry marsh into a steeply sloping meadow from which there was a view of the whole inlet — or would have been if sight had not been limited to a moving object at fifty yards. Just above us in the next field I heard the comfortable munching of a herd of cattle.

"I think I was followed," she said. "But we're all right here."

I did not take her very seriously. Anyone on a night like that would imagine a follower. I myself while waiting had felt — fantastically rather than in fear — a presence brooding over the creek, extensive and indifferent. England is so old and one cannot tell what insignia the ancients have left for us. A boy such as I, brought up on the bare downs where once there was a city, is bound to be aware of them. At school of course we would frighten each other with wild exaggerations; but out after dark, sometimes alone, sometimes with my very sensible father, I learned that one should recognize without trying to understand. That attitude seemed quite acceptable to the long-dead leaver of the spiritual mark. A man's love of his land may be as indestructible as any other love.

"You've been alone since the tide went out?" I asked.

"Oh, I didn't mean that! One is never alone."

I thought that a most revealing statement from a girl whose view of religion was presumably Marxist. I did not have to ask what she meant.

"How did you come?"

Earlier in the day John had brought out supplies and hidden them in a spot close to my landing place where Alwyn always picked them up. Tessa herself had chosen to ride out in the evening, intending to return at dawn. Nobody who happened to see her would imagine she had been out all night. She had tied up her mare fairly close to the cover where Eudora parked her car. It occurred to me that if anyone examined this ground in daylight, the tire tracks would reveal a number of recent comings and goings.

She settled down to wait for the bottom of the tide. All was quiet until the mare — perhaps disturbed by the sudden pearly quality of the night — whinnied a question at her. Tessa was busy comforting and quietening her when there were movements low down in nearby undergrowth. Badger, she thought. The sound was not repeated until she heard me sploshing ashore. Somebody else had heard it and now was definitely on the move. She crept down to the hard shale and padded ahead to warn me.

"Are the police on to Alwyn?" I asked.

"No. Eudora and I are sure they aren't. They think Alwyn is making for London or a port. It's you, Adrian. Somebody else has been making inquiries about Willie."

"But they couldn't possibly know I am here."

She told me that her admirable Tommy Bostock had called her up saying that he had had a visit from a detective who wanted her to confirm that she had bought a blue, military frockcoat for someone called Willie. Tommy had told the man that he knew nothing about a blue coat but that a Willie Yonell existed all right and was a friend of hers in Devon.

"When you bought the coat, did you leave your name and address?"

"Yes. I hadn't enough money, so I paid by check."

Then at last the reason why I was expected around the estuary was unmistakable. Somebody keeping an eye on Whatcombe Street had noticed the new arrival in the blue coat and was perhaps getting ready to question him when he vanished. But the coat remained. So the "Military Club sort of bloke," pretending that the coat might have been his, stopped Ciampra on the street and found out from the label the shop where it had been bought and who bought it.

Tessa. Friend of the enigmatic Rachel. Frequent visits to Whatcombe Street. Her political opinions far over to the left. Ciampra, I remembered, had even believed she might be mixed up in the Mornix escape. Well worth investigation. But by whom?

Special Branch and MI5 had at that time no more interest in her or the highly respectable Eudora, whatever might have been the enthusiasms of her youth. The KGB must know all about Tessa from Rachel and knew enough about me because I had confessed as much as I felt could safely enter their files. Indeed I was their agent in a small way of business. So this continual interest in me must stem from the mysterious Marghiloman. He alone could guess that Willie Yonell was Ionel Petrescu. And his methods followed a pattern. The visit to Tommy Bostock was the second time that his people had passed themselves off as British police.

Yes, it was me they were after, not Alwyn — me, the trawlerman off the Russian fleet who was so perfunctorily cleared by MI5. Marghiloman first kills two birds with one stone. He sends his suspect down to Devon with a first-class excuse for getting on intimate terms with the aunt and cousin of a traitor; at the same time he gets confirmation that Alwyn Rory really is in Moscow. Suspect then vanishes, but turns up — of all places! — at Whatcombe Street, convincingly disguised by Tessa.

Charts, he asked me about — charts of the remote Kingsbridge Estuary. What the hell were we supposed to be landing there or sending off from there? It was a monstrous edifice of suspicion which would hang together very reasonably on paper — always provided the compiler of the file stuck to paper and prejudice and either knew very little of the human beings involved or insisted on disbelieving what he was told.

"We have to get Alwyn out of here. It's become the worst possible spot for him," I said.

"But where can he go?"

"Wherever he meant to before he decided to expose Rachel — if we can get him there."

"Will he listen to you?"

"Not me or even you and Eudora. He's blind obstinate."

There was no sign at all of the unknown. He must have been waiting hopefully near the bank of the creek or perhaps keeping an eye on the mare until Tessa returned to her. He was probably unaware that he had been spotted. From his position we could not have been visible when we ran for it.

"Are you going back to London?" I asked after a silence.

"No! I told my firm I was ill. I can't bear it any more."

"Accountancy?"

"That! No, it's no worse than anything else — proving to capitalists that they haven't made a profit when they did and that they made the hell of a profit when they didn't! Money doesn't mean a thing any more, Adrian. For the state and industry and the individual it is simply debt, and debt is whatever the economists say it is and every two years they change their minds. I'm sick of them and their tame politicians, sick of crooks who don't care and idealists who don't understand. And if they did understand they'd be more desperate than ever, for they'd see that the world they want is this. I've discovered that I am selfish."

"You? I wish you were."

"Well, I am. The only way out Voltaire could see was to cultivate one's garden. So I'm going to. There's no means of giving all this to millions of townsmen who wouldn't be content with it anyway. So I might as well enjoy peace and keep a patch of sanity in the world."

I was reluctant to stop listening to her deep-toned, disillusioned voice, but the tide was on the turn and I had to pick up the supplies and go.

"You can't go now," she said. "You can't risk that spy spotting you, and it's the end for Alwyn if he does."

Perhaps I accepted that too easily. But there was no denying that the interested party who was watching the mare must have heard me sploshing ashore.

"And your patch of sanity will be here?" I asked.

It was hard to believe that anyone shared the silver-misted night with us except the bullocks I had glimpsed beyond the hedge and whatever little animal was plopping in and out of the stream.

"Oh, anywhere! Anywhere with honesty of purpose and men swearing happily and trees in the night and things that you watch grow day by day. All this!" she repeated with a catch in her voice.

"But you shouldn't be sad about it."

"I'm not. It's only that here and now is a meaning. And you know it and I know it."

"I haven't said so."

"It's not necessary. Speech covers things up. The sound of it is what matters. Tell me something in Romanian!"

I told her plenty in Romanian, for I was free to say exactly what I thought of her and what I might have said if I had been anything but a Willie with no future and a hardly recommendable past. I kept my voice low and steady, fairly impassionate as if I were reciting poetry. Once I was.

"You see? You didn't understand a word."

"And you'll see that I did. I know it was what I wanted you to say to me."

There is no need to go into what happened then. As she once — much later — had the impertinence to point out, it must have been one of the very few occasions when an International Marxist and an agent of the KGB were completely united.

When we returned into our lives — or out of them, according to how you look at it — the first of the dawn was on us and the creek filling and there could be no reaching of Alwyn and Rachel till the following night. Our unknown companion was cautiously on the move. He passed quite close to us, bending low among the rushes and aiming for the higher ground. His game was obvious. He did not want Tessa to know that she had been observed; so he was not going to risk running into us by taking the track which we normally used. When there was no more cover he cut straight up towards the road, trusting to the semi-darkness to conceal his movements — which it would have done if we had still been on the other side of the creek. He found a gap in the hedge above us and climbed over. I heard a rip and a muffled exclamation as his trousers caught on hidden barbed wire.

There was great excitement among the bullocks who thought a more serious breakfast than grass had arrived early. The whole score of them charged towards him, and then I saw his head and shoulders outlined against the sky as he climbed on something. It amused me that this sewer rat, perhaps very effective with his guns and bugs and walkie-talkies and God knows what, should be completely at sea among the normal occupations of honest men. I told Tessa to stay where she was and ran downstream — taking a chance that he would see me, but he was too busy waving at the bullocks — then into dead ground and up the hill until I found a gate.

I advanced upon him across the field. Confidence, truculence and a near-empty bag of fertilizer which I found by the gate represented agricultural authority. He was standing precariously on a field roller in front of a semicircle of two-year-old Red Devon bullocks prime for market. A youngish man he was, of indeterminate class, with a face as clean-cut and keen as an advertisement for after-shave. He was efficiently dressed in a leather jacket and sweater, carrying a small pack and wearing a beret. I gave him the speech of my youth, for I was never any good at Devon.

"What be doin' 'ere? Aafter rabbits, be 'ee or aafter my beasts?"

"Call 'em off!" he begged. "Call 'em off!"

I shooed them a few yards away, all but one who put his lovely wet muzzle in my hand and added convincing local color.

"You own this land?" he asked.

"I does. And me faather before me."

"I am a police officer," he announced, coming down from the roller.

I could have bet any money he was going to say that.

"Not from around these parts you ain't."

"No. From London. There's been some queer goings-on down here."

"And there's bin a pack of tomfools askin' questions. You'll be one of them Special Branch coppers?"

"Yes. Yes, that's what I am."

"Well, they giv I the word so I should reckernize 'em."

"What word?"

"That's for 'ee to say."

"Well, we don't all know it."

"You tell I what un was or I'll set the beasts on 'ee. Coom, me beauties!" I called. "Coom! Coom!"

It must have been near enough to the farmer's feeding call, for those splendid, obliging bullocks put their heads down and their tails up and came.

"I'll shoot," he warned me, getting back on the roller.

"What with?"

He pulled out an automatic — more, I think, to show me that he was armed than with any intention of blazing away at Red Devons.

"Got a license for that there?" I asked.

"I don't need a license. I'm working with your police, I tell you. Ever heard of the CIA?"

I had, but as hardly more than a Communist's bogeyman. At my college we had to endure weekly lectures on international affairs. I remembered one of the pundits telling us of the incredible cavortings of the CIA in Latin America which, he said, had been more forceful propaganda for socialism than anything the USSR had thought up. At the time it sounded to me more like a typically Romanian dig at the Russians than a statement of fact.

This fellow, however, was no American and I told him so.

"They train British to do the job for them here."

"Duty, like?"

"Duty."

"Communists and such?"

"And such! And plenty of them."

"Well, we ain't got none 'ere. And if they Socialists want my vote they must raise the milk prices. But I'll 'elp 'ee."

"How far does your land go?" he asked.

"Down to top o' creek."

"Are you out much after dark?"

149

"I ain't out aafter dark but before light I am. And a good thing too, with 'ee muckin' about on me land and threatenin' to shoot me beasts."

He said he never meant to, that the gun was just for personal protection. By God, I was enjoying myself!

"Protection 'gin who?"

"Have you come across any foreigner around here, speaking broken English?"

"What's 'is name?"

"Ionel Petrescu. Sometimes called Willie."

"Two other fellas was aaskin' about 'im some time back. What do 'ee want 'im for? 'E can't 'elp bein' a furriner."

"When I tell you that he came off the Russian trawler fleet, you'll guess what we want him for."

"Anchor 'em in Goodshelter Creek, like? Not enough water!"

"Enough for a small boat at night. Did you ever hear of Alwyn Rory?"

" 'Im that let the spy go?"

"He knows this coast. I wouldn't be surprised if he escaped from here."

"Naa! They was arl aafter un, but didn't find un."

"What about his aunt and her daughter? Ever see them here?"

"Mrs. 'illiard? Ah, I'd like to see un 'ere, but 'tis out of 'er country. Good, 'ard-workin' pack she's got and they foxes are killin' of my lambs. What's wrong with daughter? Lives in London, don't she?"

"She rode down to the creek last night and her horse is still there. What do you think she's up to?"

"Same as the rest of 'em. Meetin' 'er sweet'eart. Where be to if I let 'ee go?"

"Off to Plymouth."

"Comin' again?"

"If I do, there'll be more than one of us."

"Not on my land there won't."

"Ten quid any use to you?"

"I'll 'ave no Americans frittin' me beasts like they does on the flicks. I'll set the police on 'em, I will!"

"I'll make it twenty if you move your cattle out of the valley and keep your mouth shut."

" 'And it over, mister, and we'll shake on it."

A generous lot, the CIA agents! That made seventy altogether which I'd had off this chap and Marghiloman. I pocketed his twenty and led him to the gate followed by the ferocious herd. He said he had a bicycle up on the main road, so I gave him such bucolic and complicated directions how to reach it that he would never suspect I hadn't the least idea how to reach it myself.

I rejoined my darling Tessa and sent her back alone to recover her mare in case my benefactor should catch a glimpse of us together. It was now full dawn; one of Alwyn's peepholes ought to allow him to see her riding openly home up the Cousin's Cross track. He could infer that something had gone wrong but that there was no immediate danger.

We arranged that Eudora should meet me on the bracken path about midday. I could walk there openly. The police had probably never heard of Ionel Petrescu and certainly didn't want him. The CIA appeared to have fallen back for reorganization. I had to admit that the instinct proper to very experienced crooks had led them correctly, though starting from preposterous evidence. Petrescu could afford to laugh at them — or would have done if not too indignant to laugh — but they were dangerously close to the bigger, far more triumphant capture of the traitor whom they believed to be in Moscow. It was going to be difficult to extricate him, and what to do with Rachel was beyond me.

Eudora was tucked away off the path with some very welcome lunch, her pile of white hair showing among the bracken like the scut of a giant rabbit. She said that she had heard as much of my story as I had had time to tell Tessa and now wanted the rest of it. Tessa herself was busy at the house making some essential preparations for Alwyn's escape.

When she had got it all from me, expanded and clarified by her acute questions, she was appalled. My own reaction was British indignation mixed with a Romanian tolerance of normal government iniquities, but hers was cold anger at this secret interference by her country of birth in the affairs of her country by adoption. That Tessa should have attracted suspicion did not surprise her; it was too much to expect such an earnest and romantic agency to understand the contempt with which MI5 regarded parlor revolutionaries. As for me, she understood both her countries well enough to guess at what had happened. MI5 had told their solemn allies that I was of no importance and had not swum ashore from any fishing fleet, skating over my long and unusual life story which alone could explain the whole thing. And they were dead certain to have been too professionally mysterious, impatient and therefore not believed.

"But me!" she exclaimed. "Still little violent Eudora, the scourge of Wall Street and the FBI! Willie, let's sell my story to the papers! *I Was Stalin's Mistress* — how's that for a title? What would they think of it here in Devon?"

"The joke of the century if it wasn't for Alwyn. But as it is . . ."

"As it is, you press a button in the White House and up comes some smirking, fat-bellied bloodhound with a gun in his pants and Eudora's file all alone on a tea trolley. Willie, listen to me! Sometimes my Puritan ancestors speak through me! In my day America was terrified lest the masses should be corrupted by communism. And what has happened? It's not the masses but the governing class which has been corrupted. The lying of the state — straight from Russia! Conform or be suspected — straight from Russia! The end justifies any means. That's an old one, but where did the CIA get it from?

152

Straight from Russia, and the KGB at that! The threat — well, it exists all right, but you meet it proudly with the morals of long civilization not with those of the scum of the earth. By God, they are worse than Franco! I'll bet you that if I went back to Spain he'd ask me to a party and talk horses with me like a Christian gentleman and wouldn't even have me searched before I came in."

I was left gasping by this tirade. If that was the fire and splendor of Eudora's youth, there must have been a whole cabinet of files on her, not one.

"And has it occurred to you," she went on, "that my Kill-a-Commie-for-Christ compatriots will have found out by this afternoon that you were not the nineteenth-century farmer you pretended to be, which wouldn't have taken in anyone except a nice, clean American boy or some bloody Fascist from Surbiton recruited to throw the money around with a nice, clean English accent?"

"You think they won't believe him, Mrs. Hilliard?"

"I am quite sure of it, Willie. That gang of arrogant thugs is efficient and somebody is talking to the real owner of those bullocks right now. I have to get Alwyn away in broad daylight. And by the grace of God the South Devon Agricultural Show is tomorrow!"

I waited for her to develop that obscure remark, but got no explanation. She began packing up the picnic basket and looked me over severely.

"Willie, daughters do their best to deceive their mothers but they make the mistake of trying too hard."

"Yes, Mrs. Hilliard."

"You could have drawn off that skeezicks of the capitalist KGB and let her ride home instead of staying out all night."

"Possibly, Mrs. Hilliard."

"Are you aware that she is a girl of decided character, and when she knows what she wants she'll take it?"

"More or less, Mrs. Hilliard."

"Well, don't let yourself be bullied like that Tommy Bostock. And another thing, Willie! Aren't you supposed to be an agent of the KGB?"

My mouth was full of rabbit and pigeon pie. I mumbled unhappily that yes, in a sense I was, expecting to be on the receiving end of more of her invective. I did not realize that this accusation was a complete and deliberate change of subject.

"Well, here's their little friend, Rachel, disappeared. Alwyn's whereabouts is unknown, but he's probably not far off. Ionel Petrescu is on the spot ready to do anything for five hundred quid. If I were running the KGB which," she added savagely, "I should sometimes enjoy, I'd get in touch with him pronto."

I objected that it was only thirty-six hours since Rachel's postgraduate partner bolted, and he was going to report that the Customs had nearly caught them. The yacht's master could only say how the operation failed and that he had got clear away without being questioned.

"Which gives you just time to vanish before the KGB joins the CIA in wanting to put you through the hoops, Willie. Don't bother about leaving Tessa and me to face the music! We're sweet innocents. We have never heard of Alwyn since he escaped to Russia. So there's no music to face provided he isn't caught."

That was a very big "provided." I pointed out that I was the only person concerned in whom British security had no interest — which could be invaluable — and that she and Tessa needed help to get Alwyn away. I added a comment on what the CIA and KGB could go and do to themselves.

"Willie, we are not in the hunting field. But if that's the way you feel — can you ride?"

"No. I never have."

"Well, you're going to, and sidesaddle. And you've brought it on yourself."

We went separately down the hill: she to the house, I after a safe interval to John's cottage. Soon she turned up carrying a vast quantity of dark blue cloth, two top hats and two veils.

"We're getting Alwyn out now," she said. "It's one hell of a risk! I'm just gambling that we react quicker than Great Powers."

"But the tide is high."

"And right for an afternoon swim. So long as he can slip into the water unobserved he can cross the creek and no one will think anything of it. Now take off everything but your shirt and underpants and ma will dress the blushing bride."

They were two riding habits she had brought which had belonged to the well-built Mrs. Rory, Alwyn's mother. She was relieved to find that mine had to be padded out with a cushion, and so the other should not be far out for the broader Alwyn. Top hat, veil and John's riding boots completed the costume. I fell over the immense skirt as soon as I moved and she showed me how to gather it up in one hand. Then she made me sit down while she painted and powdered me like a dockside whore.

"Now, Willie, pay attention! You and Alwyn are going to the South Devon Agricultural Show where you have entered for the Ladies' Hunters. I daren't go with you. If I'm spotted, it could give the game away. So you're on your own except for my guardian angel. Alwyn can sing falsetto. Let him do the talking if any. You don't speak English at all. You can give girlish squeaks in a foreign language if you like. I think you both should be obscure foreigners. Visiting Arabs perhaps. No, they'd have Arab horses. Make it Persian noblewomen! Cousins of the Shah. Mother and daughter. You still look a bit masculine under your veil, Willie, but never mind that! I guess they have wrong hormones in Persia like anywhere else."

Speed and decision — that was Eudora, and age had not slowed her down. I have been told that she was too impulsive to be a good Master of Foxhounds, but for her opponents in

Spain and America she must have been as fast and elusive as a fly. I'll bet that file on the tea trolley was more full of attempts to oust her than any actual connection with the target.

Tessa and John had gone ahead two hours earlier with the horses. We loaded the car with Alwyn's habit and two side saddles, and at the last moment I remembered scissors and a razor for his beard. Then we shot through Molesworthy and twenty minutes later left the car in the usual screened parking place. Nobody was about. Eudora was prepared to bluff it out if anyone was. All she dreaded at this point was the police.

During the weeks which Alwyn had spent in the derelict she had worked out a fairly safe method of communication. First she showed herself on the foreshore, her unmistakable figure dreamily enjoying sunshine on water which reflected the valley green in its own deeper green. As soon as she had given Alwyn time to notice her and made sure that no casual passerby was immediately opposite, she retreated into a gap between bushes and hoisted a notice in large letters black on green. Her message was SWIM NOW.

Meanwhile she sent me up the slope where I found the horses in a clearing, Tessa giggling and John's grin splitting his face; they had been watching my progress with that damned skirt in both hands. When we had fetched the side-saddles and all other necessaries from the car they put me on Tessa's quiet mare and arranged my flow of cloth, assuring me that for a beginner sidesaddle was much safer than riding astride. So long as I kept my right leg over the pommel and my left under the third pommel I could not fall off. It did indeed seem impossible provided the mare herself did not fall. How to unlock myself then was beyond me.

Always walk, they told me, and concentrate on keeping the hands low and the body upright; then if I passed anyone at all knowledgeable I would not look utterly ignorant. In an emergency I was not to trot, which I should find vilely uncomfortable, but canter. They showed me how to communicate with the unfortunate animal — the aids, they called them — but warned me not to try to be too clever. I could trust my horse to do whatever Alwyn's did. I should also remember that I would have the hell of a job mounting without help, let alone arranging my skirt.

After half an hour of this Alwyn came running and dripping up the hill. John quickly cut off his beard and shaved him. Eudora went to work on him as she had on me, producing an enameled, frightening, old harridan under the veil who would have been sure of at least a Highly Commended because the judges would not dare give her less.

Meanwhile I told him the events of the night — or those which concerned him. To my astonishment he was utterly loyal to the CIA and not in the least indignant.

"You none of you understand them, not even you, Eudora," he said. "If it pleases them to treat this ancient land as a banana republic who cares? We have only to be polite. They can't do any harm. They started off by investigating our labor troubles and arriving at the most fascinating fiction. Then they began getting in the hair of MI5, for they don't trust our security or anyone else's. I've no doubt that, as you told Willie, we just laughed off the question of Petrescu and said he wasn't a Romanian at all. But they wanted to know for sure and they kept on after him. And if you think Russian submarines and Russian trawlers are a joke, you have another think coming. That's where the real battle of the cold war is today, and Mornix and I were in the front line."

"And it was the CIA who framed you, not the KGB," Eudora said.

"Nonsense! It's inconceivable. I know they forced the investigation on our people, but from their point of view they were justified. I knew Rachel. I introduced her to her Minister. And they were right — she was a Russian agent. I couldn't tell them what we were up to in the Mornix case. The feeding to a spy of false and correct information was a little too subtle for them. Of course I was suspect to them, and of course Willie is! Now, can you keep Rachel quiet for a day or two?"

"I shall keep her very quiet, Alwyn."

"And where will our clothes be? Where will John collect the horses?"

"A horse box will meet you on the lane below Berrystone Rock. Not mine. Police might have the number. Forrest's box."

"I can't let him take that risk for me."

"He is taking no risk, Alwyn. I have lent two horses to Persian friends of mine. He has kindly agreed to drive them to the show. If the police ever get on to him, how should he have known who they really were? He will have your clothes and will put you out wherever you like. Then he will drive straight back with the horses and tell me where you are and how I can reach you."

III

Eudora and Tessa kissed us and dropped our veils — bridal veils in a way for we were setting off into an unforeseeable future. Sometimes on tracks, mostly on by-roads, we rode to the north, passed by a few cars and fascinated holiday-makers but without a sight of police as far as the village of Frogmore at the head of its creek which we could not avoid. There we walked our horses slowly, I trying to sit like a statue as ordered. A police car parked in a side street paid no attention to us beyond curiosity. According to Alwyn, it was probably posted in Frogmore to stop him breaking out to the southwest in case he was still somewhere near Molesworthy.

But there was an incident which bothered me more than

this first evidence of road controls. In Frogmore, playing happily around the garden of a pub, were two children who looked vaguely familiar. At a table with beer in front of him was their father. He was three-quarters turned away from me, but that was enough, given the children. He was the pleasant fellow from the Russian Naval Attaché's office whom I had met in the zoo. It was a safe guess that Rachel had reported her meeting with Tessa in Frogmore and that he knew how to read a map imaginatively. Alwyn was not surprised at his presence in the district. Though the movements of Iron Curtain diplomats were limited, they could hardly be refused permission for an innocent family holiday. He did not think that the fantastic uniform worn by class-ridden, imperialist horsewomen was likely to interest him.

About sunset we were circling Berrystone Rock but came on no horse box. Eventually we dismounted — I with skirt hung up on the pommels to reveal hairy, male legs above the boots — and settled down to wait and wait. Our situation was very tricky. If we were seen it was going to be hard to explain why a county dowager and niece — experience had shown that Eudora's Persians were an unnecessary complication — all togged up for a horse show, should have got themselves benighted on the way, tethered their horses, and taken to cover instead of walking to some well-traveled road and yowling for help in whatever disaster had struck them. Eudora or her quick-thinking guardian angel had gambled that there would be no interested observers after sunset; but to set off in the morning, crumpled, bristles showing through worn makeup, horses looking as if they too had never been put to bed, was asking for trouble.

About midnight we at last saw the lights of a car on the farm track which circled our miniature peak. It could be the police or it could be rescue, so we heaved those abominable skirts over our heads and very cautiously approached. The

159

occupants of the car were standing in the beam of dipped headlights in order to be recognized. They were John Penpole and Forrest.

Unsure of what story the innkeeper had been told, Alwyn confined his remarks to the least possible greeting, his falsetto sounding very like a bad-tempered old lady with bronchitis. Forrest was too much of a John Bull for that nonsense. He said straight out:

"Mr. Alwyn, I only want your word that you are innocent."

"My word of honor, old friend."

"Then cheerful does it!"

He asked nothing about me. At first he thought I was really a woman and, I suspect, scented romance.

He explained that with best will in the world he dared not pick us up with his horse box. A police check was known to be on the two main roads between Totnes and Dartmoor which he would have to follow before crossing. He reckoned that the police would be satisfied after glancing into the cab and the back and seeing two ladies and two horses, but they might make a note of the number of the box. He was sure to be observed leaving Molesworthy and returning, and he could think of no story which would not lead to further investigation of Eudora and himself.

Car lights were switched off, horses unsaddled, fed and watered. We then held a council of war. The pair had decided for us, quite rightly, that while our disguise might pass just to reach Berrystone Rock we would never get away with it on a long day's journey. Food for the horses or alternatively asking someone's permission to put them out to grass was going to be impossible. Our only hope was to continue as a couple of hearty fellows on a riding tour, for which they had brought the necessary change of clothing. If sometime, when the heat was off, we were to telephone Forrest he would find a plausible excuse for driving his horse box out of Molesworthy empty

160

and returning with it empty — having discreetly unloaded the horses at the far end of the bracken path.

There seemed nothing else for it. I suggested, however, that I alone should continue as a woman until we were past all likely road controls. I had three good reasons for this. First: that when the third pommel was between my legs I felt as secure as a baby in a basket; second: that at a distance my superb outfit would add an unquestionable note of social distinction and we could pass as Lady Enid Paddington-Penzance followed by her respectful groom. And the third reason was that if we were stopped Alwyn could gallop like a highwayman for any safety he could find while Lady Enid was being shamefully disrobed by the police.

They doubtfully approved this plan. John, foreseeing unexpected movement with the instinct of an experienced Huntsman, had brought out powder and a powder puff belonging to Amy — I never dreamed that she used any — and a short, toy moustache, rather wider than Hitler's, which was merely comic at close quarters but possibly effective if we did not pass police too near. At any rate it was the only disguise Alwyn would have besides his glasses and his graying hair.

"But what'll ye do with the extra saddle?" John asked.

It would be essential when I returned to manhood, but we certainly could not carry it.

"You'll have to drop it on us, John, and take the sidesaddle back," Alwyn said. "We daren't telephone you or Mrs. Hilliard, so we must fix a rendezvous. Let's say in the valley of the Otter. Day after tomorrow in the afternoon. We ought to be able to make it by then if we get there at all."

They drove off, and we dozed a little till dawn. When and how to start off was the next problem. We must not pass any police so early that they would be suspicious nor leave Berrystone Rock so late that we risked being caught out by the farmer on whose land we were. There was no cover to hide us, so we simply had to mount and stand still or walk in circles ready to move off as soon as anyone was in sight. When we saw some early riser gaping at us from a distance, we took refuge in woodland outside Harberton. At eight we set out.

We had to cross two main roads, which might have been easy enough if we did not also have to cross the main railway line to Cornwall which ran between them and parallel. This limited possible routes to three. One of them led us too close to Totnes; another involved too long a ride down the Plymouth road; the third and nearest had the advantage of taking us straight into fairly wild country, but if there were police at the bridge over the line we should have to pass them close to.

We were able to reconnoiter this road from above. Police were checking traffic, but far enough away for Alwyn to use his absurd moustache with safety. The lady and her groom crossed without incident. Once out of sight I stopped to powder my face and to arrange top hat, veil and skirt. I passed Alwyn's careful inspection and we rode on towards the railway bridge saying nothing and very nervous. The bridge was unguarded and we crossed it exchanging a glance of relief. But just ahead, at the junction with the second main road, was a police car very well placed. Any traffic turning back on sighting it would immediately be suspect.

Our only hope was an isolated church on the right of our route. Just conceivably it could be our destination — lady of the manor dropping in to dust the pews or arrange the flowers or grab the vicar's surplice for its monthly wash. There was no easy way for a horse to enter the churchyard, so Alwyn dismounted and told me to hold his gelding while he walked round the church out of sight of the police. We had no time at all to prepare any plan and I had not the least idea what he meant to do; nor at that moment had he. Meanwhile I sat like a picturesque statue of largish maidenhood, erect and keeping my hands low as instructed.

He said afterwards that his vague idea was to swipe something from the church — flowers or a choirboy's collar or whatever presented itself — hand it to me very formally, and ride back. I think his sacrilegious plan might have been too obvious. A much better one was provided by a fast freight train roaring and rumbling under the bridge. His gelding, admirable in traffic but with no experience of the railway age down in Molesworthy, became alarmed. So did I, for I had no idea how to hold one horse while keeping my seat on another. The police were watching our sidling and swerving with interest, no doubt in the hope that I would fall off and they could come to the help of beauty in distress, but my groom came dashing out of the churchyard, hissed at me to let go the reins and — safely covered by our circlings — made some sort of indecent assault on the gelding with the point of a pocket knife.

It took off towards the main road with him in pursuit. A cop gallantly leapt out of the car to hold up the traffic and Alwyn and horse bolted across the road. Then came a really brilliant touch. Instead of moving on and leaving me to follow he led the gelding back over the road, tipping his cap to the driver of the car as he passed with the horse's neck partly obscuring his face. He mounted and we returned the way he had come. I suppose that when all the flurry was over the police must have wondered what the hell our church business was, but our behavior, however eccentric, was in keeping with village life and its inexplicable ways.

There was now nothing for it but to follow the road westwards sometimes on the verge, sometimes making circuits through the lanes. Road and rail were alongside each other and we had a chance to inspect the next bridge before committing ourselves. Once across, we took to the hills and wooded valleys on the edge of Dartmoor where no one said more than a polite good morning to the veiled lady and her groom, though we must have aroused curiosity among villagers who would know that we had not come from any of the big houses in the district. In the evening we went into hiding not far short of Crediton, horses dead tired, ourselves hungry and thirsty. Alwyn risked entering a pub in a village through which we had not passed, returning with cider and sandwiches. The horses had to put up with a stream and woodland grass.

The next day we started at dawn, not caring who saw us out so early for we were now beyond easy explanation. Our bred-in-the-bone country setting was worthless. I couldn't see my aristocratic little face in a mirror because we hadn't one, but I knew very well that I must look like a dusty circus ringmaster impersonating his only equestrienne who was off sick. I said so — a weary crack to improve breakfastless morale — and Alwyn remembered it. As for him, his bristles were coming along fine, and the last thing he resembled was a smart groom in attendance.

We got away with it partly by using major roads where there were hardly any pedestrians and cars passed us too fast for close inspection. But villages had to be avoided by awkward detours where we cantered past anyone we met. Once we were stopped by a tweedy, squirish gent bursting with officious curiosity and once by a farmer who wanted a chat. On both occasions Alwyn made use of my fantasy, saying sharply: "Chipperfield's Circus. On ahead. Trying to catch up," touched his cap, and cantered on.

We came down into the valley of the Otter soon after midday, crossing the river by a footbridge so that we did not have to pass through the village of Upottery. A compact copse a few hundred yards from road and river provided temporary cover — inadequate but good enough until John Penpole should appear with another saddle and much-needed food for men and horses.

For the time being we had broken all contact with the police, and it was at last worthwhile to discuss the future. Alwyn had now no longer any doubt that he must leave the country.

164

In his professional career he had had dealings with Bristol and its port of Avonmouth and considered that he knew the loopholes of security well enough to bribe a seaman to stow him away or even get a job on a banana boat; but there could be no deciding on our destination until we had news and clothes from Molesworthy. We were also likely to run short of money. Alwyn had a few soaked notes with which he had swum ashore and I had the CIA's twenty quid for moving my cattle and keeping out of the way.

In the late afternoon we saw Tessa, not John, driving slowly up the valley. She parked close to the river and waited — a solitary figure engaged in the innocent and ecstatic contemplation which was peculiar to the family when considering illegalities. No doubt the pose was so effective because it was half sincere.

We waited to see that she was not followed and then Alwyn went down to her. The bank of the river was safer than many more lonely settings since no one in sight had the least interest in anybody else. A chap was fishing his way upstream without any luck and on the grass was an attractive picnic party, mother and father still dozing after a heavy lunch and their young getting the feel of a strange countryside like any other family band of anthropoids.

Tessa and Alwyn returned to the copse carrying a basket under a load of John's old clothes and a rug, but no saddle. Anyone curious about them would have assumed that the pair were bound for a campsite higher up the slope. Reluctant to be seen by my Tessa as the bedraggled clown I felt and was, I took off habit and hat and received her with a curtsey in shirt and skirt. She laughed but there was no smile in it. Too obviously both horses and ourselves were in desperate need of rescue

While we fell upon the meat and drink in her picnic basket she told us that Molesworthy was again a center of interest to the police. Neither Eudora nor John dared to make any move

165

beyond ordinary daily routine. She herself was not suspect —
perhaps because she had been resident in London and stead-
ily working in an office during nearly the whole period of
Alwyn's disappearance — and she had proved by several
pointless journeys that she was not followed.

She and Eudora had decided that very soon questions were
going to be asked about the lady and her groom and that we
ought to leave the horses and continue on foot.

"Forrest and the horse box are at Honiton," she said. "I
shall telephone him as soon as I'm out of the valley and tell
him where to find you. He'll go back by the northern route
and unload the horses at the far end of the bracken path tomorrow morning. So he leaves Molesworthy empty and comes
back empty. On the way he will go and inspect a hunter which
was advertised and won't buy it. That's his excuse for the
journey."

"And Rachel?" Alwyn asked.

"I don't know. But Eudora is quite calm. There's enough
food and drink in the derelict and she's keeping a close eye on
her."

With Eudora more under suspicion than ever, Alwyn could
never take the risk of telephoning or writing; the only news of
him they could get for a very long while would be from me
after we had separated. Remembering how quick and unsatisfactory had been the former goodbye between the cousins I
pretended that I was nervous lest she might have been followed. There was another road running along the top of the
ridge from which the whole valley could be watched and I
wanted to be sure that no car was waiting there. Alwyn protested that if there was anyone up there he still couldn't see
into the copse, but Tessa gave me an unexpected, unmistakable smile of gratitude. Half of me was jealous of their devotion to each other.

I gave them the time it took me to climb up and down, and
in fact I did see a car parked some way back on the upper

road. So far as I could tell at the distance the occupants were not engaged in any visible activity, which could mean that they were just sitting. Townsmen on holiday seem very willing to do that — preferably with the windows shut — but a man on the run does not ignore other possibilities.

When I came back Tessa and Alwyn were lazing side by side on a patch of grass leaf-dappled by sunlight. I had the impression that both had somehow managed to look forward beyond danger and exile.

"We were talking about Adrian Gurney," Alwyn said. "Eudora and Tessa are going to need him. It's the end of me, you see."

I replied that I would do my best and make myself useful. I understood him as meaning a job on the estate, but my voice tailed away. It was impossible. Inevitably there would be local scandal. The relations of Tessa with an obscure employee could not be hidden.

"I think you should bring yourself up to date in agriculture," he went on. "A year will be enough considering your childhood and the Romanian training. I have asked Eudora to arrange it. After that you must all three see where your future lies. Not in South Devon. Somewhere in your own country where you are just Adrian Gurney and your father is remembered."

Possibly I did not look too happy about that either. There would be no Tessa any more.

"There's nothing I cannot tell Alwyn," she said.

Guilt. Embarrassment. Compared to Tessa I was preposterously old-fashioned. But they were both smiling at me.

"I have always wanted for her someone who could share her loves that matter," Alwyn said, "but more down to earth, more able than I to make use of the world. *Débrouillard*, as the French say."

I may have answered, being still young, that I didn't think there was any character much better than his own.

"In so many things, Willie, I am a coward. I hide from life. You and Tessa do not."

He was not fair to himself, but there was some truth in what he said. Who else would have run instinctively to the hiding places of boyhood? Knowing the ways and expectations of policemen — plain or secret — he could appreciate the safety of such refuge and at the same time ignore discomfort in the satisfaction of return to what used to be. But then, revolting against being a mere hunted animal, he would indulge in the burst of energy and rashness which had sent me to Whatcombe Street and laid the trap for Rachel.

"I approve, and Eudora will blink twice and ask Sack and also approve. I don't suppose any family has ever known a prospective son-in-law as well as we all know you — if that's what you both go on wanting, and it doesn't matter if you don't."

A bit fast, all that, in normal society. But there in the valley of the Otter it was hardly normal. She and I knew what we felt and hoped, but what the humiliated admirer of Rachel and the disreputable Ionel Petrescu could say to each other was limited until some catalyst combined us back into our true selves. Alwyn was the catalyst, forced now or never by what she had told him. He was not a man to object to an affair between us; indeed he might have welcomed it. What swung him over the edge to the "bless you, my children" stuff was that he could foresee no quick end to the affair and wanted to give us courage.

I raised and kissed Tessa's hand. Neither romanticism nor formality. There was Alwyn's last goodbye to her to come and I was shy of intruding my emotion — a sensitivity which did not belong to the Latin but to the English peasant I am.

When she had driven away with all the clothes of the former groom and lady safely locked in the trunk, we sat for some time talking, reluctant to move away from the presence she had left behind.

168

"What's the next move, Willie?" he asked at last. "Down to the Vale of Taunton and then along the coast?"

I suggested sticking to the hills and working our way around to somewhere near Bath, partly because it was the sort of country I knew far better than tumbled Devon which never gave a man a straight run at anything, partly that I distrusted the Somerset lowlands where the ditches and rivers made it hard to get off the roads, and police had only to watch the bridges if they ever had any idea where we were. Walking over the high grass and sleeping in any rough shelter we were most unlikely to draw any attention to ourselves.

"You'll have to tackle the port alone. I'll be no more use to you there," I said. "But meanwhile I can go into pubs, shops, police stations, anywhere. Nobody wants me."

There must have been some considerable interval between that bold statement and the appearance of the slow-moving car on the valley road, though memory, which dramatizes everything, insists there was none. Those two fair children were in the back, and the driver was my naval friend from the Russian Embassy. At first sight it seemed incredible. Then I remembered Eudora's remark that if she were running the KGB she'd get in touch with agent Petrescu pronto. Obviously he had decided, unlike the police, that Tessa's movements were those most likely to be revealing and had followed her up himself. He must have seen the parked car from the upper road and wondered whom she was visiting.

"But we'll be away and gone for good as soon as he stops," I said to Alwyn. "He hasn't a hope of finding us."

"He knows that. I think he only wants you to see him if you are here."

"What for?"

"In case you have anything to report. No other agent has been in direct touch with Eudora. You told your boatwoman that you would try."

"But how does he know I did?"

"Five hundred pounds would be real money to Petrescu. And like a clever little Romanian he has killed two birds with one stone. It's an old saying that the way to the daughter is through the mother."

That pricked my conscience unjustly, though he was only pointing out what the KGB might believe. I replied coldly that I could never have been seen with Tessa by any agent of the KGB and that he was wrong. He paid no attention to this flat statement. He was hot on the trail — an experienced hound following the scent from cell to cell of his own mind.

"By God, he's after Rachel, not you!" he exclaimed at last. "Tessa was her loyal friend. Tessa took her to the birthday hut. When the attempt to collar me failed and Rachel vanished, it's ten to one she would have appealed to Tessa. That's why Tessa's car was the one to watch. He wants to get in touch with Rachel urgently. She would know what really happened three nights ago."

Three nights. It seemed like weeks since the yacht had failed to capture him. The KGB had reacted with the utmost speed, posting a respectable and presentable diplomat at the strategic point of Frogmore and presumably planting some minor agent to keep watch in Molesworthy. But they had not moved so fast as Eudora.

"You're sure he's not after you?"

"He'd hardly expect me to come down and talk to him. And that's what he is up to. I recognize it."

"Suppose I let him find me instead of Rachel?"

"Why the devil should you?"

"Because it was me Tessa came out to meet, not Rachel. As you said, Petrescu has got the daughter and could do with five hundred quid as well."

"You'll never get away with it."

"But I can. I'm no mystery. He knows every damn thing about me except that I am Adrian Gurney from Caulby."

"It's a hell of a coincidence from his point of view."

"No, it isn't. If he follows Tessa about, he's quite likely to run into her boyfriend. And that little Romanian, friend of her mother, is a very possible candidate."

"How will you explain what you are doing up the valley of the Otter?"

"I thought you might tell me that."

"What do you want from him?"

"I want to deliver my report. And we must get him away from here before Forrest arrives with the horse box."

That clinched it. Alwyn still doubted if I was a good enough actor, but he had to let me go.

"Then tell him there are too many police around Molesworthy for your taste — which he must know already — so you took a bus to Honiton and then telephoned Tessa to meet you here. And stick to Russian! For heaven's sake don't forget that you speak little English!"

That was a wise flash of advice. After all the urgent talking of the last few days I could easily have forgotten.

Leaving Alwyn where he was, in cover and with a view of the road, I started to walk up the valley and met the car coming back. It stopped and the driver leaned out of the window as if to ask a question. He recognized me of course, but not a muscle of eyes or mouth gave it away.

"Good evening — I mean, good afternoon," I said.

He did not bother with the reply but took a quick look up and down the road and told me to get in. We then drove down to the river where Tessa had waited. The boys went off to play on the banks of the Otter. I hoped they wouldn't fall in. They seemed well accustomed to being turned loose while Daddy talked to strangers.

I gave him my story of being alarmed by police searching for Alwyn Rory and that Tessa had told me of this private spot where we could meet for a long afternoon — which was more credible than that I should have telephoned her. He swallowed the lot and passed immediately to a description of Rachel,

171

asking whether I had seen such a woman or if the Hilliards, Miss or Mrs., had appeared at all agitated. I said they had not.

"When did you yourself leave Molesworthy?"

"Yesterday afternoon."

"Where were you staying?"

"Mrs. Hilliard offered me a room over the kennels."

I translate our conversation into English, but none too exactly. Kennels, for example. I did not know the Russian word and we got into a thorough muddle over my being sent off to sleep with the dogs.

"Did you have a talk with her?"

"Yes. I have the information which a certain lady asked me to find out. When I recognized you and your sons I thought you must be looking for me."

"You are not so important as that, Petrescu. What information was it?"

"The nature of the evidence against Rory, which was so strong that he ran away."

"It is no longer required."

"But there was a question of a reward."

"It will not be withheld if your information conforms with what we know."

"The Special Tribunal discovered that Rory had received a sum of money through a Swiss bank. When the British traced that payment back, it was found that it had been paid from an account known to have been opened by the KGB. He had no defense except a ridiculous story that he didn't look at his bank accounts and had no knowledge of the payment."

My naval friend made no remark immediately, apparently interested in a rise of trout. Eventually he said:

"Ionel Petrescu, am I right in thinking that you left your country because you did not like the method of government?"

"More or less. I wanted freedom."

"From what?"

"Well, police for one thing. A man can't spit without some bluecap asking him why."

"That will not last for ever."

"It's lasted a hell of a time."

"And you believed there were no secret police, no dirty tricks in the West, eh?"

"That's it."

"Then I will open your eyes to what goes on, and when you have realized that the brutalities of government are the same everywhere you will perhaps return to your country and become a useful citizen. We will see you come to no harm. Have you heard of the CIA, Petrescu?"

I replied that I had read about it in newspapers.

"You know that it operates outside America to protect capitalist interests just as we do, for example, in Romania for the sake of our common defense?"

I was not happy about the way this friendly interrogation was going. All I wanted was to be forgotten by both those bands of trespassers in my country. Sometime a return to the identity of Adrian Gurney would ensure that; but meanwhile it seemed to be agreed and settled that I was a KGB agent.

"Your Marghiloman worked for this CIA," he went on. "It was his duty to supervise Romanians who had defected to England and were suspect."

"The devil it was!"

"Marghiloman is now controlled by us, thanks to the information you gave us about him, dear Petrescu. If you get the money you have deserved, it may be from his hands. In future would you be willing to report anything you notice or can find out about him?"

"Very willingly."

"Where are you going to now?"

Another question which I could not afford to answer and gave me no time to think.

"I am going to look for work in the fields."

"Not very convenient as cover. But perhaps our people can handle it."

That was too much for Petrescu and far too much for me. I said I had agreed to do a single job but that I was not going to be a full time agent.

"It is only Marghiloman that we wish you to make friends with and keep an eye on."

"He's a double agent?"

"You could put it that way, but it would be inadvisable for him to do any doubling. He must obey orders. Now, is there anywhere he might expect to find you?"

"Yes. You may remember he had me followed from Swindon to the Marlborough Downs. He may think I have business there."

"What was your business there?"

"I told you. I wanted to lose him. So I took the first train I saw from London and it went to Swindon. I never dreamed he had put an agent on the station to watch me."

"What do you suppose he thought you were doing there?"

"I don't know. It's between both seas. It might have been where I kept the bombs for loading on the trawlers."

"Dear Petrescu, you and I can afford a sense of humor. Others cannot. Remember that! Give me a date and a time!"

If we were to avoid the more closely populated lowlands and keep to the high grass we should eventually arrive on Salisbury Plain — say, five days if we walked all the way and never risked a lift or a bus. Time was no object and it did not matter whether Alwyn made his dash for Bristol from there or from the Downs. I remembered the lonely upland crossed by the Ridge Way. It would be easy to find and a convincing spot for a rendezvous. It might also play on Marghiloman's nerves a bit.

"He is to drive to Avebury and leave the village and its Stone Circle by the Herepath running east. Where it ends he will have half a mile or so to walk. I will wait for him where

the Herepath crosses the Ridge Way, two green roads inter-
secting. He can't miss it. No one will pay any attention to us.
Up there they are used to archaeologists on the prowl.

That strained my Russian to the limit. I doubt if they have
the green roads of English downland, or are the caravan
routes east of the Caspian green after the rains? At any rate I
had to do a lot of explaining and write down the names for
him. He must have realized that such exact knowledge of
country by a refugee needed explanation, but he said nothing.
We arranged the meeting for midday in six days' time.

He collected his children and drove off. As soon as I was
sure that he was well on the road to Exeter I returned to
Alwyn and made my report. He had no objection to approaching Bristol from the east, but thought I had been too bold in
arranging to meet Marghiloman. I pointed out that he was a
colleague of mine, however unwilling, in the KGB and that I
was sure to get something out of him which would be of use to
MI5 or to us — perhaps clear evidence which would prove
Alwyn's innocence. I also said that I seemed fairly certain to
receive five hundred pounds and that he would find it an invaluable help towards getting on board a ship. He refused to
accept anything from me.

"You will, or I'll give it to a fund for destitute refugees," I
told him. "I'd choke every time I bought a drink with KGB
money. But you can take it with a good conscience and use it
for your private cold war."

"We'll see. Personally I think they'll run you like a credit
account — pay in a little and demand more goods."

It was prudent to move off straightaway without waiting for
Forrest. We made the horses comfortable and took to the
Blackdown Hills — now two nondescript travelers minding
their own business and, we hoped, hardly worth a glance from
the police once we were further away from their zone of oper-
ations.

This was not country that either of us knew. We could only

keep the setting sun more or less behind us until nightfall, making use of far too many roads. We had had the devil's own luck with the weather, but now it had broken. The driving, gray rain of the West Country poured down, and we took shelter under the remains of a corrugated iron roof more or less supported by three good posts and one broken. Our only comfort was the remains of Tessa's picnic — cold beef sandwiches and three bottles of claret. We drank the lot and woke up in the morning with fuzzy heads and added depression. It was still raining.

When it cleared we climbed sulkily uphill into heather and began munching bilberries for breakfast. They acted as a pick-me-up — or perhaps our spirits were revived by this windy ridge from which, down the Vale of Taunton, we could see the sand-clouded waters of the Bristol Channel and to the south blue Lyme Bay. For me it was still another marriage to my land and for Alwyn a last embrace before divorce. We were both very silent throughout the morning.

I was glad to see that he looked a lot more scruffy and unrecognizable — unwashed, short of sleep and in John's old clothes which fitted badly. The only trouble I foresaw was that it would be difficult for anyone curious about him to place him, not a tramp, not an underpaid schoolteacher on holiday, not a farmer. Neither farmers nor their workers ever walked anywhere.

"Who's on strike?" Alwyn asked.

"I don't know. I haven't seen a paper for days."

It was not a bad idea. I went down to the little town of Chard and bought newspapers and some much-needed maps, together with a warm loaf and butter. We settled down to decide a route and invent our identities. As usual car workers were on strike. The production line tempted us no more than it did them. There was also an unofficial strike among dockers at Southampton. Dockers, we felt, would do very well — a sturdy lot quite likely to stretch their legs in the countryside. Alwyn's Devon dialect came to him so naturally that he could speak it without effort. I myself was tired of Wiltshire, broken English, Russian, Romanian and what-have-you and afraid I might easily slip up in any emergency. So I decided to be a clerk with standard English.

The next day took us through the lovely Dorset country by Beaminster and Cattistock. It was a Sunday and distant church bells continued to praise the gift of life even if there was no longer much of a congregation underneath them. We found it hard to remember that we were hunted men.

Coming down into Cerne Abbas the Giant faced us — that nobly phallic demi-god cut in the chalk. It was new to us both and started me off with memories of the Marlborough Downs where we were going, bare except for the whispering grass and the tombs, temples, forts and ditches which so affected my boy's sense of the continuity of our land.

"Not melancholy?" Alwyn asked.

"Not to me or my father. They were our friends and ancestors. He used to say that if we felt their presence in our time, it was sacred."

"Presences. Yes. Closed, dark, the silence of the tide bringing presences more mindless than yours. Adrian, those weeks in the derelict were hell. There was no coming out of the tomb for me except sometimes to talk to Eudora."

Lulled into security we put up for the night in a cottage outside the village owned by a garrulous dame in her fifties — one of those women who desperately want to belong to an outer world and conceive it in terms of their daily paper. She hung about after our supper, talking and talking. She said she had a son who was a Southampton docker and gave us his name. We had already committed ourselves to our identities and we said, a little too soon, that we did not know him. He turned out to be one of the leaders of the strike. Alwyn had

177

been too clever. Choose a natural, common, convincing part and you are all the more likely to run up against the real thing!

No amount of "oh yes, of course" could put it right. We were marked down as a pair of disreputable, unwashed liars. She burned the breakfast bacon deliberately, and though we parted on outwardly cordial terms I could see she had dreams of appearing on TV as the unmasker of two wanted burglars.

She had asked us where we were off to now. Back to Southampton, we said, by train from Dorchester. There would be a bus to Dorchester in five minutes she yapped triumphantly. No wriggling out of that. We had to take it. Dorchester was a dangerous center of roads to and from the west, and the last place we wanted to be seen. So we got off at the next village, which meant that the bus driver would remember us if asked.

We were annoyed but not worried. Alwyn thought that our old-fashioned, innocent method of transport made us fairly safe. A criminal hardly ever walked, stealing a car or fixing false license plates and disappearing into the mass rather than into the country. It was also in our favor that there were two of us. The police were hot after Alwyn Rory but knew nothing of Ionel Petrescu.

Part right he was and part wrong, as we found out tramping northwards along the crest of Woolland Down with half of Dorset spread out below us and the other half glimpsed down wooded valleys. The road through the grass was narrow and open and entirely without traffic until we saw a police car coming up behind us. It stopped and a cop got out to talk to us. He wanted to know if we had stayed the night in Cerne Abbas. Yes, we had. Dockers? Yes, we were.

"There's a good lady thinks you aren't."

Alwyn said nothing. I could see that he feared the game was up and that he was waiting to hear what evidence the police had before committing himself. Myself I was without his sense of guilt and could appreciate more readily that it was a hundred to one the police were as bored with the woman as we were.

"Only pulling her leg, mate! She asked if we knew her son, Jim Halran. As if we didn't, the silly bastard calling us all out for nothing! Never heard of him, I told her, not wishing to get into an argument. What did she say about us?"

"She didn't like the look of you. What made you get off the Dorchester bus?"

Fortunately I had bought a paper. That inspired me — that and dread of being searched. My passport in the name of Adrian Gurney was in my pocket. Dorset police would remember who he was, or rather had been.

"Because as soon as we opened the paper we saw the strike was still on. So we changed our minds and thought we'd go to Salisbury. Better train service home from there, too! Did you think we'd bust into the Bank of England or what?"

"Just checking up on you. It's a man and a woman we're looking for."

Alwyn cheered up.

"Like we to take us'n shirts off, mate?" he asked. "What's they done?"

"Don't know except that it's big stuff."

He described us perfectly — a woman riding sidesaddle and a well-dressed groom. They might be on foot now, and she might be dressed as a man. We should keep our eyes open and run down to the nearest police station if we saw them on our way to Salisbury. Now on friendly terms, he wanted to know why we were on strike when we were earning three times what he did. Alwyn dealt with that one in his broadest Devon — a fiery and convincing defense of a man's right to strike whenever he bloody well pleased. I suppose he had read enough reports in his time on unrest in the docks to know just where Communist influence began and ended.

When the police car had driven away we sat on the grass to get our breath back and wished to God we had saved a bottle of that claret.

"How the hell did they get on to Lady Enid?" I asked.

He explained that it was certainly due to the search for Rachel, who could well be with Alwyn Rory.

"Suppose our Chipperfield's Circus story reached the police. They might have thought nothing of it if the circus had been in the district, but it wasn't. Then wide inquiries bring in a mass of reports when and where the pair were seen. Description of groom fits me. Description of lady sounds all wrong for Rachel, but her face could not be seen clearly under the veil and informants were vague. The incident at the church highly suspicious."

He added that Forrest and the horses must have got safely home, or the police would not still be looking for a pair of riders. He thought we could be more confident after what we had learned. Rory was with Rachel or he was alone. But it would be as well to sleep rough in the future and clean ourselves up at streams or in public baths so that we looked respectable. I must be clean-shaven and we must buy a clothes-brush.

That was the last word we ever had with the police. Whatever they were looking for, it was not two honest and perhaps envied pedestrians; and probably they had decided that to continue an intensive search for Rory in the West Country was not worth the organization required. When we were crossing Salisbury Plain he was very tempted to make his dash for Bristol, but then considered that the longer he delayed, the less port police would be on their toes. He had also come around to my way of thinking and was hoping to make good use of any information which Marghiloman — who was no amateur spy like Rachel — might be persuaded to divulge.

I had to look a fairly clean and neutral Petrescu for the interview with my KGB colleague, so when we had worked our way around Devizes I suggested that I should spend a night under a roof. To my surprise he wanted to join me and for the same reason; preparing for the meeting

"But suppose he recognizes you?"

"Why should he? His interest is in Petrescu and refugees. I think the CIA picked the right man for that job, but he's not big enough to have been employed on dynamite like the Mornix-Rory case. I'll see what the setup is when we get there."

We found beds for the night, of course not using our dockers-on-strike line. Alwyn produced the most convincing bit of lying I had ever heard from him. He claimed that our car had broken down in Devizes and that he had managed to find accommodation there for his wife and children. He and I, being short of money, had decided to sleep rough when we came across the bed-and-breakfast notice and thought we might just afford it. It was the sort of trouble which might hit anyone returning from a cheap holiday in a cheap, second-hand car, a shy, pathetic story accepted with a kindness which made us slightly ashamed of ourselves. But we had left no shade of suspicion behind us if the police ever made inquiries.

In the morning, rested, well fed and with Alwyn's beard looking a little less as if he had merely omitted to shave, we started early to cheer up the wife and children. When we were out of sight of the house we turned off the Devizes road and struck across the open downs for the River Kennet. So past my father's farm and on to the Ridge Way.

It was a good day for that great sweep of rolling upland with a light wind giving intervals of cloud and sunshine so that distance, though marked by the tumuli and standing stones of the dead, was incalculable. I was puzzled because I could not see Silbury Hill where it ought to be. Under cloud it appeared as a singularly long, dark green field of roots stretching away to a point. Then the sun showed that the point was the top of our pyramid and my long field a trick of perspective. The

Grey Wethers disappeared like rabbits or were lumpy as resting sheep or stood up as boldly as five thousand years ago when our ancestors chose from them the boulders with which to build their temple.

We lay down in the grass on the reverse slope of a Long Barrow which overlooked the junction of the Ridge Way and the Herepath by which Marghiloman would come if he came at all.

"Myself I would never meet a secret agent here," Alwyn said. "It looks utterly empty but one could post a platoon so that not a man would be seen."

"Towns and parks — that's all they know. They won't picture this at all."

"Nor did I. I wish I had."

"There's nobody much about except at lambing."

"But someone ought to be detailed to watch your meeting."

I pointed out that there was no need. Petrescu and Marghiloman could be trusted to report on each other, and anyway both were expendable.

We saw Marghiloman strolling up the Herepath, stopping at intervals to get his breath back and look around him. I had the impression that he was surprised rather than suspicious — a civilized man interested by a new environment.

"Find out if he has ever seen me! If he hasn't, give me a signal by smoothing down your hair in the wind!"

Marghiloman arrived at the Ridge Way and turned a little way up it. Sliding down behind the tumulus I walked around to meet him. He greeted me with nervous politeness in the Romanian we had last spoken together. He was no longer the overbearing, confident fellow of the Charing Cross Road and I was able to dominate the interview from the start.

"It is some time since we met," he said.

"Yes. I am glad you have now been persuaded to be sensible."

"You appeared so ingenuous."

"And you a man of such distinction."

"Well, we didn't come here for compliments. I have been instructed to hand over two hundred and fifty pounds. You will be told when and where to collect the rest."

I answered without showing any disappointment that I was quite content, and counted and pocketed the money.

"This is a very strange place to meet."

"Not if one's cover is agriculture."

"You are a long way from the coast."

"Would you expect me to live on it, Mr. Marghiloman? Here I am only fifty miles from each coast."

"I see, I see. I had no idea . . . well . . . of course."

"When you kindly sent me down to Devon, did the CIA expect Rory to be there?"

"No. But they wanted confirmation that he was in Russia."

"Have you any description of him? A photograph, perhaps?"

"No. He is nothing but a name to me. You must ask about Rory higher up — if you have the right, that is. I know so little of your position, Mr. Petrescu."

I ran my fingers through my hair, and Alwyn materialized almost instantly. While we were engaged in conversation he had managed to reach a smooth, grassed bank and follow it till he was behind us.

"Good morning, Mr. Marghiloman!"

"I have the money, sir," I said in perfect English. "He is what we thought. Shall I caution him?"

"No, not yet, Petrescu. This is quite a good place to talk as long as the rain holds off. Formerly CIA and now KGB! Don't you ever consider the British at all, Marghiloman? And now disturbing a couple of amateur archaeologists at their work! What have you got to say for yourself?"

It was my English which helped to reduce Marghiloman to pulp — apparent proof that I had fooled him all along the line. He must also have appreciated that MI5 considered him so important a catch that it was worthwhile blowing Petrescu's cover as a harmless Romanian.

Alwyn was using the half-jocular, half-deadly manner of the confident interrogator. It was all the more effective because of his shabby appearance. The voice and the air of authority rang true; therefore the appearance must be for some purpose assumed.

"I have nothing to say, sir. I do not deny that I have worked for the CIA."

"Well, well! And here you are paying out to an agent of the KGB!"

"But I do not think you will wish to put me on trial."

"Quite right. We wouldn't like to upset the CIA. Do you know what those mounds are?"

"Iron Age tombs, sir."

"The round ones, yes. The long ones are neolithic. It was not so lonely a spot then as it is now."

"I do not believe MI5 would do such a thing," Marghiloman answered stoutly.

"MI5 would not dream of doing such a thing. But that was quite a pull-up for a man in his fifties. A sudden heart attack could be expected. Did the CIA recruit you in America or England?"

"In England."

"By Mr. K.?"

"I was interviewed by him. I have not seen him since."

"Your immediate chief was their Mr. F.?"

"He was."

I have honestly forgotten these names, except for the fact that Mr. K.'s was good Anglo-Saxon and Mr. F.'s sounded like Polish. Alwyn's precise knowledge of both men and their responsibilities reinforced his authority.

"And your duties were to obtain the confidence of Romanians and others who had escaped to England, to report on them and make use of them?"

"They were."

"In fact the CIA didn't trust us to do the job for them?"

"They thought you were too kindly, too easily deceived."

"What did MI5 tell them about Petrescu?"

"That they were wasting their time."

"A bit patronizing?"

"Very probably."

"It didn't occur to them that we might be watching him — also to see if he was any use?"

"It may have done so. I don't know. I can only say that my organization was instructed to keep him under observation. We noticed that he took great pains to prove that he had no connections or friends, which suggested that he had something to hide. It was then decided to use him to carry the message to Mrs. Hilliard and see how both of them reacted."

"Why Mrs. Hilliard?"

"As you know, sir, her daughter was closely connected with Miss Iwyrne and she herself was distrusted by the Americans. She was seen on more than one occasion hanging about the Kingsbridge Estuary for no obvious purpose. It was thought possible that she was receiving enemy agents dispatched by Rory."

"And all this time you were working for the KGB as well?"

"No! I swear I was not."

"When did they recruit you?"

"Only two weeks ago. They suddenly found out I was a CIA agent."

"Why did you not at once report to the CIA that they had approached you?"

"The KGB have dossiers on all of us who have come from Communist countries — Czechs, Romanians, Poles . . ."

He went on burbling about refugees and their difficulties, talking and talking in order to put off the next question which he knew must be on the way. I was sorry for the man. There was no reason why he should not have worked for the CIA and he was good at the job — good enough at any rate to fool me, and well mannered with it.

"And what was in your own dossier, Marghiloman?"

"Nothing, nothing! I mean . . . well, for these days. We all have our tastes. So little to do with daily life. The secret side. Our private necessities. But the other parties were quite willing. An older man and a boy. Fatherly, and I would do anything for them. So beautiful. So full of curiosity."

"Under the age of fourteen?"

"You understand, sir."

"I understand it's a criminal offense. And so?"

"I was framed. Witnesses. Photographs. Oh dear, how defiling!"

"And what assignments were then given to you?"

"They knew I had been involved with Mr. Petrescu and Mrs. Hilliard. Every detail. How they knew so much I cannot understand. Oh, a very harmless assignment. They told me that Rory had never worked for them and never been paid by them. It was a mystery why he should have pretended that he had escaped to Russia."

"That was the first time you knew he had not?"

"Yes. The CIA still believe he is there."

"How many of the KGB men have you seen?"

"Two. One was British, I think. The other was not. And there were men who forced their way into my flat. Oh God, that horrible little actor! Such lies! Such depravity in one so young! I wouldn't have spied for them whatever they had on me. I loathe them. But what they required me to do was harmless."

"Control yourself, Marghiloman! These things happen. Go on!"

"You know, sir, that it was the CIA who had questions asked in the House and forced the Government's hand so that a Special Tribunal had to be appointed. They have their favorite Members of Parliament just as the Russians have theirs."

"That is beside the point," Alwyn retorted with such anger that he could have given himself away. "Such sympathies are normal and proper in any discussion of foreign policy inside or outside the House. And thank God we are still free in this country to express an opinion honestly held, however damned silly! And sometimes it turns out to be right."

I had a feeling that he only just checked himself in time from adding "as in the case of Miss Iwyrne." He cleared his throat and resumed his former manner.

"And what was this harmless assignment, Mr. Marghiloman?"

"To find out from one of my colleagues what was the evidence against Rory."

"You would have had to go as high as your Mr. K. to learn that."

"No. I remembered that when the papers were full of Rory's defection, I had discussed the case with the head of another department. A minor department like mine. But it is their duty to take action when the British are too scrupulous to do so. He said to me: "Yes, we got the bastard and now they've lost him."

"By 'they' he meant MI5?"

"Yes."

"The CIA knew Rory was guilty?"

"Of course. Circumstantial evidence was overwhelming. Mrs. Hilliard who brought him up had belonged to the IWW and run guns for the anarchists in Spain. Her daughter was a friend of the suspect Rachel Iwyrne who lived at Whatcombe Street and whom he introduced to the Minister."

"What made them believe that Miss Iwyrne was a spy?"

"Her opinions, I suppose, and her friends. You do not realize what risks you take. That was why the CIA started to operate in England."

"I am aware of that. But Rory — how did they get him?"

"You don't know?"

"What I require is what you told the KGB."

"I told them the story as I heard it, sir. After Mornix escaped it occurred to my friend's department that there might be evidence in Rory's flat. Unlikely, but the flat could easily be entered, and he might have been careless. So they sent in two of their specialists in that type of work and went through his personal papers."

Both Alwyn and I saw what was coming. His face quivered just once, but he retained a control as lifeless and commanding as any of the ancient stones below us.

"They found nothing of interest but a number of unopened bank statements which they read and re-sealed," Marghiloman went on. "Rory had too large an overdraft and did not wish to remind himself of it. The CIA psychiatrist confirmed that this was a common failing. So the department arranged a payment into his account which they knew that MI5 could trace to the KGB. The plan was foolproof. If Rory spotted it and reported it, no harm was done. If he did not, it was the solid evidence which was still missing.

"I see. So that was how they got the bastard. Was your friend a reliable informant?"

"He was rather drunk. Those American martinis, you know. He should not have washed them down with the good Burgundy I provided. In vino veritas. They are very clever, but inclined to indiscretion when pleased with themselves."

"When you passed on this information to the KGB, what was their reaction?"

"They showed none. Then they gave me this job of paying Petrescu."

"Why you?"

"Probably because I could recognize him."

"So could several of their operators. Why you?"

"For God's sake, sir! I don't know."

In spite of Alwyn's rigid expression I knew him well enough by now to detect that there was something in the last two answers which had opened a new train of thought. He appeared to accept Marghiloman's statement as the end of interrogation and looked straight at me with a plausible air of consulting my opinion. But in fact his eyes did not meet mine at all; he was looking past me in the direction of the Grey Wethers. I would have turned around if I had not been frozen into immobility by the two strained faces and the silence.

"Marghiloman, you have betrayed to the KGB the fact that both the CIA and ourselves know the number of their Swiss bank account. Why did you not report to your chief when the KGB first approached you?"

"I didn't dare."

"Did you or did you not do so?"

"Not at first. I was too frightened."

"So when?"

"When I was asked to pay Petrescu."

"I see. So all you had to confess was that you were meeting him and nothing else. And they answered that if you caught Petrescu for them, they'd fly you to the United States next day in a blaze of glory."

"Very discreetly. Very discreetly, I promise you," he replied, taking Alwyn literally.

"What was the plan?"

"I was to take him down to Avebury for a drink and point him out."

"And what were they going to do with him?"

"Drive him back to London."

"Suppose he yelled?"

"He would be asleep on the journey."

"What are you going to tell them now?"

"May I tell them the truth? That Petrescu is working for you?"

"And what will you tell the KGB?"

"Nothing."

"You said you did not know why they chose you to pay

Petrescu. I suggest they wanted to see if you would double-cross them."

"But that would mean we are being watched!"

"And that they know that you or Petrescu brought a third man to the meeting. If I were you, I should get straight on that plane without talking to anyone. Now get out!"

In the clean silence of the downs after he had gone I exploded my fury at the story we had heard and my delight that he had a chance of clearing his name if ever it could be proved. He cut me short.

"Later. This is not over."

When a fold of the ground had hidden Marghiloman we moved off the skyline and into the shallow cradle of a terrace to watch what he did. Below us was the village of Avebury, trees, gray manor and gray church all within the circle of the tall, shapeless stones standing on their rampart as sentries for ever over the first temple of England. I remember thinking that the priests of that ancient society must even then have fulminated against human treachery, the sin which above all others made their newly settled life uneasy, and have preached that between Earth and the Gods there was another great naked stone, and its name was Honor.

We saw Marghiloman almost running down to the point where the green road of the Herepath became a metaled track. When he got there he hesitated, buzzing around like a bee on a windowpane, looking at the ground, looking back at the bare hillside, trotting off towards Avebury, pulling himself together and walking back.

"That's where he left his car, by God!" Alwyn exclaimed.

"The CIA has taken it?"

"No, the KGB. They know as much about double agents as anyone else."

But Marghiloman was not such a townsman as I had thought. Perhaps his youth in Romania counted and he remembered he had feet. He did not go into Avebury to look for his car. He strode casually south for the Marlborough road, quickening his pace whenever he was in dead ground. That was the last we ever saw of him. In spite of the trouble he had caused me and his infamous private amusements I hope he reached home before anyone was at his front door to receive him and to prevent him picking up his ticket and catching the first plane out.

At the time, however, I was more worried about my own future.

"If the KGB get him he'll tell them Petrescu is MI5."

"They won't believe him for a moment."

"But my unknown companion!"

"They have had a long look at him."

"How do you know?"

"I told Marghiloman how I knew. I think their operator is in among the Grey Wethers."

I protested that at quarter of a mile a watcher couldn't possibly recognize him even through glasses.

"I am sure that KGB 13 would. That's the training."

"Call in Special Branch!"

"What proof have I?"

"You can make the CIA confess."

"Can I? I doubt it. And if I can, should I? What Eudora said is true. They have learned from the KGB that the end justifies any means. But they are our allies. Their country is our shield. If this story ever comes out, Washington must be free to swear there is not a word of truth in it."

It was not the first time that I had suspected Alwyn of an indefinable death wish, and I doubted if there were any Russians whatever around little Avebury. At the most there might be sympathizers well paid to do the less dirty jobs; people like the unknown yachtsman ordered to lift Alwyn from the creek or — to take an example from the other side — like the CIA agent who feared he would be trampled into the ground by bullocks, probably a half-witted fanatic whom Whatcombe

Street would have called a Fascist beast and not been far-out.

I said it was unbelievable that they would call in their professional thugs just for me and Marghiloman.

"Rory somewhere on the run and defenseless," he replied. "Tessa likely to know where he is. You possibly knowing anything she does. Attempts to check your background — Paris, wasn't it? — up against a blank wall. On top of all that, Rachel vanished. Almost anything might turn up, and if I were running the show I'd choose operators who were well prepared for it."

"How could they get into England?"

He answered with a faint grin:

"Perhaps off the trawlers, Willie. Off the trawlers!"

Still unwilling to believe, I wanted to ask: why here? But I could answer that myself. All my lies which I had thought so good suddenly seemed amateurish. I had said to my naval officer by the Otter that Marghiloman had me followed here and therefore it would appear to him a natural choice. A weak story! How would a refugee know the locality so well? Advisable to reconnoiter the place beforehand. They would then find it suspiciously lonely. So what's Petrescu's game? Perhaps he chose it in order to see all around him. He thinks he can, but he can't, the poor, unmilitary, little crook!"

"If you're right about the Grey Wethers, why hasn't he risked a shot?" I asked.

"Because the country is too open to get rid of the corpse. Now listen, Willie! Since they could tell when it was safe to remove Marghiloman's car we know that their man up there has a walkie-talkie to communicate with companions down in Avebury. So we're in trouble. They'll stick at nothing to find out what you are doing with Alwyn Rory and how long we have been together."

We were about to move off when a station wagon came whizzing out of Avebury along the Herepath and stopped where Marghiloman's car had been. Three men got out, leaving the driver behind, and strode up the hill evidently bound for the rendezvous with Petrescu.

"The CIA has found his car, but no Marghiloman. Straight into action, American style. Always that, or an interminable conference," Alwyn said.

We were now in serious trouble. It was easy enough to lie still in the cover of tumulus or ditch; but to move was difficult, for there was no avoiding the long run of the bare grass or a skyline. If we started to make our way below the escarpment towards the Marlborough road, more or less on Marghiloman's route, we should be in full view of the driver left in the car; and if we took to the top we exposed ourselves both to the three new arrivals and Alwyn's KGB man in the Grey Wethers — unless he was now trying to bury himself in the tussocks camouflaged as a chunk of sandstone.

All the same we had to risk it. The open downs which I thought so safe had not appreciated my trust, and I longed to get down into the valley of the Kennet and across the river into country still bare and rolling, sprinkled with barrows and standing stones, but with patches of woodland where I knew every path.

We decided to go singly since the CIA party was on the lookout for two men and might not pay immediate attention to a solitary walker. Below us we could see the Stone Avenue running down from Avebury to the water and the Sanctuary, part of the avenue still standing, part dotted with concrete markers where ages less interested in the past had broken up the stones for building. A group of tourists was wandering down it from their motor coach parked at the top.

Alwyn went first, aiming to join the sightseers and walk along with them. If all was then clear he was to wait for me near the little bridge over the Kennet. Once there I guaranteed I could get him away from anything but dogs or a cavalry patrol, neither of which were available to these very cautious operators.

He walked confidently straight down the hill as if he had just come over the top. The man in the station wagon must of course have spotted him but nothing could be done about it. Then he swung south for the Stone Avenue which he reached in ten minutes. For most of the time he was in full view of anyone in Avebury, or at least of anyone standing on the high bank of the Circle. At that distance I could not make out his figure with any certainty, but I did notice that when the motor coach came down and the tourists piled in one was walking away.

By this time the CIA men had returned, having drawn a blank. They all drove back into Avebury and were lost among the trees; so it was safe to crawl up my terrace to the top of the downs. Not a soul was to be seen, but I had learned that one could not trust to eyes. However, if the KGB observer was still among the Grey Wethers he could not catch me without running. And that did not seem to be at all the style of either of these bands of missionaries creeping like cockroaches in daytime about my country, always determined not to be conspicuous.

I walked fast and openly down the Ridge Way and crossed the Marlborough road after taking a good look around. No car was there to intercept me, innocently loitering along the edge of the modern road; nor on the ancient one was anyone taking a fast and casual stroll over the short turf. But I could bet that my movements were being reported. I put an immediate end to observation by fording the Kennet, where I used to paddle as a small boy, and vanishing into fertility, hidden by the willows on the bank, the hedges bounding the water meadows and the canopy of foliage around the church and in the manor gardens.

There was no Alwyn at the bridge. After I had remained there a few minutes to give him a chance to see me, I decided to reconnoiter the corner where the lane to the village left the main road. Avoiding the lane itself, I went around by way of the Sanctuary, the small Circle close to the water which must have supplied those prehistoric settlers and their hanging fields. My father used to say that the Sanctuary was dedicated to the God of the River and that the Stone Avenue was a triumphal way along which were dragged the cartloads of great pots up to the gardens and the terraces. Mere imagination, I suppose, but one farmer is in tune with another.

The concrete plinths of the Sanctuary — I regret to say that the foundations of our house were some of the original stones — plus a few drifting foreign tourists covered my approach until I could see the road junction. At the entrance to the lane a large car was parked, colored a cheerful blue and yellow which was more vulgar than sinister. Three men and a woman were in it. I recognized the woman. I had rowed her up to Eel Pie Island on a lovely morning. The reason for her presence was obvious. She was the only available KGB operator who knew me by sight — apart from my naval friend who could not take part in so dubious an outing. They had brought her down, I take it, as a kindly thought for my welfare in case Marghiloman's intentions were ungentlemanly. Thoughts would not be so kindly now that they knew I had been in Alwyn's company.

I did not like this continuous, close contact, though I was for the moment in a populated district and could hardly be kidnapped. Indeed I had only to sing out that I was Adrian Gurney and some friend of the family would come running and swear that I hadn't changed at all. Alwyn's problem was more difficult. He must get clear away, but had to avoid being trapped in some unobservable spot and finishing up — according to him — neatly jointed and polythene-packed.

It was easy enough to guess what had happened. Alwyn's move had been spotted and the car driven down from Avebury — a mere three minutes' run — to cut him off. There was no reason why he should recognize it for what it was. The woman and the three men were talking gaily; a bottle and sandwiches were circulating. If he had not suspected the car, he was still waiting for me nearby; if he had, he might have made for the downs which were just as bare and wind swept on this side of the valley as the other and even more thickly inhabited by the dead. But I was fairly sure he would not have broken away. He was by now thoroughly suspicious of this country so different from his Devon of small fields and lush growth and would hesitate to expose himself again on the slopes. And, for another thing, he was quite unnecessarily loyal to me.

I went through the village once more, and he joined me on the main street coming quietly from the yews of the church-yard. He said he had been in the willows below the bridge and had seen me all right but wanted to be sure I was not followed. Yes, he had noticed the car and avoided it, but the occupants had had plenty of time to watch his approach to the Marl-borough road and could now have no doubt at all that he was Alwyn Rory.

"And after you had gone off towards the Sanctuary I went into the church."

"What for?" I asked, meaning that I had wasted time look-ing for him.

"Put it that my own love of country begins with two bits of wood, not a circle of stone."

For the moment the KGB were checkmated by the leafiness of an English village. They could, of course, use their speed and charge up and down the only two lanes out of the place. That, however, would give their identity away if we saw them — as was likely — and they failed to see us. Their best bet was to sit still and wait for developments, meanwhile getting their man with the walkie-talkie down from the Grey Wethers and on to high ground on our side of the valley.

We too wondered whether we might not sit still till nightfall, possibly in the village inn. That would have fixed the KGB, but we could not count on the patience of the CIA or guess what they were up to. They wanted Petrescu badly and might well use the police to detain him or play their old trick of impersonating Special Branch themselves. It stood to reason that they must have seen Marghiloman's car being driven away and only realized too late that he was not the driver. Then nobody at the rendezvous. No signs of violence. The only observers stones and tumuli, impassive and disquieting. Afterwards two men had been spotted walking away. One must be Petrescu; the other was unknown. Even at a distance they could tell that neither was Marghiloman.

"Wherever we go we should avoid the tops and be in sight of other people till darkness," Alwyn said.

"Do you feel it's safe to start off by road?"

"Provided there is occasional traffic and a cottage or two."

What I had in mind was the Wansdyke. It could be reached by a mile of road, very open and overlooked by hills on both sides, and then by another half mile where we could leave the road and take to the woodland alongside.

The Wansdyke, I told him, ran from Savernake Forest to the outskirts of Bristol — with longish gaps — and all the way it was a track, a footpath or merely a ditch. He could hide in it; he could avoid towns and villages by following it; and he had perfect cover as an amateur archaeologist studying the reason why so immense an earthwork was ever built.

"Then you'd better let me know why it was."

"Nobody knows. It means Woden's Ditch — fifth century and nothing to do with all the old friends around us. A frontier, it's said, between Saxons and Saxons or Arthur's kingdom. Armies of men must have worked at it, for it's still twenty feet deep in places. Yet they couldn't possibly defend its whole length."

"Wansdyke!" he murmured. "There's a whole world of lost hopes in the name. What a place for your presences, Willie!"

"I never noticed any. Beer and the sword don't leave presences."

It was then that we saw the station wagon which had gone up the Herepath to look for Marghiloman. Its general appearance was less commonplace than the KGB car. The driver and his three passengers looked a bit too deadpan and purposeful, lacking the gentle influence of the opposite sex. At a guess one would have taken them for a couple of bookies and their clerks or a gang of dealers — in old cars or antiques rather than livestock.

The station wagon drove slowly through the village and then turned left on a course which would take them back to the main road. They might be having a last look around before heading back to London or be scouring the country with no definite aim. They cannot have been very hopeful, for our likely move, once contact was broken, was to vanish into the green-scarred downs and wait for the KGB to collect us. They could not guess that to be picked up by the KGB in any lonely spot was the last thing we wanted.

We started out for the Wansdyke fairly confidently. There was no cover on either side of the road and no traffic; on the other hand it was not a place which an assassin would choose when a farmer's car or a delivery van might come along at any moment. On the high ground to the left a small herd of Ayrshires was grazing. A townsman could well think that somebody unseen might be keeping an eye on them and have a full view of the road.

We were not far from the T junction where we should turn right for the Wansdyke and at last have woodland on one side of us when a car came around the corner towards us. There could be no doubt that it was the station wagon doing a last sweep back through the lanes instead of giving up. No escape was possible. If we tried to bolt across country we risked being followed and caught. The CIA men had looked dangerously athletic.

"Quick! Do they know you by sight?" Alwyn asked.

"No, they can't."

Rapid-fire thinking, justifiable but disastrous. Marghiloman had implied that he was to be the Judas who would point me out. To the CIA men in Devon I had been just a name, and their operator who was watching Tessa's movements had not recognized me. But I had long forgotten those weeks in London when strangers often stopped me to ask for directions or the right time and I had been smugly satisfied that it was my kind face which attracted them.

I think Alwyn accepted my snap judgment because it was our only chance, not because he was convinced. He reminded me that he himself was safe; the chiefs of the CIA in London knew him by sight, but the rank and file did not. They had probably learned from MI5 or Special Branch that he was not in Moscow, but that was all.

The station wagon came up and stopped. Its driver leaned out and asked if he was going right for East Kennett — a transparent excuse since he must have seen the signpost two hundred yards back.

Remembering that the CIA file on Petrescu would state that he spoke only broken English, I burst into my thickest Wiltshire which I doubt if anyone under the age of sixty still speaks. They couldn't understand me, for I kept rambling on about whether they wanted the pub or a farm. Alwyn cut me short, giving the impression that I was the village idiot, and told them to keep straight on.

They did, but then stopped and stayed put for half a minute. My conjecture is that one of them insisted I was Petrescu and another asked him if he thought those peasant noises were Romanian. Meanwhile we were stepping out as fast as we dared without making it too obvious. The pro-Petrescu man must have won the argument, for the car made a sudden and decisive U-turn through the long grass at the side of the road, hit an unexpected ditch and had to back out. By that time we were around the corner and in Boreham Wood.

But far from safe. We had dropped flat only yards from the

road and could not move. Two of them entered the wood; a third ran uphill towards the northeast boundary; and the fourth patrolled the road. Calling up boyhood memories I realized that they had done the right thing. It was a small hanger on the hillside in which we were trapped. All around were open fields which we should have to cross before we could reach the Wansdyke or the West Woods — two square miles of timber where we would be safe.

No one but Alwyn could have picked the right cover for us or even spotted its possibilities at all. The trees were beech with a little fir, well spaced so that there were patches of thick undergrowth. He had stopped for an instant on entering the wood and — to my mind — wasted precious seconds looking around. What he chose was a patch of rose-bay willow herb, just high enough to conceal us, in an open glade. Our pursuers ignored it and plunged straight for the self-evident — the bramble and hazel where we must be since we had no time to go far.

When the two had moved away, now searching the length of the ragged boundary hedge, I asked Alwyn in a whisper what weapon they were carrying.

"That, Willie, is a machine pistol with a silencer. Only to persuade you to surrender without a fuss. Every intelligence organization prefers interrogation."

Up to that point I had never, I think, taken his extreme caution seriously. Now at last I did. He spotted my misgivings though they were only expressed by silence.

"Just as much to comfort himself as to pot at you," he added. "Always remember that in action!"

He asked me for a situation report on the ground which I gave him, though it would have been more use to a small boy bird-nesting than two men clinging to cover which would just about do for a rabbit.

"I see. Eudora and the pack at the top of the hanger, John at the northeast corner and the Whips on the road. We can't break out without someone yelling Gone Away. But we'll last out the season yet, Willie."

All this hunting stuff was to comfort the raw recruit in his first experience of lethal weapons — artificial but it worked. The two had now stopped searching the hedge and were climbing up through the wood. At any moment they might decide that they had gone far enough and cut straight back to the car. If they did and looked down on our patch of willow herb they were bound to see us. We were only hidden from eyes on a level with us or below us.

We could not tell what the third man on the east side of the wood was doing — Eudora and the pack, as Alwyn called him — but even if we could reach that side we certainly could not leave it. I remembered a wide strip of bare down with a cart track running down the middle, passable for a car. To return to the road where the sentry was alert and continually on the move was equally impossible.

So our only hope was to try for the Wansdyke itself, although that involved crossing some two hundred yards of field which might be stubble or might be grass but was open to the road. If the man patrolling it was near the T junction when we started we might just make the Wansdyke; if he was coming towards us we hadn't a chance. And we could not watch him without exposing ourselves.

We crouched down and used the wretched cover of the thin boundary hedge until it turned away from the road and we could stand up. The two searchers in the wood had done what we expected and cut back to the station wagon, beating out the undergrowth all the way. Giving them time enough to get well into the trees, we took to the open and started to race across what turned out to be stubble. The bank of the Wansdyke was a light green wall in front of us, looking like the edge of another wood though it was a bare forty yards wide with more open country beyond. We were nearly there when the man on the road came around the corner and saw us. He shouted to us to stop and began to run. He could not fire even if he wanted to. A tractor and trailer were in sight and he had to consider the susceptibilities of the natives.

Crossing the Wansdyke by road you would notice our side of it only as a small copse with a deep dell in it; on the other side it was shallow and treeless, filled up by centuries of rain washing down the banks but still a work too large and smooth to be formed by water or by grubbing up some immense hawthorn hedge. That was the stretch of the ditch we intended to follow after dark, sweeping westwards over the downs past tombs and earthworks already three thousand years old when it was dug, until we came down at dawn into softer, well-timbered country where we could separate — he towards Bristol, I grabbing the first bus or train which went anywhere at all.

As soon as we hit the leafy bottom of the Wansdyke we hurried up it and then climbed the bank to see what was going on to the north of us. The two men who had been searching our wood had come out at the top of it and joined their companion. We had been right in assuming that we could never escape into the West Woods there. The fourth man who had kept watch on the road had now taken the station wagon up the cart track and was bumping over the open ground towards the others. Their tactics were plain. They probably did not know what the belt of trees was in which we had taken shelter, but they could see that it led up to the West Woods. They were dashing to cut us off and at the same time get a clearer view of the country.

They had in fact cut us off, but they could stay up there waiting for us as long as they liked. Twilight was now not far away and the bottom of the ditch was in shadow. We remained on the bank, safe in that mysterious line of defense, gazing at the long run of the Wansdyke on the other side of the road as it climbed towards the high ground and the continuation of the Ridge Way. Alwyn said that it looked like a modern tank trap.

"If the bank was then sheer it would have stopped cavalry — always assuming that intelligence reports from enemy territory were accurate enough to get the swordsmen up in time to the right spot."

He looked at the blank skyline to the west as if tanks or perhaps Arthur's cataphracts might be massing unseen behind it with a clear run down to the ditch.

"That's our problem, too, Willie — local intelligence in the shape of a walkie-talkie. The KGB must now recognize the CIA station wagon which went up to look for Marghiloman. The CIA have no reason to recognize theirs."

"Avebury parking lot?"

"No, they would have been much too careful and looked like any other visitors."

"Since they are in the same line of business, the CIA must know there is a KGB car about somewhere."

"Yes, they do know now. But when they came to Avebury it was just to grab Petrescu and they were not prepared for competition. The Russians were. That man who was among the Grey Wethers — where would you post him so that he could overlook the country on this side of the Kennet?"

"The Long Barrow which you saw from the road or up on the Ridge Way bang opposite to us."

"If he was there in time, he'd see us on the road and he'd notice some odd goings-on afterwards. But would he have seen us crossing the field to here?"

"From the Ridge Way, yes, if he was watching."

"How much would he see of the Wansdyke?"

"I should think just the belt of beeches and nothing of the ditch."

The CIA had left the lower end of the Wansdyke wide open for our escape. They realized, I suppose, that a lot of good it would do us; if we broke cover there they must see us either on the road or climbing up to the desolate Ridge Way where they could probably run us down without much fear of interruption. The essential from their point of view was to cut us off from the woodland. I was inclined to try for the hills, though doubtful if Alwyn could stand the pace. But it was not that which set him against it. He was still obsessed by the need to avoid any emptiness where the KGB could get at him without any witness.

The evening silence was absolute. I had the impression that the CIA agents were not confident away from city streets. Though they had plunged fast and intelligently at the opportunity we had given them, they were now showing extreme caution. They may have been unduly disconcerted by the covered way of the Wansdyke which required three men to search it efficiently — one down the middle and one on each bank in case we broke out over the side. That left only the fourth man to keep watch on the upper end.

We were beginning to hope that the stalemate would last till nightfall when we heard a car stop at the road end of the Wansdyke and remain there. I crept along the bank to look at it and found the three men and the boatwoman in the pleasant dell at the foot of the ditch, again innocently picnicking. Very cautious. No aggression. No reconnaissance until they had some idea what they were reconnoitering. It was a brilliant move and a neat piece of mapreading. The blue and yellow car, after receiving the lookout's news of all this significant hide-and-seek, had made a considerable circle at speed and had come up from the south so that it never passed the T junction. The CIA party would have noticed it coming up the road, then lost it to sight and assumed it had gone on towards Marlborough. Alwyn was right in his guess that they would not recognize it.

As all was quiet, one of the men left the picnic, went some

way up the Wansdyke, and lay prone on the north bank. From that position he could give warning of anyone coming down the bottom of the ditch. He could not see the edge of the West Woods. He did not have to. Any unexpected movement there could be at once reported by the walkie-talkie up on the Ridge Way. Or thereabouts. I have always wondered in what dimple of the dead the watcher made himself comfortable.

We ourselves moved a little further uphill and lay down on the outer side of the opposite bank, our heads high enough to see the bottom but well concealed behind seedlings of elder. Alwyn was as tense as an animal uncertain whether to charge, his nostrils slightly flared and quivering. I had seen that expression before — for example, when I invaded his privacy at the birthday hut.

"Beer and the sword do leave presences, Willie," he said.

"Yes? I could do with some beer."

"You will have that tomorrow."

I remember that he said "you," not "we." At the time I saw no special meaning in it.

"He left red anger behind."

"Who did?"

"Do I know? I only feel. Isn't that what you meant by a presence? He fought berserk in Woden's Ditch. It was his land, not theirs."

I suppose the red anger had mounted up in him — against himself during those weeks in the darkness of the derelict when he must have wondered whether he should not come out of hiding and challenge his fate, win or lose. Now in his mind, as well, were the images of our journey through the fairest, calmest counties of England until we came to my hills where the first of us cut terraces for their corn and knew their home for a home, building for the gods and honoring their dead. So all the afternoon since the meeting with Marghiloman he must have been dreaming of revenge. But revenge is the wrong word. He was not that sort of man. I would call it protest — the ultimate and only protest against two gangs of infidel trespassers.

"He was without hope as I am, Willie. His sword will not be hard to get. Lie still where you are and never move! Watch and remember and drink my health in the beer tomorrow!"

He crawled down the reverse side of the ditch and along the trunk of the fallen beech where he became completely invisible among the foliage. The Russian — if he was a Russian — went back to his picnic party silently and springily over the carpet of dead leaves. We had seen him very wisely inspect the tree when he first passed it and he now walked under it without more thought.

I saw Alwyn dive with outstretched arms so that one hand closed immediately over the man's mouth before he could make a sound. The other hand seemed to hit the back of his neck, but the attack was as fast as the swoop of a hawk and hard to analyze. At any rate the fellow lay there motionless on his stomach with his head back at a most unnatural angle.

Meanwhile Alwyn had picked up his complicated weapon and was striding fast over the soft, brown floor of the Wansdyke. The KGB party took a little time to react, for they were still sitting close to the roadside and could not see the beech which crossed the ditch. They heard the thud of the fall but it was followed by nothing.

Alwyn was now out of my sight. He must have emerged from cover close to the edge of the West Wood and the waiting station wagon. I imagine that he deliberately showed himself and turned back in simulated panic when he was seen. I heard the pack crashing after him down the middle of the Wansdyke and at last realized, helpless and appalled, what his intention was. The presence? It could be. I only know that the hunted Alwyn now blazed with the same fury as that figment of a warrior who had hurled away his shield in defiance and fought, naked and red, in the twilight of the ditch.

The picnic party held a hasty conference. It must have been clear to them that they had at last trapped Rory in just such a private spot as they had hoped; on the other hand an embarrassing confrontation with their opposite numbers seemed to be on the cards. The boatwoman stood by the car innocently packing up the picnic. Her two companions advanced cautiously up the ditch. When they saw the body beneath the tree they drew their guns and ran to him, one bending down and covered by the other.

At that moment Alwyn appeared with the four CIA men close behind him. He turned, took out the Russian gun from under his coat and fired a short burst at them. He could not possibly have missed at so close a range but he did. Deliberately, of course. Allies should be treated with tact and courtesy at all times. He then swung around and killed one of the astonished Russians — one only — with a single shot. The other plunged for the cover of massive beech roots and riddled Alwyn with rapid fire which shattered the head of one of the CIA agents and dropped another. Their two companions flung themselves behind trees and continued the battle. I have no experience of war, but I think I would prefer honest bangs to the sharp and terrifying sibilation of the silencers.

Desultory shots died away, and discretion took over. Both sides were quiet, waiting to see if any despised peasant of the host country had been attracted. But in the depths of the Wansdyke silencers were effective. Some homing farmer, not too far off, may have wondered that a sudden gust of wind, funneling up the dyke, should have so swished the leaves, but continued on his way to his family, his supper and the racket of his television. I think, to judge by what followed, that it was as well for him that he did. Once upon a time they would have said he had been snatched by fairies.

Myself I had been fairly safe where I was, out of the line of fire as Alwyn knew I would be. Resting my head on my arms I mourned for him, trying to reconcile that blood-soaked corpse with my friend so quickly responsive, and I began to wonder how well he had foreseen the efficiency of both sides at clearing up their more inconvenient necessities of state.

It was my boatwoman who, with feminine common sense, made the first move. She was Russian all right — possibly an unsuspected refugee with complete freedom of movement. From my side of the bank and uncomfortably close to me she shouted in English:

"You bloody fools! You could have had the police on the lot of us."

I don't think she realized that it was Alwyn who had provoked the battle. I was near to hysteria anyway and her remark nearly made me sob with laughter out loud. The overriding anxiety was lest the Law should suddenly appear from some Wiltshire Sinai in the shape of two grave young policemen, unarmed but inviolate.

There was a silence. I thought I heard whispering from the cover on the other side of the ditch, but it may have been holly leaves using the light wind to settle down for the night. Soon a voice asked:

"Have you a car?"

"Yes. And we know you have."

"Get on with it then! We'll pick up ours."

The CIA carried their two dead up the ditch. The messier casualty left a trail behind, but they did not bother about that. They were quite right. The floor of leaves was red-brown anyway, and the carrion crows would deal with the brains at dawn. If he was British, I suppose they had to produce some story of a death at sea where his body probably ended up; if American, it might be harder to tidy up the matter in view of the national custom of shipping home those dead on service. A waxwork head, perhaps. Lips of the living would never detect the difference.

They mentioned Petrescu. I gathered that he had slipped away into the woods while his companion provided the daring diversion. There was no conversation between the two sides. KGB 13 had no reason to say who Petrescu's dead companion was. I am sure that they assumed the CIA knew who he was, for never at any time in the future did they dare to claim he was in Russia as Alwyn always feared they would. That, too, must have been in his mind. He had once said to me that he did not have to live so long as he made it impossible for the Russians to claim he was alive.

Together with his two victims he was removed by the boat-woman and the only remaining picnicker. I could not see their arrangements. No doubt the boot of the car was reasonably well prepared in case of accidents to Marghiloman or myself. But three bodies were a lot for that blue and yellow sedan; as soon as it was dark they must have dropped the overspill in a secluded spot and telephoned to some very unwilling friend to come out with a van and pick it up. The CIA, expecting only a drugged Petrescu, must also have had trouble with space though the station wagon was more commodious and the two empty seats could be folded back. An innocent load of sweet hay gathered from any wayside stack might have been their answer.

There at the Wansdyke I left that much-wanted trawlerman from the Russian fleet. Nobody has ever wanted him since or, I am sure, hoped that he might turn up. He walked away and lay shocked and in tears on the smoothly sloping tomb of some other nameless occupant until at dawn he took a train from Swindon and became Adrian Gurney.

IV

I arrived in Worcestershire and at once found profitable work picking fruit for the market. I was dazed by the problem of how to get in touch with Tessa and Eudora, desperately anxious in Molesworthy and without news. I could not know whether telephones were tapped and letters opened — justifiable activities if Rachel was still missing and Alwyn suspected of abducting her. It may be that my mind was too tired for any more ingenuities and that I was clinging to mechanical, open-air labor to save me from thinking.

After a week I recovered the power to make a plan and wrote to Forrest at Molesworthy under the letterhead of The Black Bear — the village pub where I sat in the evening with fellow workers, or alone and drinking too much. I asked him if he would care to receive a free trial case of our home-bottled cider — the pub did not make any but I reckoned no one would investigate — and thanked him for his kindness to our representative when he was in the district. I signed the letter Adrian Gurney, saying that I was usually in after working hours and would be glad to see him or any friend of his. Forrest could have no idea who Adrian Gurney was, but he'd be at Cleder's Priory with the mysterious letter half an hour after receiving it.

I expected them in the evening two days later — a miserable evening of utter indecision. I did not want to be caught in The Black Bear unavoidably drinking. I could think of no excuse for hanging about alone in the village street. I did not know by what road they would come or how to break the news. Eventually, I waited, skulking in cover as if expecting Marghiloman, by a crossroads which I was sure they must pass. When they did not, I returned to The Black Bear where I found Tessa nervously waiting in the parking lot.

It was too public a place for emotion, and I was still inhibited by anxiety lest she might have been followed; so I got quickly into the car and directed her to a quiet spot among the nearby orchards where we could talk. When we were clear of the village she stopped and for a moment was in my arms, but the Wansdyke was still behind my eyes.

"Has he escaped?" she asked.

I told her that he was dead. She took that in silence, a dry-eyed statue hardly listening to the beginnings of my too fast, incoherent story.

"Eudora knew it. I think she wants you to herself, which is why she didn't come."

"Or couldn't bear to see me. How did she know?"

"They were very close always."

After more of our journey and its end I tried to explain that when he left my side on the bank of the Wansdyke I could have no idea of what he intended.

"And you don't even know what they have done with his body!" she exclaimed.

"What does his body matter? He carries with him what it loved."

Poor comfort — but I did not know how to cherish her, vaguely understanding that no comfort was possible and that her mind was in the same chaos as my own, drifting in the past with no hold on the present. She must have felt subconsciously that her passionate grief for Alwyn was a disloyalty to me and her love of me a disloyalty to Alwyn. Neither could be expressed.

I asked her if it was safe for Eudora to meet me. She replied that it was, in a tone which suggested the complete triviality of safety.

"And Rachel?"

"She has gone. That's all I know."

Tessa drove me back to the village and left me there, saying that she must return to Eudora at once. I felt guilt and desolation, for I knew she would be crying her eyes out by the roadside and I would not be with her to help, nor knew how to help.

No word came from Eudora. In my mood of depression I told myself that there never would be, though common sense — as far as there was any left — assured me that so long as she was at home she would take care that there should be no detectable communication between Adrian Gurney and Cleder's Priory.

On the fourth day after Tessa had gone I had at last a wire from London.

"Staying at the Ritz drop everything and come: Eudora."

I sent my reply and left — after pleading illness in the family since I wanted to be sure of getting my job back when I returned. My kindly employer, who must have quietly noticed my melancholy, told me I'd never have to look for a job so long as he was in business and I should cheer up and not worry. Cheer up I could not, but his words at least gave me back some self-confidence.

The Eudora I now met was a woman I had never known before. At Molesworthy I could not think of her as anything but pure English in her tastes and manner of living, but now in London she looked the American *grande dame*, dressed all in black — the only and very private sign of her mourning. The air of decision and the humorous eyes were the same as ever and yet authority and distinction were more evident. Heads turned in curiosity about her as she crossed the foyer to meet her shabby friend.

She did not use words to put me at ease. She gathered me up and kissed me like a son. I was in her world again. I had no other, and it was still there for me.

As soon as we were up in her room I asked her how Tessa was.

"My poor Willie! I sent you Tessa so that you could comfort each other. But I should have known you are both too young and too straight."

"She was so cold."

"What did you expect? That Tessa would throw her arms around you and scream 'thank God you're safe'?"

"Where is she?"

"I have persuaded her to go back to London and her friends."

"But she has changed. She has grown out of all that."

"Yes, dear Willie. So she will be sure at last where she belongs."

"At Molesworthy?"

"Never at Molesworthy. For many reasons I cannot bear it any more. I am going back to America."

I asked her why and she replied that she had no other duty any longer.

"When I was young, I was in revolt against the exploitation of the helpless," she said. "Now that I am growing old, I am in revolt once more — against all the conduct we are accepting, Willie. The plain citizen is no angel. Never has been. But if we allow his moral sense to waste away, we're going to have a culture of devils where no man can trust another's word or hand. Such money as I have will be used to stop the rot."

And a very formidable opponent she would be, I thought, always a law to herself in friendship or vengeance.

"But I shall leave one sound investment here which Alwyn wished — a farm in our West Country with the most reliable tenant I can find. That happens to be you. It's a straight business transaction, Willie. You won't have learned anything about farm tenancies in Romania, but they'll become very familiar to you after a year's training here. You'll pay me rent because you'll have to, and it will be lent back to you for the few years that you are likely to need it. That's settled. Now, tell me calmly about his death."

It was easier this time to relate the whole story of our journey and the Wansdyke, for she understood every facet of Alwyn's character, even that defenseless side which he concealed from Tessa.

"Was it suicide, Willie?" she asked.

"No, never! He was like the warrior he dreamed of. He wanted to kill, not to die. But if it cost him his life, he didn't care."

"His own justice," she said. "Sometimes when one defends what one loves there is no other way."

"And Rachel? Where is she?"

"I don't know. The last time I went to see how she was getting on I found only Sack."

"Sack?"

"He must have crawled into the derelict when I brought her food. There was only a foot or two of water and I was so frightened of the boat being stranded on the mud that in the hurry I never noticed he had gone."

"But if Rachel was alone with Sack in the dark she would have jumped out!"

"I am very much afraid that may have happened — and she would not know that one had to slack off the mooring to hit hard bottom."

"She didn't yell for help?"

"She must have hoped to escape quietly. Perhaps she went on expecting to find her feet on something solid till it was too late."

"Sack is all right?" I asked after a pause.

"In the best of health, dear. But he is not fond of hotels. I shall leave him with you till I have a home. Afterwards, later, Tessa too. And, Willie, among those presences of your England, remember Alwyn!"

More Mysteries from Penguin

Margery Allingham
THE CRIME AT BLACK DUDLEY
MR CAMPION AND OTHERS
POLICE AT THE FUNERAL

Freeman Wills Crofts
THE CHEYNE MYSTERY
INSPECTOR FRENCH'S GREATEST CASE

Sir Arthur Conan Doyle
THE MEMOIRS OF SHERLOCK HOLMES

Nicolas Freeling
BECAUSE OF THE CATS
DRESSING OF DIAMOND

Michael Innes
AN AWKWARD LIE
FROM LONDON FAR
HAMLET, REVENGE!
WHAT HAPPENED AT HAZELWOOD

Jack London
THE ASSASSINATION BUREAU, LTD.

Patricia Moyes
BLACK WIDOWER
THE CURIOUS AFFAIR OF THE THIRD DOG

Georges Simenon
MAIGRET AT THE CROSSROADS
MAIGRET MYSTIFIED
and many other Maigret titles

Julian Symons
THE MAN WHO KILLED HIMSELF
THE MAN WHO LOST HIS WIFE
THE MAN WHOSE DREAMS CAME TRUE

Geoffrey Household

ROGUE MALE

His mission was revenge, and revenge means assassination. In return he'll be cruelly tortured, tracked by secret agents, followed by the police, relentlessly pursued by a ruthless killer. They'll hunt him like a wild beast, and to survive he'll have to think and live like a rogue male. "A tale of adventure, suspense, even mystery, for whose sheer thrilling quality one may seek long to find a parallel . . . and in its sparse, tense, desperately alive narrative it will keep, long after the last page is finished, its hold from the first page upon the reader's mind"—*The New York Times Book Review*.

WATCHER IN THE SHADOWS

Watcher in the Shadows is the story of a manhunt, of a protracted duel fought out in London and in the English countryside by two of the most accomplished and deadly intelligence officers to have survived World War II. One of them is a Viennese who served in the British Intelligence; the other is a dangerous fanatic who has already murdered three men. Their duel begins ten years after V-E Day, and they bring to it every ounce of the cunning and courage on which their lives depend. "A thriller of the highest quality, always credible, well written, solidly grounded in locale (rural England) and character"—Anthony Boucher, *The New York Times Book Review*. "Fully up to current standards of savagery"—*The New Yorker*. "Recommended through a megaphone"—Francis Iles, *Guardian*.

Lionel Davidson

THE ROSE OF TIBET

The Rose of Tibet is a story of adventure on the roof of the world, before and during the Chinese invasion. Charles Houston, a London artist, goes out to seek news of his brother, reported dead in Tibet. In India a Sherpa boy tells him of Europeans recently encountered in the mountains, and the two set off for the forbidden monastery of Yamdring. Their extraordinary reception there, after weeks in the killing cold, Houston's romance with a reincarnated she-devil, and their violent and tragic efforts to escape the Chinese with a fortune in gems are told with that amalgam of humor, romance, and incredulity that make Lionel Davidson the perfect storyteller for today. "I hadn't realized how much I had missed the genuine adventure story—not thriller, not detective, without social significance—until I read *The Rose of Tibet*"—Graham Greene.

Other titles by Lionel Davidson available
from Penguin Books:

Making Good Again

The Night of Wenceslas

Peter Lovesey

A CASE OF SPIRITS

Sergeant Cribb was warned that discretion was needed
in this case of burglary. The risqué oil painting that had
vanished belonged to Dr. Probert's secret gallery of naked
nymphs and goddesses. Dr. Probert was a member of the
Royal Society, a man of eminence and reputation, but
he had been dabbling in the occult, Victorian style.
There was reason to think that those who contrived
spirits might also have contrived burglary. And much
worse was to follow. Violent death interrupted a "spiritual" session in Dr. Probert's house—and the police
marched in. Sergeant Cribb and Constable Thackeray,
that indomitable pair from Scotland Yard, pursue their
clues in their usual down-to-earth and orderly manner,
but the weird characters and suspects among whom they
move are only "down to earth" when it suits them. Peter
Lovesey presents a rich picture of the eccentricities of
ESP in Victorian times, when it flourished as widely as
it does today. This literate and stylish entertainment
provides amusement for all and a challenging murder
mystery for connoisseurs of crime.

Also by Peter Lovesey:

The Tick of Death

Elizabeth Ferrars

HANGED MAN'S HOUSE

Distraught after the violent death of her husband, Valerie Bayne had come to live with her brother Edmund in his quiet village in the English countryside. She had hoped to find a retreat from the world and a chance to rebuild her shattered life—but what she found was murder. It was Valerie who found Charles Gair's body swinging from a beam in his cottage. That discovery unlocked the secrets of Charles's sordid and violent past, secrets that threatened to destroy the lives of those who had survived Charles as well. There was Hugh Rundell, whose wife, Debbie, had deserted him years before but still plagued him with intermittent letters. There was Hugh's seventeen-year-old daughter, Isobel, whose relationship with the hostile and arrogant young Ivor Hayden alarmed and infuriated her father. Valerie, Edmund, Hugh, Debbie, Isobel, Ivor—all had certain secrets that police Superintendent Patrick Dunn's investigation of Charles's death threatened to expose. Each one of them had reason to fight his probing. Valerie, however, found the desire to live, and love, awakened within her once more. If only the mounting rash of horrifying discoveries —and corpses—didn't destroy them all first.

Other titles by Elizabeth Ferrars available
from Penguin Books:

Breath of Suspicion

The Small World of Murder